A JESSIE BLACK LEGAL THRILLER

by

Larry A. Winters

In loving memory of Uncle Richie,
you are missed

1.

Jessie sensed something was wrong the moment she saw the girl, who stood in the doorway of the interview room looking too young to be a second-year law student. Her clothing—jeans and a baggy sweater—were way too casual for an interview. Her hands were not clutching a fancy-looking portfolio full of writing samples and extra copies of her resume. Her hair, long and brown, fell in messy ringlets around her face and down her back—a far cry from the carefully controlled styles of most interviewees. She seemed to hurry into the room and close the door with jerky, nervous energy. It wasn't the nervousness of a typical Ivy League law student seeking a summer position. Hers was a different kind of nervousness. A more raw, desperate kind.

Jessie glanced down at the resume on the table in front of her. Her first interviewee was not due for another ten minutes. "Are you Madeline Grady?"

"Are you a prosecutor?"

Jessie watched the girl twist her fingers together in another display of nervousness. Definitely not

1

Madeline Grady. Probably not a student at all. But if not, why was she here? Who would want to sneak into the Penn Law fall on-campus recruiting other than an aspiring lawyer? "Why don't you sit down?"

The girl stepped further into the room and closed the door behind her, seeming to notice her surroundings for the first time. The interview room was small and austere, with plain, eggshell-white walls, stiff-backed swivel chairs, and a rectangular table. No prints on the walls. No windows. The table was bare except for a manila folder in which Jessie had brought copies of the resumes of the students she would be meeting today, and next to the folder, her cup of coffee. Jessie had already gulped it down, but the coffee smell lingered in the air.

The girl sat in one of the swivel chairs. "Are you okay?" Jessie said.

"Why do you ask that?" The girl's eyes flashed. They were green eyes, a shade not much different than her own. As out of place as she looked here, the girl also seemed strangely familiar. Had Jessie seen her somewhere before?

"You just seem like you're in the wrong place. Is there someone I can call for you?"

"I'm in the right place. I mean, if you're a prosecutor. It said on the directory that the DA's office is doing interviews in this room."

"Yes, I'm an assistant district attorney. Jessica Black." She hesitated, then added, "You can call me Jessie."

"Good." The girl tucked a strand of hair behind her ear.

"What's your name?" The longer Jessie watched the girl, the stronger her instinct became that she had seen her before. But she couldn't recall where or when that had been.

"Carrie."

"Well, Carrie, how can I help you? We don't have much time before my first interview."

Jessie glanced at her watch. She had no doubt Madeline Grady would be prompt. In her experience, Penn Law students tended to take their careers very seriously. Jessie certainly had, when she'd been a student here.

She remembered her own interviews, which had taken place in the same venue—the Leonard A. Lauder Career Center, located in the McNeil Building, a cube-like structure on the picturesque Locust Walk. It was here that law firms, government agencies, and other employers conducted first round interviews with first and second-year law students. The summer positions were critical, as they often led to permanent positions after graduation. The students vied for them fiercely.

Jessie's calendar wasn't quite as jam-packed as most of the interviewers' today. Not surprisingly, the demand for cushy, high-paying summer associate gigs in giant law firms was higher than the demand for summer internships at the Philadelphia district attorney's office. But Jessie had no problem with that. She wasn't interested in talking to students focused on prestigious names and high salaries. She wanted to meet the students eager for courtroom experience and a chance to make a difference. She'd been doing these interviews for years. Not much surprised her at this point. But she had not been expecting her day to begin with a strange girl appearing unannounced in her interview room.

"Carrie," she prompted, when the girl didn't respond, "why are you looking for a prosecutor?"

A hardness entered the girl's eyes. "My father was murdered and the police are letting the woman who killed him get away with it. It's not right. Someone needs to do something!"

It occurred to Jessie that this could be some kind of prank—there were some jokers in her office and among her friends at the university—but she didn't think so. The girl's face was so intense it was hard to maintain eye-contact.

"This happened here in Philly?"

"Yes! You don't even know about it? And you're a prosecutor?" Carrie's face flushed. Her fingers twisted together with more urgency. Jessie reached out and touched the girl's hands, stilling them.

"There are a lot of murders in this city. Too many for me to be familiar with every one of them. I know that's an awful thing to think about, but it's true."

Carrie's gaze lowered and she seemed to look at Jessie's hand covering her own, but she made no move to pull away. A second later, her eyes returned to Jessie's, and some of the hardness dissipated.

"My father's murder was on the news. It's *still* on the news. I hate it. It's like they're celebrating his death. Like it's a good thing. It seems like every day those reporters find a new way to say something terrible about him. And meanwhile the woman who killed him...." The girl's voice seemed to catch in her throat.

"I'm not sure I understand," Jessie said. "Why would reporters say something terrible about a murder victim—" Then she got it. Suddenly, she recognized this girl, and everything fell into place. "You're talking about Corbin Keeley."

It was true that the media couldn't get enough of Keeley, and also true that they'd painted him as a villain—and not for the first time. But that was for good reason, as far as Jessie was concerned. At the time of his death, Corbin Keeley had been a city councilman, a position he'd held for many years. The first time he'd been vilified by the media had been three or four years ago, when rumors had surfaced in the news that during his marriage—which had ended in a supposedly amicable divorce—he'd beaten his wife savagely. Somehow he'd managed to keep the abuse a secret until a photograph of his ex-wife taken during their marriage had been discovered by the ex-wife's sister and leaked to the media. Jessie still remembered it—dark bruising had covered most of her face, one of her eyes had been swollen shut, her jaw had looked huge with swelling. And yet, Keeley had survived the torrent of outrage. He was a career politician, with clout and powerful connections. His ex-wife's vocal denials of the abuse had probably helped to some extent, too, although Jessie had not found her believable. Keeley had managed to cling to his office despite the scandal.

Now the media had returned to the subject years later, but this time, survival wasn't an option for Keeley. No amount of influence could shield him from a bullet. According to what she'd heard around the office and on the news, about a month ago, his new girlfriend had attempted to break up with him, and Keeley had gone into a rage. Unlike his ex-wife or any of the other women he might have battered during his life, this girlfriend had a gun. And she used it. After his death, when he was no longer politically useful, his former allies and connections distanced themselves from him, leaving the whole mess to the police and the DA's office to sort out. The official conclusion had been that the shooting was in self-defense, and the girlfriend, a woman named Brooke Raines, had not been charged with a crime.

"You're his daughter?" Jessie said. She recalled now that Keeley had had a teenage daughter with his ex-wife. Was her name Carrie? Yes—*Caroline*. Caroline Keeley.

Carrie nodded. The girl finally pulled her hands away from Jessie's. She wiped her eyes.

"I don't think I'm the right person to talk to," Jessie said carefully. "I sympathize with the pain you must be feeling at the loss of your father, but—"

"I don't want sympathy. I want Brooke Raines to

go to prison. She killed my dad. Isn't that what prosecutors are supposed to do—send killers to prison?"

"Your father's case wasn't that straightforward, Carrie. I can give you the phone number of the police—"

"My mom and I talked to the police. A hundred times. They won't listen to us." Carrie shook her head and looked away, lips trembling. "And the DA's office? They won't even return our calls. That's why I had to come here. It was the only way to get one of you fucking people to talk to me."

The girl's use of the F-word, which she flung bitterly from her lips, did not shock Jessie as much as the mention of her mother. She was familiar enough with the case to know that Keeley's ex-wife had admitted, after his death, that the injuries in the photograph had been inflicted by Keeley. That information had supported the decision not to charge Brooke Raines.

"Carrie, are you aware that your mother confirmed to the police that during their marriage, your father had been … violent with her on more than one occasion?"

"You don't need to tiptoe around it. My dad beat my mom. But he never beat this other woman. After my mom left him, my dad got help. He stopped drinking and he learned to control his anger and—" She stopped abruptly, maybe because she could read the skepticism in Jessie's face. "I *know* he didn't hurt

Brooke Raines."

Jessie hesitated, then said, "How can you know that?"

"You're not listening to me. What he did to my mom, that's not relevant now! He's not like that anymore. He changed!"

Jessie raised her hands, palms outward. "Okay. I understand that you believe that. And it's natural that you would *want* to believe that, because he's your father. But you don't know for sure that he never attacked Brooke Raines, do you? She claims he did, and that on the night of his death, he would have killed her if she hadn't defended herself."

"It's not true!"

Jessie tried to remember the details of the case. "They were fighting because she broke up with him. I've worked on domestic violence cases before. The threat of a breakup is a common trigger."

"She's a liar," Carrie said.

A loud rapping on the door made both of them turn. Jessie remembered her interview. Madeline Grady, a 2-L looking for a summer internship at the DA's office, was waiting on the other side of the door. Jessie felt her jaw tighten. An interview for a summer job seemed absurdly inconsequential next to the subject she and Carrie were discussing, and she didn't want to dismiss this girl who was in such obvious emotional turmoil. But she had other responsibilities, too.

"Carrie, let me give you my business card, okay?

You can call me later, and we can continue—"

"No. I'm not leaving until you agree to prosecute that woman."

"I can't agree to that. Even if I wanted to, I don't have the authority to make that decision right now."

"Even if you wanted to?" Carrie echoed. "Meaning, you *don't* want to."

Another few knocks, louder this time.

"It's not about what I want. It's about the law. You've heard the phrase 'innocent until proven guilty,' right? If we were to prosecute Brooke Raines, we would need to prove beyond a reasonable doubt that she did not act in self-defense. Proving a negative is difficult enough even when the facts are in our favor. In this case, the facts are *not* in our favor. The evidence supports Ms. Raines's statement. And your father's history speaks for itself."

"His *history*. The past. The police are wrong," Carrie said. "Or they're dirty."

"I work with the detectives in the Homicide Division every day. They're good people."

"You work with the detective on my dad's case? Kyle Fulco?"

"No. I mean, I know his name, but I haven't had an opportunity to work directly with him yet."

"He's an idiot," Carrie said. "Or corrupt."

Jessie shook her head. "I can tell you that's not true."

"Can you?" Carrie said. "Did you talk to any

witnesses? Did you see any evidence?"

A third round of knocking was too much for Jessie to ignore. "Give me a second." She stood from her chair, crossed the small interview room, and opened the door a crack. A young woman in a blue suit stood just outside the door, portfolio in hand and anxiety on her face. "I'm sorry," Jessie said. "I just need a few more minutes, okay?"

The woman nodded—*what choice did she have?*—and Jessie closed the door. She turned to Carrie, who had also stood from her chair.

"You're right that I didn't talk to any witnesses myself," Jessie said slowly, "and I didn't personally see the evidence. But I can tell you that the police did their job. Now, I'm sorry, but I need to ask you to leave. I have an interview and—" Carrie's face seemed to crumple in on itself. Jessie found herself reaching for her arm. "Look, you have my number. If you have any other questions, or just want to talk, call me."

"You don't even care about the truth."

Jessie opened the door, and, with a final look that was equal parts anger and despair, Carrie Keeley hurried out past the waiting law student, almost knocking the portfolio out of the woman's hand. Madeline Grady watched the departing teenager with confusion.

"Come on in," Jessie said. "I'm sorry about the delay."

Jessie came around the table and returned to her own seat. She picked up the resume and prepared to ask the first question she asked of all the students seeking internships with the DA's office: "So, Madeline, why don't you start by telling me why you want to be a prosecutor?"

She didn't hear the woman's answer, though, because in her head, she was asking the same question of herself.

2.

"It sounds like the interviews went well," Warren Williams said the next morning.

He'd asked her to meet in his office, ostensibly so she could fill him in on the previous day's recruiting efforts, but more likely—she suspected—so she could assure him that losing a whole day to interviewing would not impact her cases. She didn't hold his indifference against him. She knew that as the head of the Homicide Unit, he was under constant pressure to demonstrate the efficiency of his division.

Warren looked like a man under constant pressure. Overweight, balding, perpetually red-eyed and tired—he looked like a man with the weight of the world on his shoulders. And maybe that's what it felt like to run the most high-profile unit in the DA's office, constantly under scrutiny. As ambitious as she was, Jessie didn't envy him his job. She loved being a prosecutor, but preferred to steer clear of the political aspects of the office.

"Yes," she said. "I think we're going to have a good program this summer."

"Great. And regarding your caseload, everything is still on track, right?"

"Everything's on track."

He nodded and turned to his computer. She looked around. He seemed to have picked up a new habit. This time, herbal tea—a variety she'd never heard of but that she guessed, knowing Warren, was the cornerstone of his latest weight loss program. Six used tea bags leaned in a soggy heap on a napkin next to a mug in which a seventh was steeping. An odor like sweaty socks wafted from his mug. On another day, she might have offered a snarky observation, but today, she pretended not to notice.

Warren's eyes followed her gaze. He abruptly swept the used tea bags into a trash can by his desk. "Is there something else you want to talk about?"

She considered telling him about her encounter with Corbin Keeley's daughter, but stopped herself before the words came out. His face looked waxy, and lines seemed etched in his doughy skin. The DA, Jesus Rivera, would be up for reelection soon, and she knew that made Warren's job even more stressful than usual. There was something else holding her back, too. Jessie wasn't sure herself what to think of the encounter. She was still processing it. The night before, she'd been unable to get Carrie's voice out of her head, and in her mind's eye, she'd kept seeing that horrible photograph of Keeley's ex-wife.

"No, I better get back to work."

She walked down the hall to her own office.

When she'd told Warren that everything was on track, that hadn't been quite true. The Penn Law on-campus interviews had consumed a whole day, and that was time she would need to scramble to make up. Her PC was full of documents that needed reviewing, briefs that needed writing, and emails that needed answering. And her phone was already ringing.

She recognized the internal extension and picked up. "Jessie Black."

"Hey, Jessie. There are some people here to see you. Carrie Keeley and Maynard Travers. They say you're expecting them?"

Jessie let out a breath. Maybe giving the girl her business card had not been her brightest idea. Should she turn her away? She considered that, but found herself unable to do it. "Tell them I'll be ready in a minute. Let me grab a conference room."

"When I gave you my card, I wasn't expecting you to drop by the next morning," Jessie said as she ushered her visitors into a conference room. "I'm not sure there's anything I can tell you that I didn't already say yesterday. And don't you have school?"

Carrie shrugged. "School kind of sucks when the death of your woman-beating dad is all over the news." She walked to one of the conference table chairs and sat down. She wore jeans and a sweater—different than the one she'd worn yesterday, but equally baggy. Her long brown hair was pulled back in a ponytail, with a few strands escaping to spiral around her face. There was no mistaking her beauty, although it was dimmed by the distress in her eyes. She didn't bother to introduce her companion, who stood stiffly by the door.

"Your name is Maynard Travers?" Jessie said. He looked too old to be one of Carrie's friends—mid-thirties at the youngest. He wore khaki pants and a plaid button-down shirt. "Are you a friend of the family?"

"Kind of." Travers shifted his weight awkwardly, then cleared his throat.

"He's my dad's sponsor," Carrie said. "From Domestic Violence Anonymous."

Jessie had heard of the program. The victim advocates who worked with the DA's office sometimes referred people to it. It was a twelve-step program similar to Alcoholics Anonymous, for men and women dealing with violent behavior.

"I didn't know Corbin Keeley participated in the program," Jessie said.

"That's the anonymous part," Carrie said, with only a trace of sarcasm in her voice. She looked at Travers. "Tell her."

The man's discomfort seemed to deepen. "I, uh." His voice faltered.

"You were Corbin's sponsor?" Jessie prompted.

"Everyone in the program gets one—someone with experience, available to help with the process. I've been in the program for, ah, six years. I was Corbin's sponsor for about a year. Before him, I was sponsor for a couple other guys. I'm here because Carrie wants me to tell you what I told her. Corbin stuck to the program. Better than anyone I'd sponsored before. He was really dedicated to making it work. He never missed a meeting. He studied all of the literature. He even did the prayers. I do not believe the stories on the news. I don't believe Corbin was hurting his new girlfriend."

"Okay?" Carrie said, as if this settled everything. "Do you believe me now? Brooke Raines is a murderer. Are you going to prosecute her?"

Jessie looked from Carrie to Travers, and back to Carrie, gathering her thoughts. "I appreciate that you came to see me. Mr. Travers, I appreciate your candor and your willingness to share this sensitive information. But the police already conducted an investigation. They concluded that the shooting was in self-defense. I'm sorry, but that's not something I can brush aside just because you don't believe it's true."

Carrie launched from her chair. Her face twisted in anger. "This is bullshit! I'm telling you the truth, and you don't care. This whole system, it's a joke! You don't care about justice. You certainly don't care about my dad."

Before Jessie could respond, Carrie shoved past her, flung the conference room door open, and left. Maynard Travers offered a sheepish shrug.

"Sorry about that," he said. "She's a kid, you know? She doesn't understand how things work in the real world. I'll make sure she gets home okay."

After they were gone, Jessie returned to her office too distraught to focus on her work. She was angry with herself, frustrated. A teenage girl in pain had come to her for help, and how had she handled it? Terribly. Even worse than that, Travers's words echoed in her mind: *She doesn't understand how things work in the real world.* Implying that in the real world, a daughter shouldn't expect justice for her father. That wasn't something she wanted Carrie Keeley to understand. It wasn't what Jessie believed.

She chewed her lip. She knew she should try to put all of this out of her head and focus on her work—on the murder cases, all of them supported by police investigations, that she needed to handle. But she couldn't.

3.

Jessie thanked her Uber driver and hiked up the walk to Carrie Keeley's house. Carrie lived with her mother in a large colonial in Manayunk, a pleasant neighborhood in the northwestern section of the city. When Jessie had called Nina Long (the former Ms. Keeley, who'd reverted to her maiden name after the divorce), the woman had seemed cold and distant, but had reluctantly agreed to a visit when pressed. Now, as the car sped away and she faced the house, she wondered if coming here had been a bad idea.

Everything's on track, she'd told Warren earlier that day. But what track, exactly?

The front door opened. Carrie Keeley stood in the doorway. As Jessie approached her, the girl tucked a stray curl behind her ear. "My mom said you were coming. Did you change your mind? About my dad?"

"I didn't like how we left off this morning. I want to talk."

Carrie frowned, but took a step backward and beckoned Jessie into the house. Jessie followed her through a small foyer and into a kitchen. Everything about the room felt expensive, from the smooth hardwood floors to the custom cabinets. Stainless steel appliances gleamed under bright lights. There was a woman seated at the table. She looked to be in her late-forties or early fifties. She regarded Jessie with pursed lips and a tightened jaw.

"This is my mom," Carrie said.

Jessie approached the woman and extended a hand. "We spoke on the phone. I'm Jessie Black."

"Yes." The older woman shook her hand, but did not rise from her seat. She had close-cut brown hair, a slightly lighter shade than her daughter's. Carrie pulled out the chair next to her mother, causing its legs to squeal against the floor. The woman flinched, but Carrie didn't seem to notice. She dropped into the chair next to her. Side-by-side, the similarity in their faces was so striking that Jessie would have guessed they were mother and daughter even if she hadn't already known.

Jessie sat down across from them. Nina Long's face looked smooth, flawless, but in her mind, Jessie could also see her face the way it had looked in the photograph that had burned itself into her memory. She realized she was staring, looked away, and cleared her throat.

"I understand Carrie tried to convince you that Corbin was murdered," the woman said. She had a clipped, almost aristocratic manner of speech, and Jessie imagined she'd filled her role well as the wife of a city councilman before she'd divorced him. "I told her that would be a waste of time, but...." She shrugged, as if to say, *kids, what can you do?*

"It's never a waste of time to speak your mind," Jessie said.

"Well, maybe not. But no one is going to bring charges against that woman, are they?" Nina seemed calm, but Jessie noticed her hands vibrating where they rested on the table, betraying at least some emotion beneath the smooth veneer. And there was something ... skittish about her. Like the way she'd flinched at the sound of the chair a moment before. Jessie had observed that sort of body language in other victims of domestic abuse, so seeing it now didn't surprise her, but it did make her sad. Here was a woman who was clearly still suffering, yet her daughter was focused on avenging the man who'd terrorized her.

Carrie looked from her mother to Jessie, and her eyes flashed. "I don't know what you're doing here unless you're willing to prosecute my dad's murderer!"

Nina shot her daughter a warning look. "Carrie—"

Jessie said, "It's okay." She offered a sympathetic smile to both women. Neither returned it.

"Why don't you tell us why you *are* here," Nina said.

"Thanks." Jessie felt like she was in unexplored territory. After over a decade in the DA's office, she was used to talking to the family and friends of homicide victims. Forming good relationships with these survivors was both critical to her work as a prosecutor and personally fulfilling to her. Any death of a loved one was emotionally traumatic, but a murder increased the trauma to another level. The people left behind were emotionally devastated. There wasn't much Jessie could do for them—she was a lawyer, not a therapist—but she always did what she could. She listened to them, even when their shock made communication difficult. She made sure to keep them apprised of the case on a daily basis and to check in with them after even the most routine hearings, whether the news was good or bad. She scheduled sessions for them with victim advocates. She gave them tours of the courtroom and prepped them for what they would hear and see there. Most importantly, she made sure they understood that she was on their side. That she was fighting for them and for the victim they loved. But she couldn't say any of that today. And she didn't know what to say instead.

"You're the one who asked for this meeting," Nina said after a few seconds of awkward silence.

"I'm here because Carrie is clearly very upset about the decision not to prosecute Brooke Raines. It's important to me that she—that both of you— understand the facts. This is a case of self-defense, which, under the law—"

"No, it's not," Nina said.

"What?" Jessie came up short. She'd expected to face more resistance from Carrie, but had assumed that Nina, as a victim of Corbin Keeley's violence, would understand the unpleasant reality of the situation. Her ex-husband hadn't changed. If anything, he'd gotten worse.

"The self-defense claim is a lie," Nina said. "Just like Carrie told you."

"How can you of all people say that?"

Nina's stare was unwavering. "Because I know Corbin. I know how hard he worked to change, after our divorce. He stopped drinking. He joined a program. He changed. This woman he was dating, Brooke Raines, is lying. And the police are simply taking her at her word, assuming she's telling the truth because of Corbin's sordid past."

"The police didn't simply take her at her word, or assume anything," Jessie said. "There was a full investigation."

"How do you know?"

Jessie opened her mouth to answer, but no words came. How did she know? "Why would Brooke Raines lie? If Corbin Keeley really changed, like you believe, why would she feel the need for a gun? Why would she shoot him?"

Nina offered another shrug. "Good questions. Did the police ask them?"

"I don't think the police asked *any* questions," Carrie said.

Jessie felt tendrils of doubt in her mind. How could these women be so utterly confident that the police had gotten it wrong? Siding with a loved one was natural, but Nina had personally experienced Keeley's attacks, and still seemed certain that Raines couldn't have been justified in shooting him. Were they in denial? The thought was frightening.

"I'm sure the police did their job," she said, "but if it would make you feel better, I can talk to the lead detective and take a look at the police report. I can come back to you after I've seen exactly what the police found and how they reached their conclusion, and then I'll be able to tell you firsthand how thorough the investigation was."

A look of relief filled Carrie's face. "Thank you!"

Nina, looking less enthusiastic, simply nodded.

"But," Jessie said, "you need to consider carefully whether you really want me to do this."

"You know I want you to," Carrie said.

"Think about this for a minute. If I find what I expect to find, that the evidence supports self-defense, that would mean that your father, as much as you love him, wasn't able to change. Some people can't conquer their demons, no matter how hard they try. Do you really want to learn that your father couldn't conquer his?"

"I won't need to," Carrie said, "because you're going to find out that Brooke Raines's story is a lie."

"Nina...." Jessie said, looking to the girl's mother.

Nina did not look concerned. "We're not afraid of the truth."

Jessie nodded. "Then I guess I have some work to do on this. I'll be in touch soon."

She forced a confident smile, but on the inside, she wondered what the hell she was doing. She wasn't a psychiatrist. Would her intervention help the women—which was what she wanted—or would she only wind up making things worse? Rising from the table, she knew that whatever the answer was, there was no turning back now. She was committed.

4.

The Roundhouse, the headquarters of the Philadelphia Police Department, had acquired its nickname by virtue of its curving shape. The building had become as familiar to Jessie as the DA's office and the courthouse. It was here that the police built the evidentiary foundations of the cases she handled. Or, in the case of Corbin Keeley's death, *didn't handle.*

She rode a creaking elevator that smelled of body odor and disinfectant, walked past an overflowing trash can and a wall of wanted posters, and entered the Homicide Division's squad room. Only about a quarter of the desks were being used at the moment—murder was a nonstop business in Philly, and most of the detectives were out at crime scenes, hunting down witnesses, or testifying in court. She'd checked ahead of time to make sure the lead detective on the Keeley investigation, Detective Kyle Fulco, would be here. But she'd never met him and didn't know what he looked like.

"Jessie Black," a familiar voice boomed to her left and she jumped as a gray-haired man approached her. His was a face she recognized—Toby Novak, a veteran detective who'd been here for as long as anyone could remember.

"How are you doing, Toby?"

He smiled warmly. "Living the dream. If you stopped by to see Emily, you just missed her."

Emily Graham, another detective in the Homicide Division, was Novak's partner. When Jessie first met her during the investigation of a school shooting, she and Graham had not exactly hit it off, but the heart-wrenching case had brought them together. Now she considered Graham one of her closest friends.

"I'm actually looking for someone else," she said. "Kyle Fulco."

Novak made a face. "Full-of-shit Fulco? Look no further." He jabbed a finger in the direction of a cluster of desks to their left. At one of the desks, a man sat in a swivel chair, one shoe propped against the edge of the desk, twirling a pen between his fingers as he stared into a boxy monitor that looked older than Toby. "Right over there," Novak said. "Hard at work as usual."

"I called earlier and told him I'd be stopping by."

"I'm sure he appreciated an excuse to hang around and surf the web all day."

Jessie studied Novak's wry expression and tried to guess if his criticism was serious or just sarcastic cop humor. She couldn't tell. His words might mean nothing. She'd known cops who shared a bond stronger than blood but who spent their days ribbing one another mercilessly. Still, given her reasons for being here, his dismissive tone troubled her. "Full-of-shit Fulco?"

Novak shrugged. "He doesn't seem to mind the nickname."

"I'm sure he loves it," she said dryly.

She crossed the squad room. Fulco seemed to sense her approach, dropping his foot from the desk and turning to watch her. When she reached his work area, he rose from the chair and extended his hand. "I guess you're Jessie?"

They shook. "Good to meet you," she said.

"Likewise. I've heard good things about you."

"Really?" She thought it best not to mention what she'd just heard about him from Toby Novak.

"You're the rising star at the DA's office, right?"

"I don't know about that." She hoped he couldn't see the blush she felt in her neck and cheeks. She'd worked hard to advance through the ranks at the DA's office to become a homicide prosecutor, but even though she knew she was good at what she did, she still felt like she was fighting hard to justify her place there every day.

A crooked grin formed on his narrow face. "On the phone, you said you wanted to talk about Keeley?"

"Yes, if you have a few minutes. Could you walk me through the investigation?"

His smile faded slightly. "Everything's in my report."

"I know, but I'd like to hear it from you."

"Why? You think I missed something?"

"No." The conversation was veering in a bad direction. She forced a smile. "I'm sure you were thorough—especially with a high-profile case involving the shooting of a city councilman. The reason I'm here is someone close to Keeley approached me. They're ... well, they seem in denial about Keeley. About what he was capable of. I want to assure them that our reasons for not charging his shooter are sound."

"So assure them."

"I will. After you bring me up to speed."

"Is that really necessary?"

"I know it's a strange request. Can you humor me on this? I'll owe you a favor."

"Okay. I guess I have some time." Fulco sighed and dropped back into his chair. He gestured for her to take a seat near him. She wheeled a chair away from a vacant desk and sat facing him. "This was October 14," he said. "A Friday. I got a call at about 9:45 at night."

"Was your partner with you?"

"I don't have a partner. Used to. Al Kubacki. He retired, and they haven't assigned me a new one yet."

That seemed unusual, but thinking about his nickname again, she supposed people weren't lining up around the block to volunteer.

"You got a call...."

"You really want every detail? Step by step?"

"If you don't mind."

28

He let out another sigh. "There was a shooting behind Bistro Cannata. That's spelled two Ns, one T. It's a fancy restaurant in the Market East neighborhood."

"I'm familiar with it," Jessie said.

"Yeah?" Fulco arched an eyebrow. "You ever eaten there?"

"Once."

"Well. Look at you."

Jessie ignored his tone. "What did you find at the scene?"

"According to the uniforms who called it in, the vic was Corbin Keeley. I'd never heard of him, but apparently he was a big deal. A city councilman. I don't know what a councilman does, much less what their names are. I guess they write laws for the city or something."

"Close enough." It was a little more complicated than that. They were elected officials who acted as the legislative branch of local government, voting on measures to address the city's needs—infrastructure, growth, strategic planning. Before his death, Corbin Keeley had been the councilman representing District 2, which covered part of Center City, South and Southwest Philly, the stadium area, the airport, and other neighborhoods. Jessie doubted Fulco was in the mood for a civics lecture, so she kept the information to herself.

"Well, anyway, I get to Bistro Cannata," Fulco said. "First thing I see is news vans. Typical, right? You can have ten gang members gunned down in West Philly and maybe a few reporters will show up at the Roundhouse later for a canned statement, but one politician gets his brains blown out by a hot blonde at a fancy restaurant near City Hall, you get a circus at the crime scene."

"You found Brooke Raines attractive?"

Fulco looked startled. "What?"

"You called her 'hot.' Were you attracted to her?"

His eyes narrowed. "What are you implying? That I let her looks affect my judgment?"

"No, I didn't say that."

"I'm attracted to a lot of women. I'm attracted to you. Doesn't mean anything, okay?"

"Fine," she said, embarrassed now and wanting to change the subject. "Do you think the press contaminated the scene?" This was always a concern. Even a minor disturbance of a crime scene by the media or other unauthorized people could lead to the exclusion of evidence at trial.

Fulco shook his head. "The uniforms did a good job corralling the vultures. Not that it matters, right? No trial, so we don't have to worry about contamination."

She didn't want him to jump ahead. "What happened after you arrived at Bistro Cannata?"

"Well, like I said, the scene had already been secured by the first officers—two uniforms, doing their best to keep the reporters and the rubberneckers away from the corpse. The names of the uniforms are in my report, but if you want me to look them up...."

"That's okay. What happened next?"

"I examined the scene. Body on the ground. Bullet hole in the head, right here." He pointed to a spot just above his left eyebrow. "Blood on the pavement. The rock—what was left of it—on the ground at the base of the wall. One of the uniforms—"

"Hold on. What rock?"

His back seemed to stiffen. "You didn't read my report."

"I haven't had time. I will."

He let out another beleaguered sigh. "After he chased her outside, Keeley tried to brain her with a rock. He threw it at her. It hit the wall of the building and broke into pieces. Just missed her head."

Jessie took this detail in. "How big was the rock?"

Fulco shrugged and made a fist. "About the size of my hand."

"Were his prints on it?"

"No, but we won't need prints. No trial, remember?"

"You didn't know that at the time."

"I figured it out pretty quick. While I'm standing there over the body, thinking about bullet trajectories and blood spatter and all that, one of the uniforms walks over and introduces me to a woman who admits to being the shooter."

"Brooke Raines," Jessie said.

"Right. Young and blonde. *Attractive.* Half Keeley's age, if that."

"You disapprove of Keeley's relationship with a younger woman?"

"What I know now about the guy? I disapprove of his relationship with *any* woman."

The lack of objectivity troubled her, but she let it go for the moment. "What did you do?"

Fulco's eyebrows lifted. "What do you think? I told the uniforms to get witness statements from the people in the restaurant, and I took Ms. Raines back to the Roundhouse to get her confession ASAP. Someone wants to confess to a shooting, you don't take them the scenic route."

"You *Mirandized* her?"

"Of course."

"She didn't want a lawyer?"

"Nope. She just wanted to tell me her side of the story. Which, as it turns out, was pretty compelling. Keeley had been physically abusive with her for months. She had enough, tried to break up with him, and he became enraged. He chased her out of the restaurant and attacked her with the rock and she shot him in self-defense."

"Why was she carrying a gun?"

"Because she was afraid of him. She knew he'd get angry."

"Were there any witnesses?"

"To the actual shooting in the parking lot? No one

came forward."

"Did you look for any?"

Fulco's expression shifted. His eyes narrowed and he sounded more guarded as he said, "There wasn't a need."

"No one canvassed the neighborhood for other witnesses?"

"Why are you asking that?"

"I just want to make sure I have the whole story."

"Uh-huh. Well, we have plenty of witnesses inside the restaurant. They didn't see the shooting, but they saw Keeley and Raines arguing and they saw Keeley chase Raines out the door. Does that give you the whole story?"

"What about video cameras? Anything pointed at the parking lot?"

"Yeah, there was one. A jewelry store next to the parking lot had a camera aimed at the street outside its door. Real out-of-date piece of crap, but still functional. The footage is grainy, but the real problem is the camera wasn't pointed in the right direction. You can kind of see some of the parking lot, and maybe glimpse Raines and Keeley pass through its field of view for a second, but that's it. The action went down out of the camera's view."

"Does it clearly show Raines's life was in danger?"

"I just told you. It doesn't show anything."

"I'd like to watch it."

"Great. I'll have a copy sent to your office."

"Did Raines's medical records back up her claims of abuse?"

"Medical records? No. What, now you're doubting she was really abused?"

"I don't know. Did you arrange for a medical examination?"

Fulco shook his head. "For what? To prove Keeley beat her? We weren't looking for evidence against Keeley. He was already dead."

"But how do you know Raines was telling you the truth?"

"Because I know a domestic abuse victim when I see one, okay? Also, I put in a call to Keeley's ex. You want to know the dirt on someone, always go to the ex. After she got past the shock of hearing about his death, she admitted that he'd hit her during their marriage."

"But basically, you just took Brooke Raines's story at face value. Your conclusion that the shooting was justifiable is based almost entirely on her statement."

"No, it isn't." Fulco dug through a drawer of his desk and came back with a folder. He pulled two sheets of paper from it and slapped them down on the desk in front of Jessie. The first was a photograph of a rock, taken on the ground of what she assumed to be the crime scene. It was a big rock, probably bigger than Fulco's hand. Not a gun or a knife, but definitely a weapon if used by an enraged man intent on inflicting harm. The second piece of paper was the infamous photograph of Nina Long's battered face.

"That's Nina Long, not Brooke Raines." Jessie caught herself looking away. She forced her gaze back to the disturbing photo.

"A man who beat his wife like that, you know he beats other women, too," Fulco said.

"But that's not evidence. Not for purposes of the law."

"And like I keep saying—there's no trial, so who cares?"

"*I care.*"

He looked at her and in that moment, something changed. A line was drawn. She sensed that he'd decided she was an enemy. "I don't think I like the tone of this conversation. If you want to say something, come out and say it. You don't think I was thorough? You don't think I did my job?"

"I'm sure you did your job. But you said yourself, the media has taken an interest in this one. We need to make absolutely sure the shooting was really self-defense."

"The media is fully on board with self-defense. They *love* the idea of this wife-beating prick finally getting what he deserved. The news lives for stories like this. It's good versus evil. You know who else is on board? The police department. And the DA. You really want to take this little blonde woman who's a victim of violence and try to say she's the criminal because she killed her abuser?"

She saw the incredulous look on his face. "All I want is the truth."

"The truth is Brooke Raines shot Corbin Keeley in self-defense."

He looked certain. She wished she could feel the same way.

5.

Through the large, plate glass windows of the Acacia building's lobby, Mark Leary spotted Jessie approaching from the parking lot. He walked outside to meet her. The sky was gray and overcast, making the parking lot look even more dreary than usual, but the sight of her brought a smile to his face. They'd been dating for a few years now, but just looking at her could still lift his spirits as if the relationship were brand new. They embraced with a quick hug and kiss. The touch of her lips against his, and the warm press of her body, stirred a strong impulse to hold her tighter, kiss her more passionately, but he restrained himself. They were at his place of business, after all.

She pulled away from him, smiling, and her gaze seemed to take him in. "You must be freezing."

It was November, and he'd come outside without his coat. The wind sliced past his sport jacket. He gritted his teeth against the cold, feeling it now that she'd pointed it out. "I'm okay. You hungry?"

"Starving."

"Great. Let's go inside. I've got an hour and a half

before my next meeting."

He guided her to the corporate cafeteria, introducing her to a few colleagues along the way. They bought food at the counter and found a table for two. It was Jessie's first time seeing the expansive cafeteria that Acacia provided for its employees, and she looked impressed.

"The food's pretty good," he said as they settled into their chairs. "And the coffee beats the hell out of the machines at the Roundhouse."

Jessie's smile faltered, and he silently cursed himself for mentioning police headquarters. It seemed he couldn't go five minutes without thinking about his old job—his old life—as a homicide detective. He knew that Jessie knew that he missed being a cop, and that part of the reason he'd lost that job was because he'd disregarded orders while taking action to save her life. He didn't want her to feel bad about that. *He* certainly didn't.

"I like the jacket," she said.

"Thanks." He smiled. The dress code at Acacia was business casual, but after years wearing a suit, he'd struggled with the khakis and collared shirt most of his colleagues wore. The sport jacket—no tie—seemed like a good compromise.

"Look at you. An executive. Director of Loss Prevention."

Was she sincere, or just trying to make him feel better? He didn't know. And he wished he didn't wonder. When had he become so goddamn introspective? Too much time at a desk had given his mind too much freedom to turn inward.

"So what prompted you to meet me for lunch today?" he said. "Did one of your court appearances get canceled?"

"Actually, I wanted to talk to you about something. When you were still working homicide, did you know a detective named Kyle Fulco?" Her gaze suddenly lowered to her food. Leary studied her face, trying to read her expression. Was that a look of guilt?

"Jessie, it's okay to talk about my old job. I'm a big boy."

"Okay." She met his gaze again.

"I knew Fulco." He felt a smile come to his face. "We used to call him Full-of-shit Fulco."

"People are still calling him that."

"I guess he must still be full of shit."

Jessie's frown, utterly serious, wiped the grin off his face.

"Is he a good detective?" she said.

"Not really. He's lazy. Not very smart. Does the bare minimum to keep his job."

"Great." Her frown depended.

"What's wrong?"

"Nothing. I was just curious about him."

"There's more to it than that. Tell me what's going on."

She was clearly reluctant to do that. "You know the Corbin Keely shooting?"

"Of course. The wife-beater." Leary took a bite of his sandwich, chewed, and swallowed. "His girlfriend killed him. Self-defense, right? He attacked her?"

"That's what the girlfriend told the police."

"The police think differently?"

"No. But if Fulco's as lazy as you say he is.... I don't know. I feel like maybe someone needs to take another look. Maybe I need to."

"Hold on." Leary felt his chest constrict. He lowered her voice, hoping no one in the cafeteria had overheard them. "Keeley's already a huge embarrassment to the city. If the decision's been made not to prosecute Raines, then you don't want to question that. You don't want to go against the PPD and the DA's office. That's what I did, and look what happened to me."

"I know." Jessie let out a sigh and leaned back in her chair. "But Keeley's daughter approached me the other day. Her name is Carrie. She doesn't believe her father was hurting Brooke Raines. She thinks the whole self-defense claim is a lie, and that Keeley was murdered."

"Why would she approach *you*?"

"Because no one else would listen."

"What did you tell her?"

"I promised her and her mother that I would check over the police file, make sure the self-defense claim was supported by a thorough investigation."

"Why would you promise that?"

Jessie offered a weak smile. "I don't know. I guess it's just the way I am."

He nodded grimly. He couldn't argue with that, and he wouldn't want her to change. "It sounds like the girl is in serious denial. I mean, come on. She thinks the girlfriend lied about the abuse just so she could kill Keeley? That puts us squarely in the conspiracy theory zone."

"I know."

Leary sighed. "It's not ideal, but if you made the promise.... Just let her down easy. Tell her you talked to Fulco and read the file and everything checks out."

Jessie moved her fork around her plate. "That's the problem. I'm not sure everything *does* check out." Her gaze rose to meet his, and he could see from the turmoil in her beautiful green eyes that she was struggling with this. "I'm not saying I agree with Carrie. Her father beat her mother brutally. I mean, he was a monster. The idea that a few years later, he could have changed completely and become a new man incapable of that kind of violence? I understand why Carrie would want to believe that, and his ex-wife, to a lesser extent. They loved him. But I don't believe it."

"It's much more likely that Keeley didn't change," he agreed.

"Right. But...." Her voice trailed off, and she looked at her plate again.

"Something tells me I'm not going to like what you're about to say."

"The law on self-defense in Pennsylvania is clear. It's established. Use of deadly force is only justifiable when the person believes it's necessary to protect herself against the imminent use of unlawful force by the other person. And it must be proportional. If somebody threatens to punch you, you can't pull a knife to defend yourself. I'm not sure the facts here—at least the ones Fulco told me—really support self-defense. Raines broke up with Keeley, and he got mad. He chased her out of a restaurant and threw a rock at her. She responded by shooting him in the head."

Leary felt his eyebrows arch. He saw her point. "Was it a really big rock?"

"It was a decent-sized rock. The point is, I probably shouldn't have agreed to look into this case in the first place, but now that I have, as an assistant district attorney, I think it's my obligation to make sure that Brooke Raines isn't walking away after engaging in criminal behavior."

The feeling of unease returned to Leary's stomach. "Maybe it's not a textbook example of self-defense, Jessie, but you need to think about the big picture. Corbin Keeley is hated by a lot of people as a violent, abusive man who got away with terrorizing his wife because of his political connections. People are happy that he finally got what was coming to him. If the police or the DA's office go after Raines, people are going to ask why they didn't go after Keeley years ago. Do you see where I'm going with this?

Prosecuting Raines is politically dangerous."

Jessie frowned. "I hate politics."

"I know. So stay out of this mess. Tell the girl that the police investigation was handled appropriately and that there's nothing more to it."

Jessie looked at him with a knowing and sad smile. "I can't do that yet. Not until I believe it myself."

Exactly what he knew she was going to say. "Fine. I'll help you, then."

"No." She shook her head. "That would make it worse. You're not a cop anymore. You're a civilian. It would be totally inappropriate to bring you into this. And, aside from that, I—" She cut herself off abruptly.

"What, Jessie?" He sensed she was treading carefully around him again. "What were you going to say?"

"I don't think getting involved with this would be good for you psychologically. I know the transition from cop to civilian hasn't been easy. I think you helping me on this case would be a bad idea."

"Thanks for the vote of confidence." Leary pushed away the rest of his food. His appetite was gone, for more reasons than one. He wanted to help her, but she seemed to think *he* was the one in need of help. The worst part? He wasn't sure which of them was right.

"Leary, don't.... I didn't mean to insult you."

"It's fine," he said. "Let's eat, okay? And talk about something else."

"Good idea."

They talked about a new restaurant he'd heard served amazing wings, then about the arguments she'd been having with her father about his increasingly erratic driving. They laughed over a shared memory—funny only in retrospect—of a terrifying ride to a Wawa with her dad behind the wheel. It was a good lunch.

But later, as he walked her back to her car, his mind returned to Keeley.

6.

Merging onto the highway, Dave Whittaker cursed as his phone's Bluetooth signal lost its connection to his car again. He'd have to go through the pairing process again. So frustrating.

First world problems, he thought. It was all a matter of perspective, wasn't it? He was a well-off man—hell, a rich man—getting worked up about a minor problem with his eighty-thousand-dollar car on his way to the multi-million-dollar company of which he was one of the owners. He shook his head and tried to smile at himself. But the smile wouldn't come. *I am beset by first world problems.*

He parked in his reserved space and took the elevator to his top-floor office and sat in the ergonomically optimized chair behind the enormous cherry wood desk and stared out the floor-to-ceiling windows at a breathtaking view of the Philadelphia skyline. At least, it used to take his breath away. But like so much else in life, the view that had once filled him with hope and enthusiasm and pride in his accomplishments was now just another mundane detail of his life that he barely noticed. He might as well be sitting in front of a plain wall.

His beautiful assistant brought him a steaming cup of gourmet coffee with milk and sugar stirred precisely to his tastes. The mug sat on his desk and its contents cooled.

The mug was emblazoned with the logo of his firm—the words *CBL Capital Partners* below a stylized outline of Philly. CBL originally stood for City of Brotherly Love, but now it was just some letters and they meant nothing.

Dave Whittaker sat motionless and in silence for fifteen minutes, then sipped his coffee, which was now lukewarm and disgusting. He thought, it doesn't matter how gourmet your coffee is, at room temperature it's going to taste like crap. Was that a metaphor? Maybe he was getting poetic in his middle age.

Two months ago, Dave had turned forty. The big Four-Oh. But he didn't think it was his age that was causing his sour outlook on life. He knew it wasn't his age. It was something worse. It was his conscience.

I need to confront him, he thought. *I need to challenge him, flat out.*

He glared at the closed door of his office as if his gaze could pierce the heavy wood and penetrate all he way down the hall and around the corner to Luther Goyle's office. But his body didn't move.

Am I afraid of him? That thought almost made Dave laugh. Dave had grown up in North Philly, just another poor black kid in the ghetto, until clawing his way to college and then to a career in the financial industry. His childhood had been terrible, an absolute horror-show, every stereotype you could imagine. But it had one benefit. After living through it, there wasn't much in the upper-class world that could scare him.

Goyle, on the other hand, had been born in some fancy suburb in Connecticut, spent most of his youth at an elite private school in New Hampshire, sailed through college and law school—both Ivy League, naturally—and then parked himself at a global law firm before joining CBL as its general counsel—the chief lawyer. If Goyle had ever been in a fight, Dave imagined it had involved lots of slapping.

No, he thought, *I'm not afraid of him.* And he got up from his chair and he went to talk to the man.

Dave found Luther Goyle seated behind a big desk of his own, in an office almost as large as Dave's, with a view almost as good. Not for the first time, Dave looked at the obese, pale-skinned man and thought, *bringing him on board was the biggest mistake we ever made.*

The lawyer was a full partner in their firm, but not one of the founding partners. Dave and his friend, Jack Woodside, had founded the venture capital firm together fifteen years ago. Back then, they had been a couple of twenty-something Wall Street investment bankers with more money than common sense and big dreams of doing something meaningful.

Dave and Jack had left New York and founded

CBL Capital Partners in the city of Philadelphia, where they'd both come from. The company's mission had been as simple as it had been idealistic: to give something back—and make lots of money doing it—by finding the most exciting startups in the city and funding them.

Goyle had joined them later, after the firm had grown into a significant force in the investment capital world by backing several breakout tech companies. Flush with money, CBL had gone on a hiring spree, and one of their hires had been a lawyer. After all, why continue to outsource their legal work to high-priced law firms when they could have the work done in-house? That had been the theory, anyway.

At the time, Luther Goyle had been a partner at a major law firm headquartered in Manhattan. He was known for two specialties—investment work and mergers and acquisitions. His client base included venture capital firms like CBL that funded companies, and investment firms that specialized in taking control of undervalued companies through hostile takeovers. Dave and Jack had hired him for his expertise in the former.

But it wasn't long before he got to use his skills in the latter, too.

A year or so after Goyle joined as GC, CBL hit a period of turbulence. The economy took a turn for the worse, and several of the firm's investments imploded at the same time, along with a lot of the firm's money. Goyle came to Dave and Jack with a proposition.

There was a metal manufacturing company based in Conshohocken, Pennsylvania. It was struggling, but it had valuable assets. Goyle proposed buying a controlling stake in the company—via a hostile takeover, if necessary—and then liquidating those assets. Dave and Jack protested at first. They hadn't started CBL to become corporate raiders. But Goyle was persuasive. And they needed the money to get back to the venture work they loved.

The company in Conshohocken had been their first takeover. Three-hundred-and-twenty-five jobs lost. Everyone from the CEO down to the janitorial staff. Then auctions on the equipment, the buildings, the land. After all was said and done, Goyle's scheme netted them a profit of several million dollars.

After that first takeover, they'd gone back to their core venture capital business. But they continued to struggle to make a profit on their investments. It turned out their early success had been attributable as much to luck as talent, and their luck had turned bad. Finding promising young companies and growing and nurturing them was a lot riskier, and didn't pay nearly as well, as finding ailing companies and devouring them. So they did more of that. Goyle continued to prove his value, and when he pushed to be made a partner in the firm, they'd agreed—which, Dave now realized, had been its own version of a hostile takeover.

In the short term, it had seemed like a good move. Dave and Jack got rich. And when Dave felt bad about turning away from his dream of giving back to his city, he thought about his wife and children and the beautiful house he'd provided for them along with all the other luxuries he'd never had growing up, and he figured he was doing the right thing.

Problem was, it got harder to tell himself that when people started dying.

Goyle had an iPad clutched in his meaty hands. He put it down on his desk when Dave entered, and Dave saw dense text on the screen. The fat man was always online. Dave knew he frequented several forums, Facebook groups, and email lists tracking vulnerable and undervalued companies. Stalking his next victim.

"Good morning, Dave," Goyle said. He leaned back in his chair, and the springs creaked. "You here to discuss Anders Innovations?"

"What?" Dave said. The question took him off-guard. He'd been too preoccupied with other concerns lately to focus on his actual work, and the Anders Innovations deal was the furthest thing from his mind. "No, not that."

"Okay...." Goyle's eyebrows were thin, oily-looking black lines. They rose now on his pale face, an exaggerated expression Goyle used when he wanted someone to get to the point. "What's on your mind?"

Just say it, Dave told himself. "Corbin Keeley."

The name brought a toothy smile to Goyle's face. "Yes, I've been following the story. Shocking, isn't it? The reporters say he'd been beating his girlfriend. She had to kill him in self-defense, apparently." Goyle shook his head and made a clucking sound as his smirk spread across his doughy face. "Some people just have no decency."

"Just what I was thinking."

"On the bright side," Goyle said, shrugging, "the councilman's death means a certain bill you and I are both keenly interested in is much more likely to pass. Guaranteed to, I'd almost say."

"Yes, it's very convenient."

Goyle exhaled loudly. "Do I sense some judgment in your tone?" His beady eyes seemed to drill into Dave, as if challenging him to make an accusation. *Well, challenge accepted.*

"I'm not an idiot. I know what you did. You promised me this would never happen again."

Goyle snorted a laugh. "I don't know what you're talking about, Dave. Listen, I've got a lot on my plate this morning. Why don't we chat another time?"

"Don't try to blow me off. I'm still a partner in this company, last time I checked."

"Of course you are. All the more reason to see the positive aspects of this tragic occurrence. I can see, oh, about ten million of them."

"I started this firm to help my city."

"Yes, I noticed you've got a little martyr complex going on. You should really work on getting over that, Dave. The problem with martyrs is, they usually get themselves killed."

"So now you're threatening *me?* Where does it

end, Luther?"

"Sometimes the people close to the martyrs get hurt, too. Their friends. Wives. Children."

Dave felt the skin on the back of his neck crawl. "Fuck you."

"Why don't you go and read the paperwork on Anders Innovations? Put your mind to productive use. Don't dwell so much on the negative stuff."

"I suppose I should leave the negative stuff to you, huh?"

"I think that would be best for everyone." And he picked up his iPad and returned his attention to whatever he'd been reading, leaving Dave standing there as if he'd been dismissed from the room and from the man's thoughts.

Dave felt his molars grind. His hands clenched into fists. He stood there impotently for a moment, watching Goyle read his iPad as if he weren't in the room. Then he turned and stepped toward the door.

Coward, he accused himself. *After all these years, you're nothing but a coward. Even worse, a complicit coward.*

"You know," Goyle said to his back, "your friend Jack doesn't share your ethical concerns. Maybe you should talk to him."

Could that be true? Dave had assumed he'd been the only one to discover Goyle's secret, criminal behavior. Could Jack really be aware of it, too—and worse, comfortable with it? It didn't seem possible. *Not Jack.*

"Talk to him," Goyle repeated. "Maybe he can help you get your head on straight, before you make a mistake you can't recover from. Corbin Keeley is dead and the investigation into his death is closed. Trust me—anyone who tries to open it is going to wish they hadn't."

7.

Jessie stood in the parking lot outside Bistro Cannata. She shivered against the cold and looked around. In the bright, autumn sunshine, the black asphalt, white lines, and random assortment of cars looked like any other lot in the city. The sounds of traffic and wind seemed utterly ordinary. None of the gory details from the night of the shooting were visible now—during the intervening month, all of the blood spatters had been washed away, human remains taken to the morgue, rock fragments bagged and transported to an evidence locker, and the police tape removed. She turned at the sound of a car engine. A sedan rolled into the lot and parked. Its doors opened and two men climbed out and walked past her toward the restaurant. One of them gave her a friendly nod as he walked by, probably assuming she was here for lunch and not to investigate a possible murder.

She paced the length of the parking lot, trying to visualize the crime scene. *Crime scene.* The phrase repeated in her head, and she winced. Had she started to believe that a crime had been committed? She identified the area where Keeley's body had fallen, and the section of wall where his weapon—the rock—had crashed against the bricks.

Leary's warnings were fresh in her mind. *Prosecuting Raines is politically dangerous*, he'd said. *Stay out of this mess.* He was right, but he was wrong, too. Finding out the truth was an obligation, both a professional and a moral one. She examined the rest of the parking lot and then found the jewelry store and the video camera over its entrance.

Once she was satisfied that she'd seen everything worth seeing outside—which wasn't much—she entered Bistro Cannata. Warmth and noise enveloped her the moment she stepped through the door. Being featured in TV broadcasts and news articles as the scene of a shooting had apparently not deterred people from coming here. The publicity seemed to have increased interest in the place. The dining room roared with conversation, the clinking of glasses, and the scratching of silverware. Wait staff and busboys hurried from table to table.

A hostess dressed in a black cocktail dress asked her if she had a lunch reservation.

"I'm actually here to speak with the manager. My name is Jessica Black. I'm an assistant district attorney."

The hostess glanced behind her to a door Jessie assumed led to the kitchen and back rooms of the restaurant. "Jerry is the owner. Please wait here. I'll see if he's available."

Jessie stood by the entrance as the hostess

navigated between the packed tables. Bistro Cannata was a five-star restaurant in the Market East neighborhood. Close to City Hall, it was known as a lunch and dinner destination for politicians, businessmen, and lawyers. Depending on your point of view, the decor inside was either classic or old-fashioned, the jacket-and-tie dress code either classy or pretentious. Jessie had only eaten here once, as a guest at a DA's office event. She'd found the atmosphere stuffy, but the delicious food had made up for it. She smelled that food now, and her stomach rumbled.

The hostess returned, hurrying to keep up with a man Jessie supposed was the owner. He was tall, middle-aged, with a dark complexion, close-cut, shiny black hair, and thick black eyebrows. Coming toward her quickly, with a purposeful, almost angry-looking stride, he glared at her. He wore a suit that looked fancier than ones she'd seen worn by top-tier defense attorneys.

"I'm Jerry Bonarini," he said as he reached her. He did not extend his hand. "What's this about? We're very busy with the lunch rush, as you can see."

"I only need a few minutes of your time. I'd like to ask you some questions about the night of Friday, October 14, when Councilman Keeley was shot here."

Bonarini glared at the hostess, as if she were to blame for the imposition. "No one was shot *here*. The councilman was shot outside, in a parking lot I don't own."

"I just have a few questions, Mr. Bonarini."

"I already spoke with the police. In fact, they forced me to close my restaurant for three whole hours. They asked me the same questions over and over again. They harassed my customers and my staff. It was ridiculous."

Three hours? Fulco hadn't even closed the place down for a full day to make sure no evidence was overlooked or lost?

"I'm sorry for the inconvenience," she said, since the man obviously didn't realize he'd gotten off easy. "I'm sure you can understand that when a shooting occurs, it's critical that we get all the facts. That's why I'm here now to talk to you again."

Bonarini continued to glare at her. "The shooting had nothing to do with my restaurant, Ms...."

"Black. You can call me Jessie."

"As I have said innumerable times, it occurred outside in a parking lot I don't own. And, as I understand it, the police have already resolved the matter. So what more facts could you possibly need?"

"Were you here that night?"

Bonarini's gaze strayed to the people dining in his restaurant. At a few of the closer tables, people had turned to look at him and Jessie. At the table closest to where they stood, the two men who'd walked past her outside stopped talking to stare and listen.

Bonarini pitched his voice lower. "You're causing a scene."

"That's not my intention." She wondered why he cared. The notoriety had obviously increased his lunch rush, and the people around them seemed happy to consider her arrival as free entertainment. "Is there somewhere more private where we can talk? An office in the back?"

"Am I legally required to talk to you?"

Jessie hesitated. It was only for a second, but it was apparently enough to embolden him.

"That's what I thought," he said, before she could respond. "I want you to leave my restaurant immediately. I have already spoken with the police. *At length.* I cooperated fully. I'm done."

He turned his back on her and signaled the hostess over to them with a snap of his fingers. "Angie, please call the police if this woman refuses to leave."

The hostess's eyes widened. "I thought she was with the DA's office."

"Are you questioning me?"

The woman quickly looked at her shoes.

"It's okay," Jessie said, speaking up. "I'll come back another time, when you're less busy."

"I'm always busy," Bonarini said. Then he stormed away, back to the door through which he'd come.

Angie looked at Jessie with a nervous expression, and Jessie offered what she hoped was a reassuring nod. "I'll go."

She walked outside into the sunlight, the noise of mid-day traffic, and the cold. If her objective had been to glean useful information from Jerry Bonarini, she'd failed spectacularly. *Well, that's why I'm a lawyer and not a detective.*

She was about to leave when someone cleared his throat loudly behind her.

Jessie turned. A man had come out of the restaurant. He was young and tall, and wore the black pants and shirt that seemed to be the uniform of the Bistro Cannata waiters. His long, dark hair was secured in a ponytail.

"Hey, you said you're with the DA's office, right?"

"Yes. Jessica Black." She extended her hand. He hesitated for a moment, then shook it.

"My name's Greg Clifford. You're here about the shooting?"

"Yes. I had some questions. Were you working that night?"

"I had their table."

"You waited on Keeley and Raines?" Jessie tried to keep the excitement out of her voice. *Finally, a break.*

"Yeah. Listen, I don't have much time. The lunch crowd is nuts today, and Jerry will kill me if he catches me out here. I just thought, since you're here, I should tell you something. You know, for the record."

Jessie wasn't sure what he meant. "For the record?"

"To set things straight. I saw on the news, they're saying Keeley was drinking. One website even had a whole thing about how he was rumored to be a recovering alcoholic, and he must have fallen off the wagon. But it's not true. Only his date was drinking. I know because I was the one pouring the wine."

"Keeley was sober?"

Jessie would need to double-check Fulco's report. She was pretty sure the detail that Keeley had been drinking had come from Brooke Raines's statement. Had Fulco simply taken her word for it?

"Well, I couldn't tell you that for sure," Clifford said. "But I know he wasn't drinking wine with his dinner. He ordered an ice tea and that's all he drank."

Jessie chewed her lip. If Keeley hadn't been drinking, and Raines had claimed he was, then that would be an inconsistency in her story. It might be a minor inconsistency—she could imagine a distraught woman making a mistake—but what if there were more?

"Is there anything else you can you tell me? Did you hear any of their conversation?"

"Some of it. It was awkward as hell. First few times I walked over to the table, they were talking about the weather. Then she must have broken the news that she was leaving him, because he was asking why and she was telling him she didn't want to discuss it, she just wanted out. Then she got up and left and he followed her."

"Followed or chased?" The exchange the waiter had just described didn't sound like the angry argument that had been recounted by Fulco and later reported in the news.

The waiter squinted at her. "What do you mean? I don't know. I guess he chased after her. But he wasn't running or anything. She got up and left, and then he put his napkin on the table and got up and left, too. On his way out he told the hostess he'd be back to settle up."

Keeley had paused to tell the hostess he'd be back to settle up? That didn't sound like the action of an enraged man rushing outside to hurt or kill a woman in a violent rage.

"The same hostess working now? Angie?"

Clifford nodded. "Yeah."

"Did she tell that to the police?"

The waiter shrugged. "I don't know. Jerry didn't want us talking too much, you know? A lot of our customers are political bigwigs. He said they need to know we're not eavesdropping on them, waiting to run to the police to report on them." He shrugged, and his ponytail bobbed. "Makes sense, I guess."

Jessie did not agree. In fact, the more she heard, the less seemed to make sense.

8.

After speaking with Greg Clifford outside Bistro Cannata, Jessie went back inside to ask Angie if she remembered Keeley pausing on his way out the door to tell her he would return to settle the bill. She did. Jessie thanked her and Clifford. When she left, she decided to go home rather than back to the office.

She wanted to review the police file and compare it to the information she'd just received while it was still fresh in her mind. At her apartment, she carried a folder of documents to the couch, along with a steaming cup of coffee, and folded her legs under her.

Two things she'd learned bothered her—first, that Corbin Keeley might not have been drinking alcohol the night of the shooting, and second, that he'd taken the time, while supposedly chasing a woman, to stop and tell the hostess that he would come back for the bill. These details were minor, but they disturbed her anyway—because they did not mesh with what Fulco had told her. They also didn't seem to mesh with the elements of a self-defense claim under Pennsylvania law, which required that Raines reasonably believed she was in imminent danger of death or serious bodily injury, that it was necessary to use deadly force against Keeley to prevent such harm, and that she had no ability to retreat.

The police file was thin for a homicide investigation. Apparently, Fulco had felt comfortable closing the case after only a minimal investigation. Flipping through the documents now, she found Raines's statement, a small collection of witness statements, and an autopsy report from the ME. The witness statements had been taken by the uniformed officers who'd interviewed the customers and staff of Bistro Cannata after Fulco whisked Raines away to the Roundhouse. It appeared that the detective himself had not followed up with any of those witnesses.

She flipped to those witness statements now. She was looking for evidence that would back up Fulco's conclusions and contradict what the waiter, Greg Clifford, had told her. Maybe Keeley had been seen pouring his own wine, for example, or even sneaking sips from a flask. And maybe the waiter had downplayed the violence of the altercation, or the urgency of Keeley's exit.

She read every witness statement. None of the witnesses reported seeing Keeley drink. None of the statements mentioned alcohol at all. Unfortunately, it did not appear that the police asked the question. Jessie supposed that Fulco probably had not yet learned of the role alcohol had supposedly played, so the police had not known to ask. Later, when the case appeared cut-and-dried, no one followed up.

There were numerous references to Keeley

"walking" out of the restaurant after Raines. One diner stated that Keeley spoke to the hostess on his way out, which corroborated what the waiter and hostess had told her. With regard to the argument itself, no one described any yelling or violent behavior. Keeley and Raines did not appear to have made a scene. Had the shooting not occurred, it seemed probable that no one would have remembered that they'd argued at all.

Jessie turned to a series of pages covered in feminine handwriting. Brooke Raines's statement, which Fulco had asked her to write out after she'd told them her story.

The first thing Jessie noted was how neat each line of blue ink appeared. There were barely any crossed-out words or sentences. No extra details or explanations had been crammed into the margins. Nothing to show Raines's thought process or even show that she'd been putting her thoughts to paper on the fly. If anything, the tidy writing implied the opposite. One sentence flowed to the next in logical order. It was as if Brooke Raines had already had the entire story fully composed ahead of time in her mind, and all she'd needed to do was write it down.

That might mean nothing. Brooke Raines wasn't your typical confessed killer. She was educated, probably used to writing, and her good penmanship wasn't exactly compelling evidence against her. Plus, she'd just spent a few hours verbally explaining the shooting to Fulco, so that process could have helped organize her thoughts before a pad of paper was placed in front of her.

Still, Jessie had seen many statements in her time as an assistant DA. This one, before she even read its substance, just *looked* wrong.

And its substance increased, rather than eased, her suspicions:

I decided to end the relationship at a restaurant because doing it in a public place seemed safer than alone in one of our apartments. I just wanted to end things and leave, without getting thrown against a wall or kicked in the stomach or something much worse, which I knew he was capable of. Even in public, I wasn't sure I would be safe. That's why I brought my gun. I have a license to carry concealed. You can check it. Shooting is one of my hobbies. My father got me into it when I was a teenager, and I've been target shooting for years.

She could imagine Fulco absorbing all of these details and thinking he'd won the jackpot—a homicide investigation he could close in less than a day, *no muss, no fuss*—no need to even testify in court, since no charges would be brought. A lazy cop's dream come true.

Corbin didn't take it well at all. He started to yell at me, right there at our table in the restaurant. It was scary and embarrassing, and it just reinforced to me that he was a damaged person and that I needed to get out of this toxic relationship before he hurt me really bad.

But Greg Clifford and the witnesses in the file reported a subdued argument, not the kind of yelling Raines described. Did that mean her description rose to the level of a lie? Maybe not. Jessie could only imagine what it would be like to suffer in an abusive relationship. She supposed it was possible that, subjectively, Keeley's behavior had seemed scarier and louder to Raines, who knew his violent patterns and recognized the danger signs, than to casual onlookers. She kept reading.

I realized I should have tried to stop Corbin from ordering wine. He was always at his worst when he'd been drinking.

Hadn't Clifford told her, with confidence, that only Raines had drunk the wine and that Keeley had limited himself to ice tea?

I ran out of the restaurant. When I dared to look back, I saw Corbin running after me. He was moving fast and he looked furious. I'd seen that look before, the last time he hit me. It was terrifying.

Jessie sipped coffee as she studied the words. Raines had twice used the word "run," yet that didn't seem corroborated by the witnesses.

He said he was going to kill me. He grabbed a rock off the ground and hurled it at my head. I felt it whip past my head and I saw it hit the wall of the building and I knew if it had hit me, it could have killed me. There was no way I could get to my car and get away before he reached me. I had no choice. I pulled my gun out of my purse and I shot him.

The scene that played in her mind's eye was chilling. But there were no witness statements to back it up, and the only security camera in the vicinity had failed to capture the incident. Could she really rely on

Raines's account of what had happened outside when several key details she'd given about what had happened inside the restaurant were questionable? Doubting the honesty—or at least the accuracy—of a domestic abuse victim made her feel sick to her stomach, but she couldn't ignore her instincts.

Jessie flipped through the file. The next document that caught her eye was the autopsy report from the medical examiner. The ME's language was clinical, a dry recitation of observations and measurements: *On the left upper forehead, 1/2 inch to the left of the anterior midline, there is a gunshot entry wound. This wound consists of a 5/16 inch circular hole with circumferential abrasion and slight marginal radial laceration.* Jessie skimmed the report, understanding the gist—Keeley had died from a gunshot to the head, which she already knew—but lacking the expertise to derive other clues from the language.

She had one more trip she needed to make before she could call it a day. She needed to meet with the ME.

9.

Andrew Dale, the deputy medical examiner who performed Corbin Keeley's autopsy, was working. That meant Jessie had to brave the unpleasant smell and icy air of the morgue to meet with him. No matter how many times her job required her to visit this place, its tiled floor and walls, stainless steel tables and operating room sinks, and lack of any windows or natural light always made her skin crawl.

That sensation increased tenfold when she saw what Dale had waiting for her.

Dale had laid Corbin Keeley's body on a table. Surgical stitches tugged the rubbery flesh where the autopsy incisions had been closed. There were traces of a handsome face, marred by the gunshot wound and the ME's work. His eyes stared lifelessly at the ceiling. His lips were slightly parted in a blank expression. Jessie had to force herself to look at him.

It was strange, but seeing his body—which, in death, looked utterly devoid of humanity—was the first time she saw him as a person, instead of as a woman-beating stereotype.

He's the victim. She realized that somehow, against her nature, she had forgotten this obvious fact. With the photograph of Nina Long's horribly bruised and swollen face stuck in her mind, she'd never focused on the photographs of Keeley. She'd never stopped thinking of Keeley as the aggressor, so she'd never focused on him as a victim.

Dale, a short man who always seemed to be smiling, was grinning at her now. He had a bald head that gleamed under the morgue's harsh overhead lights. "I thought I'd surprise you with a visual demonstration."

"Thanks," she said, still distracted by her thoughts. When her head cleared, she said, "I'm surprised you still have the body. Didn't the family ask for it to be released after the investigation closed?"

"No," he said. "Actually, they insisted we keep him." Dale gave Keeley's ankle an affectionate pat with a gloved hand. "They said they were in the process of persuading the police to reopen the investigation. I assume that's why you're here."

Jessie knew the morgue sometimes kept bodies for months if justified by the needs of an ongoing investigation or trial. Usually family members objected, just wanting to bury their loved ones and move on. But Carrie and her mother were not the usual family members.

"We haven't made any decisions yet," she said. She returned his smile, although doing so while standing over a corpse felt unnatural. "Just trying to be thorough."

"Right." Dale gave her a pair of gloves. The smell of latex filled her nose, mingling with the other odors of the room—chemicals and the faint stink of decay. She suppressed a gag. Dale didn't seem to notice. He gave the corpse another friendly pat. "So what can I tell you about the councilman?"

Jessie looked at the body again. Glassy, dead eyes stared back at her. "Tell me about your autopsy."

"Manner of death was homicide. Cause of death was a gunshot wound to the head." Dale gestured at the entrance wound in Keeley's forehead. "Not exactly a medical mystery."

"I guess not." Jessie wondered if she'd ever be able to speak about a victim with the detachment of Dale's matter-of-fact tone. She doubted it. The room suddenly felt chillier. "Is there anything you found interesting or unusual?"

Dale shrugged. "I don't know if I'd say that. But...." His voice trailed off.

"But what, Andrew?"

He seemed to hesitate. "This isn't a medical observation, which is why I didn't include it in my report. But I did wonder."

"Wonder about what?" She tried to keep her voice level as she urged him to continue.

"Look at the entrance wound." He pointed a gloved finger at the hole in Keeley's forehead, a few inches above his left eye. "You see the round shape and the surrounding margin of abrasion, consistent with a gunshot wound. This," he said, moving his finger around the edge of the hole, "is gunpowder stippling. You see the width of the stippling? That indicates that the bullet was fired from an intermediate range—not close-up."

"Okay...." Jessie said. "That's strange?"

"Brooke Raines claims she was fleeing from Keeley, in fear of her life, right? She ran into the parking lot. He threw a big rock at her. She got her gun out of her purse and fired at him. We know, from the body, that she fired from some distance. What are the chances of a panicked woman, firing from a distance, hitting Keeley in the head?"

"She had experience with guns. She was licensed to carry concealed, and had been for years."

Dale made a face. "Even excellent marksmen don't hit their targets when they fire in a panic—not in my experience, anyway, and I see a lot of gunshot wounds. If I were to guess, I'd say Ms. Raines pulled her gun calmly, carefully took aim, and shot him. And that's not how your typical self-defense shooting plays out, is it?"

Jessie's mouth felt dry. "No."

"And there's another thing, too," Dale said.

"What?"

"The stories in the papers keep saying Keeley had a drinking problem."

Jessie nodded. "I meant to ask you about that."

"According to the toxicology report, Keeley's

blood alcohol concentration was zero. He may have had a drinking problem, but he wasn't drinking at all on the night of his death."

"Did you tell Detective Fulco about the tox report?"

"Of course."

"What did he say?"

Dale shrugged. "By the time we got the tox results in, the case was already closed. He said it wasn't relevant."

"He said that?"

Dale nodded. "You know what they call him, right? Fulco?"

Jessie nodded. "Yeah, I'm familiar with his nickname. I guess he's not the city's most dedicated employee."

"It's not my call, obviously," Dale said with a shrug, "but if you want my opinion? You should reopen the case."

10.

Mark Leary sat in front of his computer monitor, ensconced in his cubicle on the outer edge of the cubicle farm of the fifth floor of the Acacia headquarters building. All around him, he could hear people typing, talking to each other, talking into phones. He knew some people complained that the noise and lack of privacy made concentration difficult, but he had no problem focusing. After years in the bullpen—the open-floor squad room that the detectives of the Philly PD Homicide Division used as their workspace—the cube farm felt almost familiar.

His environment wasn't stopping him from concentrating, but his mind was. Instead of keeping his attention on the task at hand—studying a compilation of shoplifting reports that he needed to review and analyze—he kept thinking about the case Jessie had told him about. The Keeley shooting.

The daughter's theory, that the self-defense claim was actually a cover for murder, was a novel—almost silly—idea. And yet, the possibility intrigued him. He could see how an intelligent murderer could pull it off. In fact, he could see how it could be pulled off pretty easily, especially with an unsympathetic victim like Corbin Keeley, with his ugly history of domestic abuse. A victim like Keeley was unlikely to generate much sympathy in a court of law or in the court of public opinion. *Yeah*, people would think, *he'd been shot in the head, but by whom? A woman half his size, and half his age, who feared for her life.* Or claimed she did.

It could be done. It could easily be done. And what really captured his attention was that he was pretty sure he'd seen it done before.

His gaze ticked to the work he should be doing—a PDF document open on his screen—but instead of reading about the wild and crazy adventures of America's shoplifters as told through statistics and the driest corporate jargon imaginable, he minimized the document and opened his web browser.

He typed in a name he hadn't thought about in years. *Lydia Wax.*

Google returned a list of search results that was longer than he would have anticipated given what he'd assumed to be a fairly uncommon name. He scrolled down the page of links—LinkedIn and Facebook profiles, a few random websites and blogs, people directories, some of which would charge a fee to conduct a public records search. His pointer hovered over one of the LinkedIn hits.

He wanted to click, but he knew he would be starting down a rabbit hole that could occupy him for the rest of the day. And that wasn't a good idea. He should be doing his job—his *real* job, the one that issued his paychecks—not dwelling on his former one.

He clicked anyway. A LinkedIn page opened and he saw immediately that the Lydia Wax in the photograph was not the Lydia Wax he was looking for. An image of *his* Lydia Wax appeared in crystal clear detail in his mind, and he was surprised that his brain had committed her face so thoroughly to memory. *It's because I knew she was lying. I always knew, even when we closed the case.*

He could still recall the night vividly. Three years ago. He and his partner at the time, Paul Strickland, were sent to a suburban house where a man had just been stabbed. They arrived to find uniformed officers securing the scene and a woman sitting at the kitchen table staring at her own blood-covered hands.

The woman had perked up when they arrived, as if she'd been waiting for them. She told them right away that she'd stabbed the man, Terence Resta, the owner of the house. The woman didn't want a lawyer. She didn't want to remain silent. She wanted to make a full confession. Leary and Strickland accommodated her, right there in the kitchen.

It was self-defense, she claimed. Resta, whom she'd been seeing for only a few months, had a horrible temper. He was jealous, irrational, and violent. That night, she had summoned her courage and told him she didn't want to see him anymore. He'd exploded, told her he was going to kill her, and pursued her through the house. Desperate, she'd grabbed the biggest knife in the block on the kitchen counter and buried it in his chest.

There had been something about Lydia Wax that made Leary suspicious. Nothing concrete. Nothing he could pinpoint in an intelligible way. But he had sensed, on an instinctive level, that she was lying to them. When Leary had shared this feeling with Strickland, his partner had shrugged it off. "It's in your head."

And her story had been plausible—even more so after Leary and Strickland did some digging and learned that a previous girlfriend of Resta's had sought a restraining order against him. And there were no witnesses. No evidence to contradict her version of events.

They had spoken to Resta's surviving family members. A brother, Leary remembered, named Chance Resta, and a mother. Both had vigorously denied that Terry Resta would ever threaten someone's life, but of course that's what they would say. They were kin, the opposite of unbiased character witnesses.

Leary had kept the investigation open as long as he could justify it, talking to everyone he could find who'd known Resta or Wax. In the end, he had found nothing to support his intangible feeling that the woman's story was false. In fact, after hearing more about Resta's temper and Wax's sweet disposition, he'd begun to doubt his initial feelings and wonder if Strickland had been right, that it had all been in his head.

They had closed the case. No charges were brought against Lydia Wax. Leary and Strickland moved on to their next dead body. Back then, there had always been a next dead body.

Three years ago. *Where are you now, Lydia?*

He clicked on the second search result on the Google page, another LinkedIn profile. Then on the third, a Facebook profile.

No picture—apparently the privacy settings attached to the account limited the display of photos to friends only—but some information was visible, including Education, which listed a high school in Plymouth Meeting, Pennsylvania—a Philly suburb—and a year of graduation—2009—which would put her at around the right age for *his* Lydia Wax.

"Mark, I'm gonna run downstairs and grab a coffee. You want to come?"

Leary jumped at the sudden interruption, then turned with what was probably a guilty expression to look at the man standing at the side of his cubicle. He forced a smile. "Thanks, but I'm too busy," he said. "Next time, okay?"

Once he was alone again, he returned his attention to his computer screen and let his mind go to work. How likely was it that there was more than one woman named Lydia Wax of the same age and who'd grown up in the Philly area? He supposed it was possible that he was looking at someone else's Facebook profile, but he didn't think so.

Great. Congratulations, No-Longer-A-Detective

Mark Leary. Now get back to work before you get fired. Someone in IT is probably monitoring everything you're doing on this computer.

He knew he should listen to the voice in his head. It was the voice of reason, and ignoring it had led to the loss of his career with the PPD. On the other hand, ignoring that voice had also led to saving Jessie's life. So, that was one point in the voice's favor.

Screw it—what's a few more minutes?

He opened a new window on his desktop and ran a second Google search. Then he picked up his phone and called the phone number on his screen.

A woman answered. "Plymouth-Whitemarsh High School, how may I direct your call?"

"My name is Mark Leary," he said. "I'm hoping you can help me track down one of your alums."

11.

After his disturbing confrontation with Luther Goyle, Dave Whittaker managed to put Corbin Keeley's death out of his mind—almost. The dead politician had a bad tendency to pop into his head at random times—distracting him in the middle of a meeting, turning the taste of a sandwich sour seconds after biting into it, tempting him to turn around rather than park at the glass and steel tower of his own company, CBL Capital Partners, where Goyle squatted like a fat spider.

I won't run away from that bastard.

The lawyer's creepy words bothered him, as did his barely-veiled threats against Dave's family. But what bothered him even more was the fat man's insinuation that Dave's best friend and original business partner, Jack Woodside, was part of the conspiracy. Could Goyle really have corrupted Jack so quickly and completely?

Dave parked in the lot at CBL's tower. He killed his Jaguar's engine and sat listening to the quiet ticking of the engine coming to rest. He couldn't stop the thoughts that were swirling in his mind.

I'm part of a criminal conspiracy. I'm a criminal. Jesus, I'm worse than that. I'm a murderer.

He popped the door and climbed out of the car. He needed to find Jack.

"Freezing," Jack said, thrusting his hands into the pockets of his overcoat. He was a man with a skinny frame—except for a paunch at his gut—and for as long as Dave had known him, he'd been sensitive to the cold. "Whatever you want to talk about, make it quick."

Dave had suggested they take a walk. This conversation wasn't one he wanted to have inside their office building. But watching his friend suffer made him question his decision. "We could take a drive. Turn on the heat."

Jack turned to study him with his clear, penetrating stare. "I don't have a lot of time. What's this about, Dave?"

"I want to talk about Luther."

Dave watched his old friend closely for a reaction. He saw none. The expression on Jack's face remained constant. He shivered, but didn't break his stride. "What about him?"

"I think—" Dave shook his head, frustrated with his own hesitancy. "I *know* he's engaged in illegal activities. And I'm not talking about playing games with the IRS or the SEC. I'm talking about—"

"I know what you're talking about." Jack's voice sounded unconcerned. Could Goyle have been telling the truth about him knowing everything and being on board with it? *No. Not Jack. No way.*

Dave stopped walking. "I don't think you do, Jack."

Jack also stopped. The two men faced each other. They had the sidewalk to themselves. The street was quiet except for a wind that whipped around their heads, making Jack lower his chin toward the warmth of his coat.

Dave took a deep breath. "I'm talking about murder. I know it sounds insane. But it's true. Luther is killing people. Arranging it, I mean."

He expected a reaction from his old friend and partner—surprise, shock, horror—but the one he received was unexpected. It was anger. "That's an outrageous accusation. And it's a disgusting thing to say about Luther."

"Jack, you need to listen to me. It's true. Corbin Keeley—"

"Was killed by a woman acting in self-defense."

"Luther set it up."

"You can't prove that," Jack said, "and no one else can either."

Dave felt like he'd been punched in the gut. For a moment, his thoughts scrambled and he couldn't speak.

"Dave, business is a rough game. You know that."

"I bet Bill Gates orders hits all the time," he responded sarcastically.

"No one ordered a hit. An abused woman defended herself, and we happened to benefit. End of story."

"Maybe for you. It's not the end of the story for me."

"What's wrong with you?" Jack said. "Don't you enjoy being wealthy? Don't you take pride in being an owner of a successful company?"

"Do you take pride in being a criminal?" Dave said.

Jack dismissed the question with a wave of his hand. "What's the expression? You're only a criminal if you get caught."

"I know that expression, Jack. I know all of them. Don't forget where I grew up. I had plenty of chances to be a criminal when I was a kid. Gangs were everywhere, and they were always recruiting. You think it was easy for me to turn my back on that money? I was a kid who had nothing. You think I didn't want a Nintendo? A good pair of Nikes? A gold chain? You think I didn't want to surprise my mother with a beautiful gift on her birthday? I did without those things because I knew the difference between right and wrong."

Jack shook his head. "You were a kid. Kids see the world in black and white. You're a man, now, Dave. The world is gray—especially the business world. Calm down. Stay focused on your job. Let Luther do his job. There's a lot of money on the horizon for us. A *lot* of money."

"Blood money."

Jack brought his hands to his face, blew on his palms, and rubbed them together. "We've been friends a long time, Dave. Please don't do something you'll regret."

Dave laughed, but it came out mirthless and choked. "So you're threatening me now, too? Are you going to remind me about my wife and kids, like Luther did? Some friend."

"I *am* your friend. And I'm not threatening you. I'm talking to you."

Dave shook his head. "Well thanks for the talk, Jack."

12.

Warren Williams called, demanding to see her. He said it was about Corbin Keeley. And he sounded angry. *Damn it.* She wasn't sure how the head of the DA's Homicide Unit had found out about her little off-the-books investigation. Maybe the owner of Bistro Cannata had complained, or Andrew Dale had made a comment about her visit to the morgue. Fulco seemed the most likely suspect. The more questions she'd asked the detective, the more pissed off he'd become. But she knew Fulco's annoyance at her refusal to leave the case alone would pale compared to Warren's. She should have told him about it the other day, when she'd had a chance to give her side of the story. *Too late now.*

Outside the door of his office, Jessie paused to steel herself for a confrontation. She took a deep, calming breath, then opened his door and entered his office. There was an explanation on her lips, but she never spoke it. She stopped abruptly, staring into the face of Jesus Rivera, the district attorney of Philadelphia.

Warren sat behind his desk with an exhausted

look on his face. Rivera, looking livelier but no happier to see her, stood in front of the desk, leaning a hip against its edge. An assortment of posters and campaign flyers had been fanned across the desk's surface.

"Hi, Jessie," the DA said. "Come in, and close the door, please."

He didn't suggest she take a seat, so she remained standing, facing the man across Warren's cramped and messy office. "What, uh...." Jessie struggled to find her voice. "I didn't realize you—"

"I like you, Jessie. I respect you. You know that. We've been through some critical cases together. You're a fantastic prosecutor and your success reflects well on the DA's office. You're a valued member of my team."

"Thank you—"

"So what the hell are you doing poking around the Corbin Keeley shooting?" If Rivera had only been angry, or indignant, she could have accepted that. But there was something more disturbing in the pinched lines of his face. He looked *disappointed.* That was harder to take.

"I can explain."

"I hope so. That's why Warren and I called you here."

"Carrie Keeley approached me the other day. Corbin Keeley's daughter. She doesn't believe that her father was killed in self-defense. She's convinced Keeley wasn't abusing his girlfriend and that the self-defense claim is a cover for murder. Her mother—Keeley's ex-wife—agrees. They're certain."

"A cover for murder?" Warren said from behind his desk. His voice was laden with sarcasm. "That's ridiculous."

"I didn't say I agreed with them," Jessie said. "But, well, I felt bad for them. So I agreed to take another look at the police report and the evidence, just to assure them."

"You shouldn't have agreed to that," Rivera said. He sighed. "But I suppose the harm is minimal. Just tell the women that the noble detectives of the Philadelphia Police Department did their job with the utmost professionalism and excellence, and we can hopefully put this behind us."

She saw Warren watching her with a wary expression. "Something tells me that's not what Jessie has in mind."

Rivera's eyes widened. "Is that right? You just said you don't agree with them."

Jessie took a breath. She knew this was a critical moment. She could back down, follow Rivera's direction, and put her questions about Corbin Keeley's death behind her. Or, she could jeopardize her job to do what she believed was right. She rolled back her shoulders. "I think the police missed some critical inconsistencies in Brooke Raines's story. I'm not saying this is an elaborate conspiracy, but I don't think it's self-defense, either. I think Keeley beat Raines, and, whether to get away from him, or to vent her rage, or both, she killed him. But that's vigilante justice. It's murder."

Rivera's gaze shot to the closed door, as if people might be listening through the wood. "The Corbin Keeley case is closed. The police department and this office made a joint decision, based on the evidence and certain other circumstances, not to charge Brooke Raines."

"The facts don't support self-defense."

Rivera's jaw clenched. "Jessie—"

"Jesus," she said, surprising herself by talking over him. "You said you like and respect me. I like and respect you, too, and one of the reasons I hold you in such ... esteem ... is because you've shown yourself again and again to be a man of integrity. Most politicians don't care about right or wrong, or justice. You do."

Warren waved at the campaign flyers on his desk. "Maybe we should put you on the reelection team." He gulped his tea. The sight of steam rising from the mug made Jessie long for coffee.

"I'm being sincere," she said.

Rivera ran a hand through his thick, black hair. "Jessie...."

"Just hear me out, okay?"

He stared at her for a few seconds. "I'm listening."

"I think we should have her arrested, and we should file criminal charges. Assign me to the case. I'll win."

Warren held up a hand. "Stop." He rubbed his temples. "Jessie, we don't want you to win. Do you watch the news? Brooke Raines is being celebrated for her bravery. You want the DA's office to *charge* her? You want us to side with an infamous wife-beater against a battered woman claiming she defended herself? During a reelection campaign? God, I can see the headlines now!"

"Warren, quiet," Rivera said.

Warren leaned back his head and closed his eyes. "You're listening to her. I can't believe this. You're being persuaded."

"This isn't about me," the DA said. Then, in a careful tone, "What I don't understand is, how did the police get it wrong?"

"The investigation was sloppy and incomplete. The lead detective, Kyle Fulco, has a reputation for being lazy, and from what I've seen, he earned it. His partner recenty retired and he handled this case on his own. There are holes in Brooke Raines's story. Fulco's quick and dirty investigation didn't uncover them, but I did find them, after only a few days of asking questions. The evidence doesn't point to self-defense. It points to murder. Even if he was abusive, that's still a crime."

Rivera rubbed his face. "My enemies are going to have a field day with this. Whether we win or lose, they'll use it against me."

Warren let out a humorless laugh. "*Whether* we win or lose? Even if Brooke Raines did murder Keeley,

I don't see us winning here. Jessie, you say her story has some holes. If we bring this to trial, maybe you chip away at the self-defense claim. Show that the use of deadly force was excessive, she could have retreated, whatever. But to what end? Maybe you get a manslaughter verdict. And that's if we're lucky and the jury doesn't just turn against us and deliver a straight not guilty verdict based purely on sympathy for Raines. You'll need to battle through a trial in which every disgusting aspect of Corbin Keeley's life gets publicly aired. Jury nullification is always a risk, but in a case like this one, it's a practical certainty."

"I understand it won't be easy," Jessie said.

"You're damn right it won't be easy," Warren said. "And you know who else it won't be easy for? This girl who made such an impression on you, and her mother. Their lives will be dragged through the mud."

She knew he was right. Prosecuting Raines would put Carrie and Nina under the microscope. Even if Jessie managed, through pretrial motions to the court, to keep the two women out of the trial, she could not control the court of public opinion. Carrie and Nina would become targets of vicious op-ed pieces, blog posts, and social media. The thought of Carrie and her mother going through hell gave her pause. But only for a moment. "They're stronger than you think."

"Are they? Remember, the ex-wife never reported the abuse, even when rumors appeared in the papers, along with a *photo* of her. She could have stopped him then, just by telling the police what he'd done. One could argue she's responsible for Raines becoming a victim of Keeley—maybe other women, too. People are going to wonder what the daughter knew, too. Think about it. You seem to like these women. Do you really want to put them through this trial, knowing what it will be like for them? Sometimes everyone's best interest is better served by prosecutorial discretion, rather than the letter of the law. We don't need to prosecute Brooke Raines. Jesus, you don't have to do this."

Rivera turned to Warren. "I think I do."

Warren looked incredulous. "Why?"

"Because I'm the DA. And it's my job to make sure even a person like Corbin Keeley receives justice."

Warren leaned back in his chair. His expression was one of fatigue. "You're the boss. For now, anyway."

"Thank you," Jessie said. "You're making the right decision."

Rivera nodded. "I sure hope so."

13.

"Are you here to tell me I was wrong?" Carrie asked.

They were in the kitchen again. Sunlight filtered through the curtained window and gave the room a warm, pleasant light, but it didn't seem to brighten the mood. Carrie sat stiffly, her face pinched with worry. Nina busied herself at the other side of the kitchen, pulling clean dishes from a dishwasher and stacking them in a cabinet.

"Should I make coffee?" Nina said.

"I'd love some." Jessie felt a rush of relief just at the thought. But Carrie didn't acknowledge her mother's words. She continued to stare at Jessie, waiting for an answer. "I'm here to tell you that the DA's office has reconsidered its decision not to prosecute Brooke Raines."

Nina, who had been spooning coffee grounds into a machine, stopped abruptly and turned to watch them.

Carrie's eyes lit up. "Thank you!"

Jessie wanted to smile along with the teenager,

but she couldn't. "I want you to be ready. Both of you. Once we do this, the media will come after you."

"That's nothing new," Carrie said. "The media has been following me around since the night my dad died. I stopped talking to them when I saw how they were slanting their coverage against him."

"It could get worse. It probably will. Reporters love the spectacle of a trial. They've already decided that Brooke Raines is the good guy. Once we attack her, we become the bad guys in their story. They might try to make you and your mom seem like enablers, like your silence resulted in other women being hurt. They may try to dig up moments from your past to make you look bad. If they can't find any, some reporters will just invent them."

The coffee machine beeped. Nina, looking relieved to have something to do, started filling mugs.

"I don't care," Carrie said. "You need to show everyone the truth. My dad deserves that."

Jessie glanced at Nina, who walked toward them, carefully carrying the coffee mugs by their handles. As she placed the mugs on the table, Jessie asked her, "How do you feel about this, Nina? You'll probably take the brunt of the public's disapproval."

"Maybe I deserve it," Nina said. "In any case, if Carrie is brave enough to do this, then I am, too. Put that woman in a prison cell where she belongs."

Jessie looked from the mother to the daughter and back again, then picked up her mug and took a sip. The hot coffee felt comforting as it rolled around her mouth and down her throat. Carrie and Nina lifted their mugs, too, and the three of them sipped. A peace descended on the kitchen. Jessie wished it would last, but she knew it would be short-lived.

14.

Whoever came up with the phrase "all publicity is good publicity" definitely wasn't an incumbent district attorney seeking reelection, or anyone working for him. Jessie could practically feel the weight of her colleagues' anxiety and disapproval as headlines like *Police and DA Seek Prison for Abuse Victim* and *Battered Woman to Stand Trial for Death of City Councilman* hit the front pages of the city's papers. News websites and legal blogs posted opinion pieces by lawyers and experts opining on the intricacies of the self-defense doctrine. A string of biting hit pieces targeting Jesus Rivera raised the question of whether his reelection—once a foregone conclusion—would be a huge misfortune for the city.

The expected personal interest stories appeared, too—numerous stories speculating about the dark, secret lives of Keeley, his ex-wife, and their daughter, reprinting the horrific photograph of Nina Long at every opportunity, and glowing accounts of Brooke Raines's work as a young, selfless nurse at the Children's Hospital. The news outlets seemed mostly uninterested in Jessie, although she saw at least one article making reference to her "once promising career." *Nice.*

Through this storm, Jessie kept her head down and worked.

The arrest also set in motion a chain of legal events. Brooke Raines was jailed, but only temporarily. A preliminary arraignment was set—a hearing at which a bail commissioner would determine whether she remained in custody pending her trial or was released.

Jessie told Carrie and Nina about the preliminary arraignment and urged them to attend. She had a tactical reason—she wanted to humanize Corbin Keeley as much as possible, given the history of domestic abuse—and a tearful ex-wife and daughter sitting in the gallery might help accomplish that. But she had a personal reason, as well. She knew that Carrie had suffered for over month with the belief that the murder of her father might go unpunished, and that she was suffering even more now, as members of the media hounded and vilified her. Jessie wanted to give the girl a chance to see Brooke Raines stand accused of her crime, and hear the bail commissioner send her to a jail cell pending her trial. She hoped it might help Carrie come to terms with her father's death.

Preliminary arraignments were conducted in a basement courtroom in the Criminal Justice Center. Jessie met the two women there.

"Over there is where members of the public can sit and observe." She pointed them toward the pewlike rows of the gallery. The seats were already filling up with media and curious spectators. No surprise. It was public information that Brooke Raines would appear today. Jessie recognized several of the reporters. Most seasoned media outlets knew better than to expect fireworks at a preliminary arraignment, even in a case like this one, but a good reporter could add drama even to a routine prelim. Despite the added pressure, Jessie was glad they were here. She would be explaining her version of the shooting today, and she wanted that version to gain traction with the press.

"It smells terrible in here," Nina said.

Jessie almost laughed. The the stale, unpleasant smell was the furthest thing from her mind. She had been doing this for so long, she no longer noticed it. "This courtroom runs twenty-four hours a day, seven days a week."

"I guess that explains it," Nina said.

She spotted Raines's defense attorney, Aidan Hughes, talking with two of the deputy sheriffs near the other side of the room. Hughes must have made a joke, because the two deputies laughed. Hughes was the kind of man who seemed able to make friends with everyone he met. He had a handsome face, a warm manner, and a gaze that seemed to convey sincerity.

Hughes boasted an impressive win record and was one of the highest paid attorneys in the Philly criminal defense bar. With a young, white, female client, and a self-defense claim, he would be going into this trial with the advantage. She might have wondered how

Brooke Raines could afford his fees, but knowing Hughes, he'd probably taken her case *pro bono*. The publicity from a high-profile trial like this one would be worth more than a fee.

The room filled up and activity began to stir around her. She watched as deputy sheriffs shepherded desperate, recently jailed men and women—accused of everything from the worst felonies to the mildest misdemeanors—into the room to wait for their turns appearing before the bail commissioner.

The bail commissioner working this shift was Howard Boggs. Boggs was known to be "tough on crime," when it came to felonies, and could generally be counted on by the DA's office to set a high bail or deny it altogether. Normally, the sight of his heavy frame at the bench was reassuring. But Jessie wasn't sure how he would respond to the circumstances of this case. Would he see Raines as Jessie wanted him to see her—as an accused murderer—or as Hughes would present her—as the real victim?

The room hushed as two deputy sheriffs brought Brooke Raines into the courtroom. It was the first time Jessie had seen the woman in person, and she almost did a double-take. Flanked by the two deputies, Raines's petite frame looked almost childlike. Her face, with big, blue eyes and a pert nose, added to an appearance that could only be described as *innocent*. She wore a plain, blue suit with low heels, which Hughes must have brought her so she could change out of the orange jumpsuit she would have been wearing in custody.

Hughes waited for her at the defense table. Jessie risked a glance at the gallery, where Carrie and Nina sat. The mother and daughter wore identical expressions—eyes staring with what looked like a mixture of anger and fascination, foreheads crinkled with concentration. Neither woman looked at Jessie. They were both riveted to Raines.

"Ms. Raines," Boggs said, reading from a sheet of paper on his podium. "I understand you've been charged with criminal homicide, and that you are asserting an affirmative defense of justifiable homicide."

Raines stood up straight. She faced the bench without any apparent nervousness. "Yes, Your Honor."

Boggs read aloud a full summary of the charges, which included first degree murder as well as lesser included charges. A wave of murmurs and whispers roiled through the gallery.

"Ms. Black," Boggs said, "would you like to begin?"

"Thank you, Your Honor," Jessie said, "given the seriousness of the offenses, the Commonwealth does not believe bail is appropriate here."

"Your Honor," Hughes said. He strode leisurely toward the judge, smiling at the bail commissioner as if Boggs were his dearest friend. "I would urge you to consider all of the circumstances here. My client is educated, she has no criminal record, and she has been—and still is—employed by the Children's

Hospital of Philadelphia, where, as a nurse, she cares for children. Moreover, despite the Commonwealth's ludicrous charges, Ms. Raines is not a cold-hearted killer. She was the victim of physical and emotional abuse at the hands of Mr. Keeley, and she only fired her gun as a last resort to defend herself."

"That's what Ms. Raines claims," Jessie said, "but her story has not been demonstrated with evidence." She knew she was walking a dangerous path by challenging the truthfulness of the abuse claims, but she thought the risk was worth taking, especially given the sympathetic way Boggs was looking at Raines. "Ms. Raines is accused of intentionally shooting an unarmed man in a public location."

Hughes shook his head. "Mr. Keeley was armed with a rock and he attempted to use it as a deadly weapon. Even without the rock, he was physically much more powerful than Ms. Raines and had terrorized her with violence in the past. Frankly, I'm shocked that Ms. Raines is being prosecuted here at all."

Jessie forced herself to keep her attention on the bail commissioner and to speak in a calm, reasonable voice. "Again, those claims have not been established with evidence, Your Honor. Whether or not the victim engaged in those acts is a question for trial. In the meantime, Ms. Raines presents a flight risk—she's not a Philadelphia native and has no ties to the community—and she is a danger to the public as well."

"A danger to the public?" Hughes said. He recoiled from her, as if genuinely insulted. Maybe he was. "My client has never hurt anyone. *She* was hurt—"

"She fired a gun in public and killed a man, so yes, I would call her a danger to the public."

"She has no criminal record, no history of violent acts—"

Boggs raised a hand. "Counselors, please. There's a procedure here, of which you are both well aware."

Jessie and Hughes fell silent.

"Thank you," Boggs said dryly. "After weighing the relevant factors and considering the bail guidelines, I am ruling that the defendant Brooke Raines be released on her own recognizance pending trial."

Jessie felt dazed. ROR? That would mean Raines could walk out of here a free woman, without even a bond to pay, just by giving her word that she would appear for trial.

Hughes looked relieved. "Thank you, Your Honor."

"With all due respect, Your Honor," Jessie said, "this is a murder trial. Releasing the defendant would be unprecedented, even taking into account the factors Mr. Hughes raised."

"I think it's a well reasoned ruling," Hughes said.

Boggs knocked his gavel and they quieted again. Jessie worried that she'd gone too far and braced herself for a reprimand. But after a stretch of seconds, Boggs nodded thoughtfully. "My ROR decision stands.

Ms. Raines has no criminal record and appears to be a productive member of this community. I have no reason to doubt her claims of abuse at the hands of Mr. Keeley, and, as she has asserted a self-defense claim, it will be the Commonwealth's burden to disprove that at trial. Therefore, I am releasing Ms. Raines on her own recognizance. However," he said, looking at Jessie, "I must agree with Ms. Black that given the seriousness of the charges, there is at least some risk of flight here. I am therefore ordering that Ms. Raines be placed under house arrest and monitored via an electronic tether. Ms. Raines," he added, looking at her, "please be aware that my decision today will be revisited should you fail to comply fully with these conditions, including appearing precisely on time for all of your court appearances. Am I understood?"

"Yes, Your Honor," Raines said. And in a quieter voice, "Thank you."

"Okay," Boggs said, "let's move along to our next case."

Jessie stepped away from the counsel table. House arrest with an ankle bracelet? For an accused murderer? It wasn't the result she'd expected, and she had a feeling it would only be the first of many surprises.

15.

While Jessie was arguing in preliminary arraignment court, Leary was skipping work to investigate a three-year-old case. Since Jessie's involvement with the Corbin Keeley case began, he couldn't get the similar case from his own past out of his mind. Back then, he'd found Lydia Wax's story about stabbing Terence Resta in self-defense suspicious, but he'd been unable to find any evidence to disprove it. Now, he found himself compelled to try again.

Bullshit. You just miss being a homicide detective, and this is your excuse to play cop again.

His thoughts scattered as he stepped out of his car at the curb in front of Terence Resta's brother's house and saw the man come out of his front door. Chance Resta wasn't a particularly big man, but he was solid. His torso was compact and hard. Leathery-looking hands hung at his sides from arms that were thick and ropy with muscle. Red-rimmed eyes glared out from beneath a sloping forehead. In a bare-knuckled fistfight with the man, Leary believed he might win, but not without significant injury.

"Get the fuck off my land!"

The front lawn of Resta's small house had frosted over in the November chill, and the man's work boots crashed violently down on the stiff grass. Resta looked older than Leary remembered. His face seemed more lined, more weathered, and his lurching gait seemed more labored. The stark changes didn't surprise Leary. He'd seen what the weight of grief could do to an otherwise healthy person.

He lifted his hands, palms out, placating. "I'm just here to talk, Mr. Resta."

"Yeah, you're good at that, aren't you? About the only thing you *are* good at, you and your fucking partner both." He spat on the grass, then looked around. "He here, too? Fucking cops."

"My partner is dead," Leary said. "And I'm not a cop anymore."

That seemed to catch Resta's attention. His bulky chest stopped heaving as his breathing slowed to a normal rate. "Sorry about your partner."

Leary nodded. "Thanks."

"Why aren't you a cop anymore? They finally fire your ass for being a shit detective?"

Leary felt his anger swell. He forced the emotion down. Resta had hit a nerve, but letting him see that wouldn't get Leary any closer to getting what he wanted.

What the hell do I want?

"I resigned. I wanted to pursue other interests."

Resta let out a derisive snort. "I bet you did. You certainly weren't interested in pursuing justice for Terry."

"That's not true. I worked your brother's case hard. My partner and I both. There wasn't any evidence that contradicted Lydia Wax's self-defense claim."

Resta shook his head, a look of disgust on his face. "You didn't find it. Doesn't mean there wasn't any."

"I agree," Leary said, and the words seemed to startle Resta. "That's why I'm here. I want to try again."

"Little late for that."

"Can we talk inside?" Leary said. "It's cold."

"You think I'm letting you in my house? I fucking hate you, Detective Asshole Mark Leary. I spent the last three years hating you and the whole worthless Philadelphia Police Department."

Leary tried to peer past him, into the house, but Resta's bulky frame blocked him. Then he remembered something. "You still restoring bikes?"

The man's expression softened slightly. "You remember that, huh?"

"Back when we were investigating your brother's case, we stopped by here a few times. You were working on a Harley Davidson, I think."

Resta nodded. "FXRT 1340 Sport Glide."

"Right. I remember. You said it was your hobby, restoring old bikes. Relaxed you." Leary didn't add that the man looked like he could use some serious relaxation right now. "That bike was from the eighties, I think."

"1987." Leary thought he glimpsed conflicting emotions behind Resta's bloodshot eyes. "I love Harleys. I'm working on a 1961 Sprint now. Beautiful—you should see her." A hint of a smile touched his face.

"I'd like to."

The smile dropped. "It's an expression. You think I want to hang out in my garage with the detective who fucked up my brother's case? Get out of here."

Leary sighed. "Look, I know you don't think much of me, but I'm actually a pretty good detective. And your brother's case has been on my mind. I think I got it wrong and I want to fix that. It's not too late, Chance. There's no statute of limitations on murder."

Resta seemed to think about it. Then, silently, he turned and led the way toward a detached garage to the left of his house. He rolled the door up, revealing a small but tidy workspace. A partially disassembled motorcycle was propped near the center of the garage.

"Nice," Leary said, looking at the bike.

"Still needs a lot of work, but she'll be a beauty when I'm done." He looked from the bike to Leary, and the warmth left his face. He leaned his bulk against a worktable and crossed his arms over his chest. "What do you want to know?"

"Has anything changed since we last spoke? Have you found or heard anything that might shed light on

Terry's death?"

"Not really. I mean, me and the guys still talk about it. Put a few drinks in us, and the subject is bound to come up, you know? We were a close group, especially back when we still had the business."

The business, Leary recalled, had been an auto repair body shop in the Fairmount neighborhood of Philly. It was a family business the Resta brothers had inherited from their parents. The brothers had hired their childhood buddies as employees—not the best business decision, and probably not the only bad one the brothers had made.

"What do you mean, 'when you still had a business?' The shop went under?"

"Nah, I sold it after Terry died. There was an interested buyer, and I didn't see the point of keeping it going without Terry."

"Who was the buyer?"

"Some company. They'd already bought up a bunch of the neighboring businesses, and they wanted ours, too. For the land, to develop it."

Leary knew they were straying from the subject of Terry Resta's relationship with Lydia Wax, but some instinct told him this information might be relevant. "What was the name of the company?"

Resta's eyes narrowed. "Just some letters. CBG, I think. No—*CBL*. Why are you asking about it? I thought you wanted to talk about the bitch who killed my brother."

"You said you sold the business after Terry died.

Would you have sold it if he was still alive?"

"No way. Terry would never have sold. He was big on carrying on the family business."

"Do you still have the paperwork from the sale? I'd like to take a look."

Resta stared at him, and Leary could see the distrust and confusion in the man's eyes. In the end, Resta shrugged. "Sure, why not? Wait here, I'll get the contract. You think ... you think Terry being killed and this company buying the business have some kind of connection?"

Leary let out a long breath. "Right now, I'm not sure what to think."

But something told him he might be on the right path.

16.

"I still don't get why this is necessary," Carrie Keeley said. Jessie stood with the girl and her mother in a hallway in the Criminal Justice Center.

Jessie had a cup of coffee in her hand, but she barely tasted it. The ramp-up to Brooke Raines's trial had entered the pretrial conference and hearing stage. It required her full attention, and she was exhausted. Carrie Keeley and Nina Long seemed determined to attend every hearing—and to understand them, too. The need to educate the women added an extra burden to Jessie's workload, but that wasn't what was tiring her. Lately, she'd been finding it difficult to sleep.

At first she'd blamed her sleeplessness on adrenaline. She told herself that with a major trial fast approaching, it was natural to be wired. But that didn't explain why she saw Nina's battered face every time she closed her eyes. It didn't explain why her gut churned when she considered the strategies she would need to use to discredit Brooke Raines's story and hide Corbin Keeley's history of domestic violence from the jurors. She'd prosecuted plenty of complicated cases—

very few criminals were purely bad, and very few victims were purely innocent—but she'd never found herself in a position like her current one. Last night, her tossing and turning had been so bad, Leary had staggered out of the bedroom and moved to the couch just to get some peace.

Jessie drained the last few drops of her coffee and took a breath, focusing on the girl. "The fact that your father beat your mother shouldn't be relevant here, but the defense is going to try to use it to support Brooke Raines's self-defense claim. There are rules of evidence I'm going to use to try to keep those facts away from the jury." From the corner of her eye, she saw Nina wince. She felt like wincing herself.

They were at the courthouse today because Jessie had filed a motion in limine. A motion in limine was a pretrial motion—the Latin actually translated to "at the threshold"—a common method for raising evidentiary issues before the beginning of a trial. Jessie's motion was to exclude evidence of Corbin Keeley's alleged abuse of Nina, and specifically to prevent Aidan Hughes from calling Nina, Carrie, or anyone else to the stand to testify about it. By raising her objection now, before a jury was empaneled, she hoped to cut off any opportunity for Hughes to use Keeley's history of violence to sway the jury.

"I thought a wife can refuse to testify about her husband," Carrie said.

The teenager had obviously been doing her best to research the complicated legal issues. "That's called the spousal privilege. One spouse can't be forced to testify against the other in a criminal matter. But it doesn't apply here. There must be a valid marriage at the time the privilege is claimed, and your parents were divorced." Jessie didn't add that even if they'd still been married at the time of Keeley's death, a widow couldn't claim the privilege, either, since death was considered a legal end to the marriage. "That's why we need to exclude the evidence on other grounds."

"I understand." Carrie didn't look fully convinced of the rationality of the law, but she nodded anyway.

"Well," Jessie said with a breath, "it's time."

She threw away her coffee cup and they entered the courtroom. Aidan Hughes was sitting at the defense table. He rose as soon as he saw her, with a big, warm smile on his face. "Good morning, Jessie."

"Hi, Aidan."

He nodded to Carrie and Nina with the same friendly smile. Neither woman looked at him. They hurried to their seats in the gallery. To Jessie, Hughes said, "You wrote a killer brief. Going up against you is never easy, I'll give you that."

"Thanks."

In a lower voice, he said, "I'm still surprised you're doing this at all. I mean, prosecuting a victim whose supposed crime was fighting for her life? Doesn't seem like your style."

Was he baiting her, or was his question sincere? Had he picked up on her conflicted feelings and decided to try to turn them to his advantage? "My style is to make sure people who commit murder are held accountable."

"My client didn't commit murder. She did what she had to do to survive—"

"What's she doing now?" Jessie had noticed the chair next to Hughes's was empty. The defendant's presence at this hearing was not mandatory, and apparently Brooke Raines had not found the subject interesting enough to justify leaving her apartment. "Did your client have a more important commitment?"

"Brooke's under an incredible amount of stress."

"She should be."

Their banter was cut short by the entrance of Judge Willard Armstrong. Armstrong was one of the younger judges in the Philly criminal court system, a forty-something-year-old who'd worked as both a federal prosecutor and a defense attorney. The experience of both perspectives seemed to have rubbed off on him. He had a reputation as a fair and thoughtful jurist.

"Okay," Armstrong said. "Let's hash this out. I reviewed both of your briefs. Ms. Black, you're first."

"Yes, Your Honor. The Commonwealth believes this is a fairly straightforward issue. We anticipate that the defense will attempt to call the victim's ex-wife, Nina Long, to the stand to testify regarding certain alleged prior acts of domestic violence by the victim. We request a ruling of inadmissibility now, in order to prevent the introduction of such evidence. As the Court knows, under Pennsylvania rules of evidence,

evidence of a person's character or trait is not admissible to prove that on a particular occasion the person acted in accordance with the character or trait. That's well-established law."

"Mr. Hughes?"

"Yes, Your Honor," Hughes said. "It's also well-established law that evidence of a victim's prior conduct—*violent* conduct in particular—*is* admissible in a self-defense context to show that the defendant's fear and apprehension were reasonable."

Jessie had anticipated this argument and was prepared for it. "That rule is only applicable if the defendant had actual knowledge of the prior conduct. And Brooke Raines did not have actual knowledge of Mr. Keeley's alleged abuse of his former spouse."

Judge Armstrong arched an eyebrow. "Do you dispute that, Mr. Hughes?"

"I don't believe the rule is that clear-cut, Your Honor. Ms. Raines was familiar with the news reports about Keeley's abuse of his ex-wife. She saw the photograph—"

"Those news reports were speculative. At the time, Nina Long denied her husband inflicted the injuries."

"She doesn't deny it now," Hughes said. "In any case, it's a gray area."

"Your Honor, it is not a gray area," Jessie said.

"It is," Hughes said, "and in a case like this one—a case in which at least two women were brutally beaten and assaulted—the court should weigh all of the factors and in the spirit of fairness and justice—"

Judge Armstrong raised a hand. "Save the theatrics for the jury, Mr. Hughes. I'm sympathetic to your client's position, but I need to interpret the law. I'm granting the Commonwealth's motion."

"Understood, Your Honor," Hughes said. "In the alternative, the defense requests the opportunity to admit the testimony of Nina Long under Rule 406 instead."

Jessie shook her head. Rule 406, the so-called habit rule, provided that evidence of a person's habit could be admitted to prove that on a particular occasion, the person acted in accordance with the habit. Hughes was trying to use the rule to slip around the prohibitions on the use of character evidence.

"Mr. Hughes is intentionally blurring the distinction between character evidence and evidence of habit," she said. "Habit requires much greater specificity—for example, that a person habitually arrives at their job at a certain time. That rule isn't applicable here, Your Honor."

"It is if we can establish that Mr. Keeley had a habit of hitting women."

She heard a gasp from the front row of the gallery, but she couldn't worry about Carrie's and Nina's feelings right now.

"That's not the type of habit the rule was intended to address," she said, "and Mr. Hughes knows it."

"Once again, I must agree with Ms. Black," Judge Armstrong said. "My ruling stands. Evidence of Mr.

Keeley's alleged prior bad conduct will not be admitted at trial." Jessie let out a quiet breath of relief, but before she could thank the judge, he continued talking. "But please note, Ms. Black, that this ruling goes both ways. The Commonwealth will not be permitted to use the testimony or either Mr. Keeley's ex-wife, or his daughter, to introduce evidence of the victim's *good* character. I won't have you painting a saintly picture of this man for the jury. Am I understood?"

"But Your Honor." Jessie quickly gathered her thoughts. The general rule in a criminal trial was that the prosecution was permitted to offer evidence of a victim's good character if the defendant first introduced evidence of the victim's bad character. Jessie knew that Hughes would introduce evidence of Keeley's bad character. There was no way he could present his client's self-defense claim if he didn't elicit testimony showing that Keeley had abused Raines. Jessie's plan had been to rebut that testimony by calling Carrie to testify about how gentle, loving, and good her father had been, or, as Armstrong had phrased it, painting a saintly picture. For a second, she saw herself through the judge's eyes and her stomach felt queasy.

"That's my ruling," Armstrong said. "You can't have it both ways. You can't present evidence of Corbin Keeley's good character unless you're willing to open the door to the defense to explore his prior bad acts as well."

"Thank you, Your Honor," Hughes said. His smile

returned, and he looked relieved as he gathered his files. He might have lost the motion he'd come to argue, but he'd won a victory nonetheless. Brooke Raines would have a chance to describe Keeley's monstrous side, and Nina and Carrie would have no choice but to watch in silence.

Jessie walked them out of the courthouse. A roar of noise rose as they pushed through the door. A crowd of sign-waving protesters surged forward, shouting at the sight of them, their faces charged with indignation. Police officers approached the crowd, attempting to push them back.

"Walk with me," Jessie said quietly. "Stay close and don't make eye contact."

They walked. The crowd grew angrier. Something wet flew past Jessie and struck Carrie's face. The girl recoiled and wiped at her cheek. "Someone spit on me!" Her face flared with anger.

"Just keep walking, Carrie," Nina said.

For a second, Jessie thought the girl might confront the protesters. But her mother tugged gently at her arm, and in the next moment, she was walking again. Jessie got them into the backseat of a taxi, then told the driver to take them home. Behind her, the protesters began to calm down. The crowd thinned as the police urged them to disperse.

A uniformed officer joined her and asked if she was okay. Jessie nodded. "Yes. Thank you." She watched the street until the taxi disappeared in traffic.

17.

After pretrial hearings, jury selection, and opening statements, the trial of Brooke Raines began in earnest. Jessie arrived early at Judge Willard Armstrong's courtroom in the Criminal Justice Center, arranged her workspace at the prosecution table, and mentally prepared for the first day of testimony.

A few minutes later, Aidan Hughes strolled in with his client at his side. Well-rested, with a smooth complexion, makeup, styled blonde hair and a flattering suit, Brooke Raines did not look like a criminal defendant in a murder trial. This was the advantage of house arrest, and Jessie knew it was more significant than it seemed. Appearances mattered. They mattered enough to sway juries and determine verdicts. Aidan Hughes knew this, too. During his opening statement, he had used every opportunity to point at his client, as if to ask, *Does this woman look like she belongs in a courtroom, much less a prison?*

Nina and Carrie entered the courtroom next. Jessie left her seat to greet them, giving a hug first to the daughter and then the mother. The hugs were genuine, not stage work, although she couldn't help

116

being aware of the gallery packed with reporters and spectators. Jessie watched the two women take their seats behind the counsel tables before she returned to her own chair.

She looked over her notes as the bailiff called the courtroom to order. A familiar surge of energy rushed through her body. No matter how many times Jessie went to trial, the thrill never got old. From her first moot court competition at Penn Law over a decade ago to the murder trial in which she found herself now, her physical and emotional responses were mostly the same—her heartbeat galloped, her nerves tingled with adrenaline, and thoughts fired rapidly through her brain. Excitement mixed with nervous fear.

Only this time, there was something else, too. A feeling of uncertainty, of not being on sure footing. Nightmares and sleeplessness still plagued her. She couldn't quite shake the feeling that she might be on the wrong side of this trial.

Judge Armstrong entered the courtroom. His black robes billowed around his lanky frame. He greeted her, Hughes, and the other people in the room, then instructed the deputies to bring in the jury.

As the jurors filed into their box on the left side of the courtroom, Jessie risked a glance over her shoulder at Nina and Carrie. She flashed them a small smile she hoped would encourage confidence in them and her both. So far, they'd come to this courtroom every day in support of the ex-husband and father they'd lost, weathering the dry legal arguments of pretrial motions and the lengthy jury selection process, not to mention the protesters outside and the media sitting behind them. Jessie knew the first real test for them had been the opening statements she and Hughes delivered yesterday. Both women had quietly cried as Jessie offered the jury the prosecution's theory of the case—that Corbin Keeley, a far from perfect person, had been murdered by the woman sitting before them. Jessie had not dared to look at Nina or Carrie during Hughes's opening statement, but as the defense lawyer outlined his theory of self-defense against a violent, abusive aggressor, she had sensed the emotional turmoil of the two women.

Today, Jessie would call her first witnesses. Criminal trial procedure was mostly mechanical, and so were Jessie's goals for the day. She planned to begin by establishing the facts of the shooting, while also chipping away at the defense's story by pointing to facts inconsistent with a self-defense scenario.

"Ms. Black, is the Commonwealth ready to call its first witness?"

Jessie rose. "Yes, Your Honor."

"Please proceed."

"Thank you, Your Honor. The Commonwealth calls Detective Kyle Fulco to the stand."

Fulco had arrived at the courthouse wearing a dark gray, pinstriped suit that made him look like the competent professional she knew he wasn't. He appeared to have taken extra time to smooth his hair in place this morning, knot his tie, and strap on a nice-looking watch—probably more time than he'd taken during his so-called investigation before reaching his conclusion. She breathed in and banished the negative thoughts. Today, she would need to present this man as an authority figure the jurors should trust.

As he took his seat at the witness stand and was sworn in, Fulco's gaze met hers. For a second or two, she saw animosity there—equal to or exceeding what she felt toward him. A moment later, the look was gone from his face and he was reciting his oath like a pro. He watched Jessie as she approached the stand, both of them hiding their feelings behind pleasant smiles.

Get him off the stand as quickly as possible.

Fulco was the lead detective—the *only* detective—in this investigation. She needed to present his testimony in order to build the foundation of her case. But did she trust him? *Hell no.*

She started with easy questions about his background and career, then got down to business. "Detective Fulco, could you please tell the jury how you became involved with the Corbin Keeley homicide?"

Fulco turned toward the jury. "After uniformed officers responded to 911 calls and secured the scene, I was sent in as the homicide detective."

"You were the lead investigator?"

"Yes."

"When was this?"

"October 14. Maybe fifteen minutes after the

scene was secured. Things move quickly when a person is shot in a public place. I drove to the scene, a parking lot outside a restaurant called Bistro Cannata, and once there, I began my investigation."

Jessie walked him through the steps of his so-called investigation, hoping they would seem more thorough to the jury than she'd found them to be. He described the murder weapon recovered at the scene, and Jessie used him to authenticate Brooke Raines's pistol and admit it into evidence.

"Did Ms. Raines deny that she used the weapon you recovered to shoot Mr. Keeley?"

"No. She told us that's what she did."

"I'd like to show the weapon to the jury, You Honor."

"Objection!" Hughes said. "Any probative value would be substantially outweighed by the danger of unfair prejudice."

A murmur ran through the gallery. She could feel the combined attention focus on the well of the courtroom, where she and Hughes now faced each other.

"Your Honor," she said, "this is a murder trial, and the weapon is highly relevant evidence. The jury should be permitted to see it. As Your Honor knows, under the rules of evidence, the court must resolve all doubt in favor of admission."

"Permission to approach the bench?" Hughes said.

Judge Armstrong waved them forward. He touched a switch on his podium that caused white noise to play from a speaker, covering their voices so the jury—and the people in the gallery—couldn't hear. "I'm inclined to agree with Ms. Black," the judge said. "The murder weapon is generally considered to be relevant evidence in a murder trial."

"Generally, maybe that's true," Hughes said. "But in this trial, we're admitting that my client shot Mr. Keeley with that gun. It's not a fact in dispute. So the only purpose for showing the gun to the jury is to try to stir up an emotional response. Fear, disgust, whatever. That's Ms. Black's goal here."

Hughes wasn't wrong. Jessie wanted the jurors to touch the weapon, to look at its cold, black shape, and to feel its weight. She wanted to drive home the reality of the case and make them focus on Raines's violence instead of Keeley's. But she also had a legal justification. "The defendant's *intent* is a fact in dispute, Your Honor. I want to give the jurors an opportunity to put themselves in Ms. Raines's place. To think about and understand what it feels like to hold her gun. A gun she brought with her on the night of the killing because she intended to use it."

Jessie kept her expression neutral as she watched the judge mull their arguments.

Judge Armstrong said, "Mr. Hughes is right that the jury is already aware of the fact that Ms. Raines used a gun to shoot Mr. Keeley. I have to agree with the defense on this one. Seeing the gun and holding it in their hands won't provide them with any additional facts, and could result in Ms. Raines's being denied a fair trial. The danger of unfair prejudice outweighs the probative value."

Jessie felt her jaw tighten. In her opinion, the judge had just made a bad ruling, and she wondered if it was indicative of his feelings about the case in general. She forced herself to smile and nod. She and Hughes returned to their courtroom positions.

"We'll move on," she said. "Detective Fulco, what did Ms. Raines tell you?"

"She told us she shot Mr. Keeley in self-defense." Jessie held her breath as Fulco went on to describe Raines's self-defense claim. If he was going to make a mistake, he would do it now. She relaxed as he delivered a dry recitation of Raines's story. The alleged drinking, the alleged pursuit out of the restaurant, the alleged confrontation in the parking lot ending in a thrown rock and a fired bullet.

"Did you find Ms. Raines's story credible?"

"At first I did. She was very convincing. But afterward, we discovered inconsistencies that led me to doubt her claims."

"Can you describe some of those inconsistencies?"

He did—conveniently omitting that Jessie had been the one to track them down. "It turned out, based on the toxicology report, that Mr. Keeley had not been drinking that night. Witnesses at the restaurant didn't report a loud argument, and they saw Keeley walk calmly out after Ms. Raines, rather than chasing her in a menacing way. No fingerprints were found on the rock he supposedly threw at her."

"Thank you, Detective."

Jessie returned to her seat, and Hughes popped up. He looked eager to put Fulco to the test.

18.

The packed gallery of the courtroom buzzed with anticipation as Aidan Hughes left the defense table, where his client sat rigidly in her chair, and strode toward the witness stand. Kyle Fulco watched him approach. A shadow of trepidation crossed the detective's face.

"Detective Fulco," Hughes said, "is it true that when you arrived at Bistro Cannata, Ms. Raines turned herself in voluntarily?"

Fulco leaned forward. His hands fidgeted. "Actually, uniformed police officers brought her over to us."

"But she had not attempted to flee the scene, isn't that correct?"

"Not as far as I know."

"And you stated that Ms. Raines immediately informed you that the shooting was an act of self-defense, correct?"

"Yes."

"She told you that she shot Mr. Keeley because he was attacking her. He had actually thrown a heavy rock at her head, which thankfully missed. She was afraid that her life was in immediate danger. Isn't that what she told you?"

"Yes, she said that."

"You interrogated Ms. Raines, did you not?"

Fulco looked uncomfortable. "Yes. As I said a moment ago, I interviewed her at police headquarters where she offered her confession."

"For how long did you interview her, approximately? One hour? Two hours?"

"Two or three hours," Fulco said.

"A long time," Hughes said. He looked at the jury, then back to Fulco. "Detective, did Ms. Raines tell you why she was afraid of Mr. Keeley?"

"Yes."

"Did Ms. Raines tell you that Mr. Keeley had threatened her, and been physically abusive with her, during their relationship?"

Fulco glanced at Jessie, hesitating. The urge to object to the question was powerful, but Jessie resisted. She could argue hearsay, relevance, undue prejudice, and a handful of other bases, but Hughes would respond with exceptions to all of her objections. She knew this because the issues had already been argued and decided in several lengthy pretrial hearings. Armstrong would allow the testimony. She had succeeded in keeping Keeley's abuse of his ex-wife out of the trial, but she couldn't hide his abusive history with Raines from the jury. She remained in her seat.

"Yes," Fulco said. "But there was no record to support her claim. Ms. Raines never called in a domestic violence complaint—"

"It was a yes or no question, Detective Fulco."

"Yes."

"During the two or three hour interrogation of Ms. Raines, did her story—that she shot Mr. Keeley because she was afraid that her life was in immediate danger—did you find that story believable?"

"At the time I did."

"And you released her, didn't you? In fact, you didn't charge Ms. Raines until about a month after the shooting, isn't that right?"

"The investigation—"

"Yes or no, please," Hughes said.

Fulco's gaze darted to Jessie, his expression a call for help. She rose from her chair and said, "Objection, Your Honor. Relevance."

"The delay between Detective Fulco's original investigation of the shooting, which did not end in criminal charges, and his sudden change of heart a month later, is relevant to the credibility of his testimony," Hughes said.

The judge seemed to consider. "I'll allow it for the time being. Please answer the question, Detective."

"Yes." Fulco bit out the word. "The arrest came later."

"A month later, correct?" Hughes said.

"About a month, yes." Fulco's gaze found Jessie

again, and for a brief second, his eyes seemed to spark with anger.

"In fact," Hughes went on, "there was a substantial—some would say suspicious—delay between the shooting, to which Ms. Raines readily confessed, and the arrest, wasn't there?"

"Objection." Jessie rose again. "Detective Fulco already testified that there was a delay. Mr. Hughes is attempting to inject argument into his questions."

"Sustained," the judge said. "Please move along, Mr. Hughes."

"No problem, Your Honor. Detective Fulco, isn't it true that the reason for this lengthy delay is that the police department, working in coordination with the district attorney's office, had originally closed the investigation based on your determination that Mr. Keeley had been shot in self-defense, and that therefore no crime had been committed?"

"That was before additional evidence came to light—"

"Yes or no, Detective."

Both Jessie and Fulco had known this moment would come. As much as Jessie wished she could spare Fulco from the embarrassment—and avoid the doubt it might instill in the jury—there was no way they could avoid the truth. Fulco would need to admit, under oath, that his original conclusion had been wrong.

"Yes."

"That seems inconsistent. I mean, first you concluded that Ms. Raines did not commit any crime, and a month later you just changed your mind completely?"

"Additional evidence came to light."

Hughes dismissed the comment with a wave. "I'll take that as a yes. Is it true that the decision to reopen the case actually came from the district attorney's office, rather than from you?"

"No. I don't take orders from—"

"The district attorney's office stepped in, didn't it, because the prosecutor in this case, Jessica Black, disagreed with your findings and believed your conclusions were incorrect?"

"Objection," Jessie said.

Hughes wasn't finished. "As I recall," he said, talking over her, "the DA is up for reelection, isn't he? Maybe he's trying to make some kind of dramatic statement, although personally I can't understand why he would target a victim of domestic abuse."

"Objection! Mr. Hughes is overstepping—"

Judge Armstrong banged his gavel until they both stopped speaking. Turning to the jurors, he said, "Ladies and gentlemen of the jury, only witnesses are allowed to offer testimony here, not lawyers. Nothing Mr. Hughes just said constitutes evidence in this case. I am instructing you to disregard what you just heard." To Hughes, he said, "This is a warning, Mr. Hughes. You only get one. Don't you dare cross the line again."

"I apologize, Your Honor. My passion got the best of me."

Armstrong offered Jessie a sympathetic look. They both knew his instruction could not erase the effect of the defense attorney's stunt on the jury. It was impossible to un-ring the bell.

Hughes turned to the witness stand, where Detective Fulco was fuming. "Thank you, Detective. No more questions."

"Ms. Black," Judge Armstrong said, "I assume the Commonwealth would like to redirect?"

"Yes, Your Honor."

"Go ahead."

Jessie approached the witness stand, hoping to accomplish some damage control. Fulco glared back at her as if she'd just destroyed his career—and maybe she had. "Detective Fulco, did you see any physical evidence that Ms. Raines had been abused by Mr. Keeley, or by anybody?"

"No, I did not."

"Any bruises on her body?"

"No."

"Any defensive wounds?"

"No."

"She told you he threw a rock at her. Did she appear to suffer any injuries from that alleged attack?"

"No."

Jessie walked back to the prosecution table, picked up a sheet of paper, and approached the witness stand again. "I'd like to introduce this document into evidence, Your Honor."

They went through the process of admitting the evidence, and Jessie placed the sheet of paper in front of Fulco. "Do you recognize this document, Detective Fulco?"

"Yes. It's Ms. Raines's intake form, from the police department. From the night of the shooting."

"Were you present for Ms. Raines's intake process?"

"Yes. I walked her through it."

"And you participated in completing the form?"

"Yes."

"As part of the intake process, was Ms. Raines photographed?"

"Yes, a mug shot was taken. It's right here." He pointed to the paper.

"Do you see any signs of bruising or other injuries in that photograph?"

"No."

"Was Ms. Raines examined for identifying marks such as tattoos, scars, birthmarks, etc.?"

"Yes, that's a routine part of the process. Marks are noted here." He pointed.

"What does it say?" Jessie said.

"It says, 'None.'"

"You wrote that, correct?"

"Yes, I wrote that."

"So, during this process, you saw no bruises or other injuries on Ms. Raines?"

"No."

"Did you check the police records to see if Brooke Raines had previously filed a complaint against Mr. Keeley for assault or any other charge?"

"I checked that, and she never did."

"Thank you, Detective Fulco. That's very helpful. I have no further questions."

Judge Armstrong looked to Hughes. "Redirect, counsel?"

Hughes jumped up and straightened his tie as he approached the stand. "Just a few questions, Detective, and then we'll let you go. Based on your experience, would you agree that it is not uncommon for women who are victims of abuse from husbands or boyfriends to suffer that abuse in silence rather than reporting their abusers?"

Fulco seemed to hesitate for a second, then sighed. "It's not uncommon, no."

"Would you agree that many victims of abuse never reach out to the police?"

"I would agree with that. It's unfortunate, but true in my experience."

Hughes nodded. "Thank you, Detective."

Fulco was excused. He stepped down from the witness stand looking shaken, but when he walked past Jessie, his gaze was clear. He tilted his face close to hers, and under his breath, he said, "Thanks for nothing."

Jessie's mouth felt dry. She forced herself to smile

at Fulco, but only for the benefit of the jury and the spectators.

19.

For Mark Leary, tracking down Lydia Wax, the suspect from his three-year-old case, had been an exercise in pure detective work. Or social engineering, he supposed, depending on how you looked at it.

On the phone with Wax's alma mater, he'd posed as a lawyer trying to reach Wax about a bequest granted to her in a will. It wasn't the most sophisticated subterfuge—he doubted it would have impressed Reggie Tuck, the only actual con artist he knew—and it was definitely a move that would have landed him in serious trouble had he still been an officer of the PPD. But it had been effective. The helpful folks at the school had fallen for it and provided him with her unlisted address.

From there, some quick internet searching had given him even more information. Google Street View gave him a curbside visual of a massive, brick-fronted house set back on a large tract of property on a quiet-looking residential street. Zillow's database estimated the property's value at just over a million dollars. Pretty interesting for a woman who, as of three years ago, had barely any savings, had never married, and had been able to leverage her community college degree only as far as sporadic bartending jobs.

Obviously, something had changed between then and now. It could be innocent—she could have married a rich guy, or started a hugely successful YouTube channel. *Or she could have been compensated for eliminating Terry Resta.* It was a mystery that Leary fully intended to solve.

The drive from Philly to Mendham, a town in northern New Jersey, took two hours. Leary enjoyed every minute of it. He could feel a surge of energy in his body and in his brain that no other feeling could match. He was on the hunt again.

He didn't warn her he was coming. He parked in her long, circular driveway, walked up to the front door, and hit the doorbell. The door opened. Her eyes widened and her lips parted. She froze in her doorway, speechless.

"Um, Detective," she said. Her look of surprise changed to a friendly smile as she recovered. "Nice to see you again. What.... Is there something I can help you with?"

"May I come in?"

She hesitated. "I guess so. I need to run in about a half hour, though. I have a yoga class." She didn't move from the doorway. "Is this about what happened with Terry?"

"Please. I've come a long way to talk to you."

"You could have just called. I've always cooperated fully with the police. You know that."

During the ride to her house, Leary had debated whether to disclose that he was no longer with the police. He had decided not to. If she was a killer, he would need all the leverage he could get to coax information out of her.

"It is about Terry. I'm following up. Routine procedure, but I like to do it in person, make sure you're okay, all of that."

"I'm fine. Really." Judging by the square footage of her house, that was an understatement.

Leary waited. After a few seconds of silence, Wax backed into her house and gestured for him to follow her inside. He smiled and came in, taking off his coat as he walked, signaling that he planned to be here for a while. He saw what might have been a flash of panic in her eyes as she led him through a foyer to a family room.

The room was big, with a high ceiling and windows overlooking the expansive, heavily wooded back of the property. A comfortable-looking couch faced matching chairs and a loveseat. A large fireplace, dark at the moment, was built into one of the walls.

"This is a beautiful house," Leary said, trying to strike a casual tone but watching her closely for a reaction. It was hard to tell because she was still walking, but he thought she might have flinched slightly. "Do you live here alone?"

"Yes. What did you want to ask me about? To be honest, I've tried to put the whole thing with Terry behind me. I don't think about it much, except when I have a nightmare once in a while. I doubt I'll remember anything now that I didn't already tell you three years ago." She closed her mouth abruptly, as if realizing she was rambling. Definitely nervous. But many people became nervous around cops—even innocent people.

"Why don't we sit?" he said. Before she could respond, he took a seat in one of the chairs.

"Right. Sure." She seemed to hesitate for a second, then lowered herself onto the loveseat. She perched on the edge, as if poised to jump.

"I don't mean to be rude, Lydia, but how can you afford this house? Did you come into money since the last time we spoke?"

She stared at him. Her expression turned angry, but he sensed that she was faking the emotion. She wasn't angry. She was scared.

"I don't see how that's any of your business."

"Did you buy it? Do you rent it from someone?"

"I got ... a loan. A mortgage. Just like anybody."

"Banks don't just hand out big mortgages anymore. They would have wanted to see your income, your savings, that sort of information."

"Listen, Detective, if you want to ask me about what happened with Terry, then ask me. I'll be as helpful as I can. But I don't want to talk about my house or my life or anything else that's personal. Okay?"

Leary shrugged. "I'm not sure why you would

have a problem talking about your house."

"Well, that's how I feel."

"Okay." Leary let out a breath. "Let's talk about what happened three years ago, then." He saw her start to relax. She leaned back against the cushion behind her. "Are you familiar with a company called CBL Capital Partners?" he said. Abruptly, her body came forward again and went rigid.

"No," she said.

"Really? You never had any contact with anyone from that company?"

He could practically see her thoughts flashing rapidly behind her eyes as she tried to guess what he might already know. "Can you tell me why you're asking?"

"It's a simple question, Lydia. Did you ever have any contact with a company called CBL Capital Partners? I don't understand why that would be difficult for you to answer. I mean, unless you're hiding something."

She stared at him. A muscle in her jaw twitched. "Are you accusing me of something?"

"No. I'm just asking questions."

"I want you to leave now."

Leary sighed and nodded. He rose from the couch, then paused, as if just thinking of something. He reached into his pocket, where earlier he'd placed a slip of paper about the size of a business card. The paper had his name and phone number. He'd considered bringing one of his old Philadelphia PD cards, but giving her one of those would mean crossing a line he wasn't ready to cross. He handed her the piece of paper instead. "If you change your mind and want to talk, give me a call."

She took the paper, but her expression was dubious. "Why would I want to talk?"

"I don't know." Leary headed toward the door. "Maybe you'll remember something about CBL. If you do, it would be better for you to give me a call and tell me yourself, than for me to figure it out on my own."

"I'll keep that in mind."

"You should." When they reached her front door, he stopped to meet her gaze again. "It was good catching up with you, Lydia. I'll be in touch."

20.

Lydia Wax stood at the window, parted the curtains, and watched Leary march down the path from her front door to the driveway. The cop opened the door of his car and slid inside. Through the window, she could just barely hear the engine roar to life. She waited. The car rolled out of her driveway and onto the street, then drove away. A moment later, the sound of the engine faded and the car was gone.

Lydia glanced at her watch, then stared at the street for a full ten minutes to make sure he didn't come back.

One of her neighbors walked her poodle past Lydia's property. Other than that, the street remained quiet. She took a step backward and let the curtain fall back into place.

Damn it.

During the first year or so after Terry's death, she'd feared a visit from the Philadelphia police, but after moving to New Jersey and not hearing a word about the incident for three years, she'd eventually stopped worrying. She had assumed she was safe—

assumed that the creepy fat man had been right about there not being any risk.

She should have known better. There was always risk.

She hurried upstairs—actually *running* through her house—to the master bedroom. She yanked open the drawer of her nightstand and shoved aside various odds and ends until she found what she was looking for. The phone. A *burner*, Goyle had called it. Purchased with prepaid minutes, as anonymous a means of communication as was possible in today's world.

She pressed the button to power it on. Nothing happened. The screen remained blank.

It's been sitting in a drawer for years. Of course it's dead.

Where the hell was the charging cable?

She searched the drawer and found nothing. Had Goyle even given her one? She lifted the phone closer and peered at the ports on its edge. It looked like a standard Micro-USB port, the same type used by a bunch of her other devices.

Clutching the burner phone, she rushed down the hallway to the fourth bedroom, which she used as a home office. On her desk, her Kindle tablet was plugged in and charging. She pulled the Micro-USB cable out of the tablet and plugged it into the phone, then tried to power it on again. This time, the phone came to life, displaying a charging icon.

When the phone had enough juice to operate, she

opened the saved numbers. There was only one, and it would connect her to one of Goyle's burner phones—assuming he still used that phone.

Holding her breath, she called him.

The phone rang once. Twice. Three times. Lydia was about to give up when the call finally connected.

A voice said, "Who is this?"

Fear swam in Lydia's stomach. She swallowed hard. "It's Lydia."

"Sorry, you have the wrong number."

Panic surged through her. "I mean Penelope," she said, practically shouting the code they'd agreed on so many years ago. "Penelope."

Silence. She looked at the phone, afraid he might have already hung up, but then the voice returned: "You're alone?"

"Yes."

"What is it?"

"A cop was just here. One of the detectives who investigated Terry's death. He came to my house."

"What is his name?"

"Leary. Mark Leary. I always felt like he didn't believe me, even back then...."

"What did he want?"

"He was asking questions. He asked me how I could afford this house. He asked me—"

She heard Goyle exhale into his side of the line. "I told you, the money can't be traced. You don't need to worry about that."

"But he's suspicious!"

"Let him be. Let his suspicion give him ulcers. He'll never find a link between the money and Terry's death."

Lydia wished she could believe Goyle, but his assurances, which had seemed so convincing three years ago, sounded hollow now. "You're wrong. He found a link."

"If that were true, you'd be in a jail cell right now. He fooled you—that's what cops do. He made you think he has information, but all he was doing was trying to get you to talk—"

"He asked me about CBL Capital Partners," Lydia said.

She heard Goyle's sharp intake of breath. The sound made her fingers tighten around the phone as the fat man's surprise added a new layer of panic. "What did you tell him?" Goyle said.

"I didn't tell him anything. I told him to leave and he did. But he'll be back. He's obviously figured out what really happened, and he'll be back. What do I do?"

Goyle was quiet for a few seconds. "Stay in your house. Don't go anywhere. Don't talk to anyone. Don't even check Facebook. I'm sending two of my people to get you. They'll bring you to my office and we'll figure this out together. Okay?"

Lydia licked her lips, which felt as dry as dust.

"Lydia?" Goyle said.

"Okay," she said. "Yes. I'll be here."

"Good."

Goyle disconnected the call. She stood at her desk with her phone in her hand, feeling paralyzed.

Goyle's words echoed in her head: *I'm sending two of my people to get you.*

Her stomach churned with nausea.

He was going to kill her. She knew it with a certainty she could not explain. It was how he solved problems— she remembered vividly the cold, businesslike manner in which he'd proposed Terry's murder to her.

She shouldn't have called him. Now, his people were coming. How much time did she have? Hours? Minutes? There was no way to know.

She reached into her pocket and withdrew the small piece of paper she'd stuffed in there earlier. Mark Leary's number. If she called him, he might turn around and race back here in time to save her. But then what? He was a cop. She was a murderer. The math wasn't hard to do.

As if in a trance, she walked back to her bedroom and entered the master bathroom. Averting her gaze from her own eyes in the mirrored medicine cabinet, she opened the cabinet door. Inside, among the bottles and cosmetics, she found a bottle of Vicodin. Her doctor had prescribed it after some minor surgery. She'd never taken the pills—the pain had not been that bad—but she'd saved them.

Better to do it myself, on my own terms, than to be taken to some deserted place by two strange men and suffer God knows what at their hands.

How many pills would it take?

She moved through her house, retracing her steps to the home office. This time, she powered on her PC and brought up Google. Goyle had warned her not to use Facebook, but he hadn't said anything about Googling the number of Vicodin pills necessary for suicide.

Her search returned a surprising number of results. She sat down and read.

Leary returned to Philadelphia with a smile on his face. He might not have acquired any hard evidence or specific information from Lydia Wax, but he'd observed enough from her voice and mannerisms to convince himself that she was hiding something. Not to mention the mini-mansion.

The stabbing of Terry Resta three years ago had not been the clear-cut act of self-defense the evidence had made it appear. Leary was starting to believe that there had been a conspiracy to murder Resta. Resta had stood in the way of CBL's plan to acquire the Resta brothers' business, and, more specifically, the land they owned on which their business was located. They had arranged to remove Terry Resta, and Lydia Wax had been the tool they'd used. Apparently, she'd been well-compensated.

The best part was that proving all of this shouldn't

be too difficult. If Lydia Wax had been smarter, or possessed of more self-restraint, she would have hidden her payout. Instead, she'd splurged on a big house. If, as Leary suspected, the money trail that ended at her Mendham address started at a bank account connected to CBL Capital Partners, then the police could start building a solid case against both CBL and Wax. Three years after the fact, Resta's murderers would be brought to justice. All because of one former detective's hard work.

Hell, they kick me off the job and I'm still the best damn homicide detective they've got.

Leary didn't stop smiling the whole way home.

21.

The trial of Brooke Raines proceeded. Jessie called Deputy Medical Examiner Andrew Dale to the witness stand, established his credentials, and asked him to explain his role in the investigation.

"I performed an autopsy on Mr. Keeley."

"Can you please summarize your findings for the jury, Dr. Dale?"

"Yes." He turned to the jury box. For the trial, he'd manage to suppress his usual smile. Looking suitably grave, he guided the jurors through his findings, starting with the age, height, and weight of the victim and then getting to the more interesting facts.

"The bullet created an entrance wound just above Mr. Keeley's left eye."

"Your Honor, at this time, I'd like to introduce a series of exhibits," Jessie said. "Images from Dr. Dale's autopsy of Mr. Keeley." She lifted two stacks of glossy photographs from a folder on the prosecution table and handed one set to Hughes and the other to the judge. She waited as both men flipped through the images.

"Your Honor, permission to approach the bench?" Hughes said.

Judge Armstrong looked from Hughes to Jessie, then waved them both forward.

Hughes met Jessie at the judge's bench, where the defense attorney slapped the photos face-down. The judge flipped the switch that emitted white noise from a speaker so that their voices would not be overheard by the rest of the courtroom. "Go ahead."

"Your Honor," Hughes said quietly, "this is the same issue as the gun. My client admits to shooting Mr. Keeley. It's not a fact in dispute. Ms. Black is obviously trying to shock and disgust the jury. These images are unnecessarily prejudicial. They are also cumulative, since Dr. Dale is here and can offer testimony describing the appearance of the victim's gunshot wound without the shock value of the actual photographs."

Jessie shook her head. "Your Honor, the photos are highly relevant and the jury, as the ultimate finders of fact in this case, are entitled to see and draw conclusions from them."

Judge Armstrong raised his hands for silence.

"I agree with Mr. Hughes," the judge said. "The jury doesn't need to see the photos."

"But Your Honor—" Jessie didn't know what to say. Hughes was right that she wanted the jury to be shocked. She wanted to disgust them. She wanted the jurors to look at the starkly lit photo of Keeley's head, showing the hole that had been punched into his skull. She wanted them to see images of his brain, which Dale had removed—the violent damage wrought by the bullet evident and horrific. She wanted them to feel sick, to gag, to squirm in their jury box. She wanted them to see Keeley as a victim.

Armstrong arched an eyebrow. "Something you want to add, Ms. Black?"

"Mr. Keeley is dead. He can't testify about what happened to him. The pain he must have felt when the defendant shot him. The surprise and fear. But his body can testify. By looking at these photos, the jury can hear him—"

"That's very poetic, but it's not a legal argument," Hughes said. "Judge...."

Armstrong nodded. "My ruling stands. Ms. Black, you'll need to make your case without using the photographs."

Jessie returned to the counsel table and reluctantly placed the photographs back in their folders. Then she took a breath and returned to face the witness stand. "Dr. Dale, a moment ago you testified that you examined Mr. Keeley's body. Can you please describe your findings for the jury in more detail?"

Dale explained the cause, mechanism, and manner of death, then walked the jury through the same analysis he'd shared with her at the morgue. He noted the stippling on Keeley's forehead and explained that it had been caused by gunpowder burns and bullet fragments. He estimated, based on the stippling, that the bullet had been fired from a distance of approximately ten feet. His testimony was dry and lacked the visceral impact of the photos, but she soldiered on anyway. What choice did she have?

"Based on your experience, is it typical for a gunshot fired in self-defense to hit such a precise target from that distance?"

"Objection," Hughes said. "Dr. Dale is a medical examiner, not a ballistics expert."

"I'll withdraw the question," Jessie said. "Dr. Dale, approximately how many victims of gunshot wounds do you see in a typical week?"

"Objection," Hughes said. "This isn't relevant."

The judge eyed Jessie warily. "I'll give you a little leeway here, but not too much. Go ahead and answer the question, please, Doctor."

"It varies. Some weeks, none, some weeks, as many as ten."

"So it's fair to say you've examined a lot of gunshot wounds?"

"Objection," Hughes said. "Ms. Black is leading the witness."

"I'm going to allow the witness to answer the question," Judge Armstrong said.

"Thank you, Your Honor." The barrage of objections was meant to disrupt her and distract the jury. Jessie hoped the tactic would backfire and annoy the jury instead. She asked the court reporter to read the question back to Dale.

Dale said, "I've examined a lot of gunshot wounds."

"How did Mr. Keeley's gunshot wound compare, in your experience, to other gunshot wounds you've examined?"

"Most of them aren't headshots, except for the ones fired at point blank range. Unless the shooter is an experienced marksman, hitting the head is difficult. Most shooters aim for the body—center mass—or just fire wildly. Especially where self-defense is concerned—"

"Your Honor," Hughes said, "I object to the witness's answer in its entirety."

Judge Armstrong sighed. "Sustained. That's enough, Dr. Dale. I think you're straying from expert opinion into speculation. Jury, please disregard the witness's answer."

Jessie felt her hands tighten into fists. She quickly opened them, hoping the jurors and spectators hadn't noticed her frustration. "Your Honor, at this time, the Commonwealth wishes to introduce additional exhibits into evidence."

The exhibits included the articles of clothing Keeley had been wearing the night he was shot—which were splashed with blood and brain tissue. Hughes objected, and they went to the judge's bench again. White noise crackled through the speaker.

"Your Honor, I'm trying to establish the facts of the murder." She heard the plaintive whine in her voice and winced inwardly.

"You're trying to prejudice the jury," Hughes said.

"I'm allowed to prejudice the jury." Now she heard anger in her voice—which was better, but still not good. She forced herself to take a breath. "The rule excludes *unfair* prejudice and then only if it *outweighs* the probative value of the evidence."

"What's probative about Keeley's clothes?" Hughes said.

Usually, the combination of autopsy photos and physical evidence from the crime scene was enough to drive home the grave reality of murder to even the most aloof jurors. In many trials, Jessie had seen firsthand the rows of pale, queasy-looking faces. But this trial, apparently, would be different.

She knew before he spoke that Judge Armstrong was ruling against her. She could live with that. The gun, crime scene photographs, and clothing would all have been helpful, but they were not necessary. She could win the case without them.

"Dr. Dale," she said, returning to the witness, "you are aware that the defendant in this case, Brooke Raines, has asserted a claim of self-defense. During your examination of Mr. Keeley's body, did you find evidence that would support that claim?"

"No. I did not find any evidence supporting Ms. Raines's defense."

"Objection," Hughes said. "Dr. Dale is not qualified—"

The judge raised a hand, cutting him off. "Dr.

Dale, just to be clear, we're talking about *medical forensic evidence.*"

"Yes, Your Honor," Dale said. "That's what I meant."

"Okay," the judge said. "Go ahead, please."

"Could you elaborate, Dr. Dale?" Jessie said.

"Ms. Raines claims that Mr. Keeley was physically abusive toward her. Generally speaking, physical violence usually leaves marks on the aggressor as well as the victim of the violence—bruises on the hands, for example, blood under the fingernails, or defensive wounds such as scratches or cuts. My examination of Mr. Keeley did not reveal any such injuries."

"So there was no physical evidence on the body to indicate Mr. Keeley had ever been in any fights with the defendant, much less a life-threatening one on the night of the murder?"

"No."

"Was a toxicology screen also performed on Mr. Keeley's body?"

"Yes. The toxicology report came back with a zero percent blood alcohol content."

"What does that mean?"

"It means Mr. Keeley was not drinking on the night of his death."

Jessie ended her direct examination of Andrew Dale on that note, hoping she'd made an impact despite the evidentiary rulings against her. She returned to her seat as Hughes rose for cross.

"Dr. Dale," Hughes said, approaching the witness, "I only have a few questions."

"Okay."

"Based on your examination of Corbin Keeley's body, can you *rule out* the possibility that Mr. Keeley physically abused my client Ms. Raines?"

Dale's gaze turned briefly to Jessie, then returned to Hughes. "Well, I mean...."

"It's a yes or no question, Doctor," Hughes said.

"No."

"And based on your examination of Corbin Keeley, can you tell the jury today that Mr. Keeley was definitely *not* shot in self-defense?"

"No."

"Thank you, Doctor. No further questions."

22.

Andrew Dale's testimony ended on Friday afternoon. After the deputy medical examiner stepped down from the witness stand, Judge Armstrong adjourned court for the week. The jurors filed out of their box. Jessie watched them closely, looking for any outward signs of their thoughts, but all she saw was relief that they were being released from their duty for a few days.

Back in her office at the DA's building, she tried to convince herself that she'd ended the first week of the trial on a high note, and that the jurors would spend the weekend questioning Brooke Raines's self-defense claim. But as Warren and Rivera had warned her, it was clear she was fighting an uphill battle. Would the jurors even question whether Raines had really been in mortal danger that night in the restaurant parking lot, with no other option but to shoot Corbin Keeley in order to save her own life? Would they consider the possibility that Raines had brought a gun with her in the expectation—maybe even the *hope*—that she'd have a chance to use it? Just getting the jurors to ask those questions was a challenge. The killing of an abusive man struck many people as a form of justice, whether or not it was a crime. Had Jessie managed to break through that belief? She didn't know.

She sat back in her chair and closed her eyes. The face of Carrie Keeley appeared in her mind. The teenage girl had broken through Jessie's prejudices and convinced her to see her father as the crime victim he was. Now Jessie owed it to Carrie to do the same with the jury.

"Hey."

Jessie looked up. Warren stood in her doorway, holding a mug. The pungent stink of his tea drifted into her office. His face looked tired, but a grim smile appeared when their eyes met. If he were anyone else, she might ask him why he was working late on a Friday, but he was Warren Williams—he spent every Friday night here. He didn't ask her, either, and probably for the same reason. She and Warren were different in many ways, and similar in even more.

"I hope you didn't come here to tell me about all the trouble I'm causing," she said.

Warren sipped from his mug. "You're causing a shit-load of trouble. Rivera's approval rating isn't just in the toilet, it's halfway to the sewage treatment facility. His advisors are going nuts. It's 24/7 damage control."

"I'm sorry."

His response was a shrug. "Don't be. If we're going to go down, I'd prefer it be because we insisted on doing our jobs—upholding the law."

She had to laugh. "You don't believe that."

"No, not really. But I know you do, and I respect that about you. I guess."

"Thank you. I guess." She tilted her chin at his mug. "Is that stuff working?"

He looked insulted. "You can't tell?"

His body looked exactly the same to her, but she said, "Looks like you lost a few pounds."

"Now you're the one saying what you don't believe. Forget the tea. Tell me about the trial. Are you making headway?"

"Maybe. It's hard to tell. Like you said, this isn't a typical case where all I need to do is prove the elements of the crime to the jury. This jury might not care if what Brooke Raines did was a crime. I need to make them care, and I'm not sure if I'm succeeding."

"Is the police department backing you up? Where's the lead detective?"

"Fulco? Probably submitting his resume to every law enforcement agency he can find."

"Too bad Leary's not with the department anymore."

"No kidding." If Leary were still on the job, he'd be all over this case, working overtime to find enough evidence to make the jury's decision a no-brainer. But Leary wasn't a cop anymore, and even though she was tempted to call him for help, she knew doing so would be a selfish move. Leary was struggling to move on and to accept life as a civilian. If she recruited his help on this case, she'd only set back his progress and cause him more pain and regret. She'd rather lose the trial—and her own job—than do that to him.

"Anyone else you can call?" Warren said.

"Actually, I think there is."

23.

When Emily Graham showed up at Jessie's office, she had a bag in her hand—white plastic over brown paper. She reached her free hand to Jessie's desk, pushed some files aside, and withdrew several containers of Chinese food. A mouthwatering aroma filled the small office.

"You're a life saver," Jessie said, "in more ways than one."

"Nope. Just a friend." Graham dropped into one of Jessie's guest chairs and pulled two sets of chopsticks from the bag. She smiled as she passed one set across the desk.

Jessie smiled back. "You certainly are that."

The two women had first met working on the case of a school shooting, an incident that had traumatized the city. They had not liked each other much at first, but trauma has a way of bringing people together. By the time they'd beaten the odds and won justice for the dead, Graham had become a close friend.

Graham leaned forward and opened one of the containers. Mongolian beef. Steam rose into her face and her short, blonde hair. Jessie opened the other container and found chicken lo mein.

"I thought we'd share," Graham said.

"You thought right. Thanks for bringing this. I didn't realize how hungry I was."

"Yeah, I figured you'd forget to eat. What's Leary up to tonight?"

"Still at work, I think."

"That's good, right? He's getting more enthusiastic about his new job?"

"I think so."

They ate in silence for a few minutes. Then Graham said, "So, I'm here. You said you wanted my advice. Safe to assume this is about the Corbin Keeley trial?"

"I knew going in that it would be a difficult case. But." She let out a sigh. "I guess I didn't realize it would be this hard."

"Probably not a great time to tell you this, but you're not the most popular prosecutor around the PPD Homicide Division right now."

"If I could have avoided embarrassing Fulco, I would have. You know that."

"No one cares about Fulco. It's the case. The detectives—especially the ones who've been around for a while—don't think you should have brought charges."

"They're wrong." Jessie felt a swell of defensiveness. She didn't like the feeling, and forced herself to push it aside. "Brooke Raines broke the law. Her shooting of Keeley wasn't self-defense."

"That's what you say." Graham jabbed her chopsticks in Jessie's direction. "But some a-hole starts hitting me, I'm not going to stand there and take it, either."

"Yeah, but would you shoot him?"

"Maybe. If he was bigger and stronger than me, and beating the hell out of me."

"Keeley wasn't beating Raines that night. The most he did was throw a rock at her, and even that hasn't been established with any evidence other than her statement. There were no prints on the rock." She stopped speaking when she saw the look of horror on Graham's face.

"Are you listening to yourself? I read her statement. She tried to leave and he tried to stop her. He was angry and she knew damn well what he was capable of when he was angry. I mean, look at that photo of the ex-wife. What would you do? Hope to God you can get to your car before he bashes your head in with a rock? Or use the gun you're licensed to carry?"

"Are you angry at me?" Jessie said. Her appetite, powerful a moment ago, was gone now.

Graham looked surprised. "No, I.... I don't know. Maybe I am." Graham put down her chopticks. "I just never thought you'd be one of those lawyers who make domestic abuse victims look like liars."

"That's not what I'm doing. The evidence—"

"Who's next? Rape victims?"

"That's not fair, Emily."

"You don't think Keeley abused her?"

"That's not the legal standard for self-defense. Her life needed to be in immediate danger at the time she killed him. In this case, it's not clear she was in *any* danger. She had no bruises. He had no marks on him. The rock had no prints. His daughter and ex-wife say he got help and changed. I even met his sponsor from Domestic Violence Anonymous."

"Men like that don't change," Graham said.

Jessie looked down at her food and felt ill. There was a tension in the room she hadn't felt since the early days of their relationship, before they'd come to trust and respect each other. She could feel Graham's stare, judgmental and offended.

"This isn't about men in general, or domestic abuse," Jessie said. She felt the need to choose her words carefully now, even with her friend. "This is about two individuals and the facts of their case. Can't you set aside your preconceptions?"

"Apparently *you* can."

"I have mixed feelings, too," Jessie said, "but the law is clear. Even if he beat her on other occasions, there was no legal justification to kill him that night. It was murder."

Graham leaned back in her chair. "When you called, you said you needed my help."

"That's right. But if you don't want to get involved

in this, I understand. I didn't realize how strong your feelings were."

Graham waved her chopsticks. "Of course I'll help."

Jessie stared at her. "I don't get it. You just told me how morally opposed you are to the whole case."

"Yes, but I've also known you long enough to know you wouldn't be prosecuting this woman without a good reason. What do you need?"

Jessie felt incredibly grateful, but also pretty guilty. "This case has the potential to ruin a lot of careers. Not just Fulco's."

"All the more reason to help you. The last thing I want is a change of regime at the DA's office. You're one of the only lawyers I can stand. Let's start from the beginning. What did you find that made you question Fulco's report?"

"You want to do this right now?" Jessie's gaze went to her clock. "Don't you have anything better to do on a Friday night?"

Graham arched a pale eyebrow. "No offense, but do you think I would be sitting with you in the DA's office, eating Chinese food from the container, if I had a hot date?"

"You might be, yeah."

Graham laughed. "Point taken. Now stop keeping me in suspense. Let's do this."

"Thanks, Emily."

Graham left hours later, and Jessie carried their

empty cartons of Chinese food to a garbage can down the hall that wouldn't stink up her office. Graham was going above and beyond for her, but chances were she wouldn't be able to find anything in the short time they had, especially over the weekend, when people were harder to reach. Jessie had to assume the detective would come up empty.

What else could she do to bolster her case? *How do you prove a negative—that circumstances justifying self-defense didn't exist?*

Maybe that was the wrong way to look at it. She didn't need to prove that something hadn't happened. Something *had* happened. Brooke Raines had shot Corbin Keeley in the parking lot behind Bistro Cannata. The questions were how it had happened, and why it had happened. If only there had been a witness to the shooting itself, someone who could testify about exactly what had happened in that parking lot.

She remembered the video taken from a surveillance camera of a neighboring jewelry store. After watching it, she had agreed with Fulco's initial assessment that it was of zero value. The angle barely captured the parking lot at the edge of the frame, and the footage was so grainy that, even if the shooting had occurred in view of the camera, she might not have even been able to tell what the grainy footage showed. Finding any suspicious details in the video—or any details at all—seemed highly unlikely.

Then again, she'd reached a point in the case where "unlikely" might be the best chance she had. It was better than nothing, at any rate.

She knew a man named Tito Vallez who worked as a video forensic specialist in the Philly PD's Digital Media Evidence Unit. If anyone could find value in the video, it would be Vallez. Glancing at her clock, she saw that the time had slipped to 9:14 PM. He'd probably be home, or out, enjoying his Friday evening like a normal person. Then again, he was young, single, and ambitious, and had been known to burn the midnight oil on interesting cases before.

She picked up her phone again. It was worth a shot.

24.

Jessie arrived at the Roundhouse at 9:30 PM and was not surprised to find the place a ghost town. Most of the detectives were off-duty at this hour, and any who were working were out in the field, staring at crime scenes that had ruined their Friday evening plans.

But video forensic specialist Tito Vallez was working. He greeted her with a warm smile and ushered her into the video lab of the Digital Media Evidence Unit, saying, "Welcome to my workshop."

"Thanks for sticking around to meet with me."

"For you, Jessie? Anytime."

Vallez was young and good-looking, pleasant to talk to, and, most importantly to Jessie, a smart and hard worker. He had a unique fashion sense. Today, he wore a blue suit that must have cost two-thousand dollars over a video game tee shirt that had probably set him back five bucks, black Vans shoes, and trendy glasses with black frames. Hardly standard cop attire, and she knew it irritated some of the old guard. But she admired his insistence on self-expression. He worked in a lab all day and rarely came into contact with the outside world. As long as he helped solve crimes and convict criminals (and wore a real suit and tie if called into court), why should anyone care if he deviated from a dress code established almost a century ago?

She pointed at his tee shirt. "*Legend of Zelda?*"

"Too hipsterish?"

"No, you wear it well."

"Thanks. Buttering me up isn't going to improve the quality of that video, though."

"Can't blame a girl for trying."

He laughed. "Come on, let's see what we can do."

She followed him to a workstation in the lab. He dropped into a chair in front of a monitor and gestured for her to take the chair next to him. The swift transition from small talk to work talk didn't surprise her. Beneath his funky clothing and flirtatious manner, Vallez was all business.

"I know it's not great quality," she said, "but I'm hoping—"

He raised a hand. "Hold on. Just to set expectations. The video isn't just 'not great quality,' okay? The video was pulled from a VHS tape—you know, the kind you rented in the 80's to watch *Sixteen Candles* at your sleepover party, and you had to remember to *Be Kind, Rewind?*"

"How old do you think I am?"

"Well, you did recognize an 8 bit image from *The*

Legend of Zelda." Vallez laughed. "Anyway, the video was recorded onto the VHS tape by a Scout Z900. Ever heard of it? No? That's because the company that made it, Quanto Systems, ceased manufacturing two decades ago. And I don't mean they just ceased manufacturing this model. I mean, they ceased manufacturing, period. They went out of business in 1997."

"I get it," Jessie said. "The video was recorded by outdated equipment, onto an outdated storage medium. Can you clean it up at all?"

"Not really. This isn't a TV cop show, where I can just stare at the screen, yell, 'Enhance!' and magically get 4K visuals. I have software that can help a little, but from a starting point as bad as this...." His voice trailed off.

"Okay," she said. "You've set my expectations appropriately low. Now, let's do what we can."

Vallez turned on the equipment in front of them. The monitor flared to life, showing what looked like a typical Windows desktop. "I digitized the video and saved it, so at least we won't have to dig a VCR out of storage." He opened a software application and started navigating its menus. The pointer moved almost too quickly to follow, so Jessie sat back in her chair and waited.

The video opened in a window at the center of the screen. It displayed the sidewalk just in front of the doors to the jewelry store from which they'd obtained the tape. A small area of the neighboring parking lot was visible at the periphery of the screen.

"These security cameras from the 1980's had terrible resolution and low frame rates," Vallez said. The disgust in his voice was almost comical. "So you're not going to be making out any fine details. By the way, what details are you even looking for? Based on the time code, the incident should be happening right ... about ... now." They watched the screen. A figure moved in and out of the frame—probably a woman, but it was hard to tell. A second figure followed her a moment later. In and out of view, and then they were staring at the static image again. "Thrilling, right?"

"The shooting is happening right now?"

"Best guess, based on the time code." Vallez paused the video. "Not very exciting when you can't see it. I can think of lots of better movies we could watch together on a Friday night."

"Can you make the video any clearer? Can you zoom in on the parking lot?"

"I can zoom in," Vallez said. "Won't help much, though. I can't turn the camera." Working the mouse, he dragged a square over the visible area of the parking lot, then clicked through some menus. The square grew to fill the window. The image became larger, but the blurriness also increased. "You want me to run the video again?"

"Yes, please."

He did. She watched the static image of the parking lot, and, as before, saw the two indistinct figures and then nothing. Vallez paused it again.

"Maybe if you tell me what you're looking for...."

"I don't know what I'm looking for."

"Should I play it again?"

She was about to say yes when she noticed something she hadn't seen before In the corner of the zoomed-in video window. She pointed to a car parked in the lot.

"Is that what I think it is?" she said.

Vallez squinted at the image. "Nissan Sentra, I think. My sis drives one."

"Not the car. The driver."

"Driver?" Vallez leaned closer to the screen. "Holy crap—you're right. Looks like a face behind the windshield. Or a dinner plate. Or a balloon."

"No, that's a person, Tito." She felt enthusiasm buzz through her. "Dinner plates and balloons don't sit in the driver's seat of a car." If there had been a person in one of the cars in the lot, that meant she might have a witness. "Can you zoom in on him?"

"This is as much zoom as the source can handle. Any more, we'll be looking at pixels the size of Lego bricks."

She was sure the blob visible behind the windshield of the car was a face, but beyond that, she couldn't discern anything. The person could be male or female, black or white, nineteen or ninety. There had to be a way to identify him or her.

Her gaze ticked from the face to the car, searching for an identifying characteristic. She was pretty sure

Vallez was right about the make and model. The car looked like a recent model Nissan Sentra. But the video was black-and-white, so she could not determine the color. There was no license plate to read, because front plates were not required in Pennsylvania—a rule she now cursed as she stared at the blank front of the car. There was a small, square sticker in the upper corner of the windshield. Maybe some kind of parking pass. "Anything you can do with that sticker?"

Vallez looked at her like she was joking.

"I need to find that car," she said.

"Well, there are other surveillance cameras in the city, right? You know you're looking for a Nissan Sentra, and you know the date and approximate time. You could check other cameras in the area, like traffic cameras, and see if any of them picked up a Nissan Sentra driving by before or after the time of this video. If one of them picked up a plate number, then bingo."

It sounded like a long shot, but it was something. "I'll try that. Thanks, Tito."

"Like I said—for you, any time."

She pulled out her phone to call Emily Graham.

25.

While Jessie was working late on the Keeley case, Leary was in his apartment, thinking about his own case. A knock at the door disturbed him. He knew from the sound of the knock—a hard, businesslike rap—that it wasn't Jessie, and there was no one else he was interested in seeing right now. He left the chain hooked in place and opened the door a crack, ready to tell whoever was there that he wasn't interested.

"Hey, Leary."

Leary froze, caught completely off-guard. His visitor was Toby Novak, Emily Graham's partner. That was unexpected, but not unwelcome. He liked Novak. He wasn't sure about the two men Novak stood in the hallway with, though. Ramrod-stiff postures, close-cropped hair, ill-fitting suits, and facial expressions that could mean either serious concentration or serious constipation. Definitely cops. What were they doing here?

"Hold on, Toby. I'll open the door."

Once his visitors were inside, Novak made introductions. "Gentlemen, this is Mark Leary. As you know, he used to be a detective at the PPD. Leary, meet Dominick Chernin and Rupert Bertie, detectives from the Mendham Township Police Department Detective Bureau, out of Jersey. They need to speak with you about an incident in their township, and since we're friends, I volunteered to coordinate."

Mendham Township? Now Leary was definitely uneasy. But he shook hands and offered each man a friendly nod, despite the feeling that they were looking at him more like a suspect than a colleague. "What's this about?"

"You're familiar with Mendham Township?" Chernin said. "It's a relatively small town in New Jersey. Police department only has fifteen people, including me and Bertie."

"If you're here, you must know I visited the town a few days ago."

Chernin rocked back on his heels. "Well, we *didn't* know you were there for sure, but thanks for telling us."

Leary cringed inwardly. It had been a while since he'd played this game, and he was getting rusty. "Let's sit down." He led them into his apartment to a small kitchenette with a table for four. Novak shrugged out of his coat, draped it over the back of a chair, and sat down. The two New Jersey cops stood stiffly for a moment, then did the same. Leary sat down last. "How can I help you?"

"One of our residents committed suicide. This was found on her body." The detective pulled a folded sheet of paper from his pocket, unfolded it, and showed it to Leary. It was a photocopy of the slip of paper he'd given to Lydia Wax showing his name and cell number.

He tried to hide any surprise. The two cops leaned forward and watched him closely. He knew they were studying his face for reactions, just as he'd studied so many suspects. His hands, under the table, gripped his legs.

"The woman you're talking about," Leary said slowly, "what's her name?"

"Lydia Wax."

"Are you sure it was suicide?"

"That's an unusual question to ask," Detective Bertie said.

"According to the autopsy, it was," Detective Chernin said. "Is there a reason to think it wouldn't be?"

"Maybe." As a former cop, Leary knew that if given the chance, these detectives would extract as much information from him as possible while revealing as little as possible of what they knew. He'd already slipped up once by admitting he'd been to their town. He didn't plan to give them any more information without receiving some in return. "How did she do it?"

Bertie let out a quiet laugh under his breath. "Mr. Leary, we'll ask the questions."

"And I'll answer them," he said, "but first I want to know what happened."

"Come on, guys," Novak said. "You can relax. Leary's one of us."

Chernin exchanged a glance with his partner, then shrugged. "Nothing dramatic. She took a bunch of pills, went to sleep, and never woke up."

"And you're sure she took the pills voluntarily?"

Bertie sighed. "There were no defensive wounds. No signs of a struggle in her bedroom or anywhere else in her house. No strange visitors."

"Other than you," Chernin said.

"Leary, what were you doing in New Jersey?" Novak said.

"I was investigating one of my own cases."

"What are you, a PI or something?" Chernin said.

"No, I mean one of my old cases, from back when I was a homicide detective. A murder case I worked three years ago. Lydia Wax killed her boyfriend, a man named Terence Resta. She stabbed him with a knife and claimed she did it in self-defense. He had been violent with her before, so her story seemed credible and no charges were ever brought in the case."

"So why were you visiting this woman three years later?" Bertie said. "In connection with a closed case? When you're not even a cop anymore?"

Leary heard the exasperation in the detective's voice. He sensed that both men were annoyed to have to deal with a suicide in their peaceful little upper class township, and even more annoyed to have to drive two hours to Philadelphia because some former cop had stuck his nose where it didn't belong. Leary could explain the whole story to them—that a new self-defense incident had triggered his memories of the three-year-old case, and that he'd never been satisfied with its resolution, and that that's why he'd made the trip to visit Lydia Wax—but he didn't like the tone of either of these New Jersey detectives, and he didn't feel like giving them an explanation.

"Did she leave a note?" Leary said.

"What?" Chernin looked even more annoyed. "You want to answer my questions, or what, Leary?"

"I'm asking you if Lydia Wax left a suicide note."

"No, she didn't. Now, you better explain your role in all this, or I'm going to get impatient and arrest you."

The threat was offered without much conviction, since everyone in the room knew that there was no basis for an arrest, and even if there were, a couple of detectives from Mendham Township, New Jersey, had no jurisdiction to arrest him in Philly.

"I told you what my involvement is. I visited Ms. Wax to follow up on my old case. I thought it was interesting that she seemed to have a lot more money than she did three years ago. I questioned her a little bit, to see if she would say anything that might undermine her original claim of self-defense."

"What, you think she murdered the guy?"

"When you found her body, did you search her phone records? Had she called anyone immediately prior to taking the pills?"

The look the two detectives gave each other told Leary everything he needed to know.

"You found something suspicious, didn't you?" Leary said. "What? A recently called number saved under a strange name? A second phone altogether?" The detectives looked at each other again. "It *was* a second phone, in addition to her main phone. One with prepaid minutes and not tied to an account, right? A burner. And I'm guessing whatever calls she made with it, those numbers led you nowhere."

"I think we've given you enough information already," Chernin said. "Too much." He got up from his chair. His partner followed suit. "We'll be in touch."

Novak shot Leary an apologetic look, then walked to the door with the two New Jersey detectives. He said, "Good seeing you, Leary. Have a good night." Then they were gone.

Leary locked up after them. No note, he thought, but the timing of Lydia Wax's suicide, and the presence of the burner phone, were as good as a confession to him. She'd killed Terry Resta, and a company called CBL Capital Partners had paid her to do it. Maybe it was time he spoke to someone at the company.

26.

If Jessie had ever had any doubts about Emily Graham's prowess as a detective, they were put to rest by the speed with which Graham obtained the license plate number of the Nissan Sentra from the parking lot outside Bistro Cannata.

Graham had taken Tito Vallez's suggestion and run with it, finding two traffic cameras that had recorded the car after it drove out of the lot minutes before the police arrived at the scene of the shooting. The car—which turned out to be silver—was registered to a person named Conrad Deprisco with an address in Center City.

Jessie and Graham drove to the house in Graham's unmarked car. The first time they reached the house, Graham drove past it and they both got a look at a small but attractive row house with a brick facade located on a quiet street in an upscale section of the city. Then Graham parked a block away.

"I'm not sure you should come in with me," Graham said.

Jessie was already unbuckling her seatbelt. "Why

wouldn't I?"

Graham drummed her fingers on the steering wheel. Her gaze seemed unusually intense, and her lips were pursed. "We don't know much about this guy, Jessie. We don't know what to expect."

They knew a little bit about him from the DMV database. He was eighteen, five-foot-eleven, with blue eyes. "Given his address, I doubt we're dealing with a gangbanger," Jessie said.

"Yeah, well, he witnessed a shooting—saw a man die—and didn't call the police or come forward with information. That's not normal behavior."

She couldn't argue with that. "Doesn't mean he's dangerous."

"Maybe it does," Graham said. "We're both experienced enough to know what it means when a witness to a crime doesn't come forward. It means they have something to hide."

"Yes, but not always related to the crime. I'm going with you."

Before Graham could object, Jessie opened the passenger-side door and climbed out of the car. She heard her friend breathe a curse before she exited the car on the driver's side. Together, they walked the block to Deprisco's house.

Graham touched her arm as they neared the house. "If anything seems suspicious, you run. Got it?"

Now that she was standing on the sidewalk, looking at the front door of the row house, Jessie felt a jolt of adrenaline and fear. Her breathing became shallow and rapid. She forced herself to take a deep breath.

She understood Graham's concern. Anything could happen in a moment like this. Nine times out of ten, a detective interviewed a potential witness without incident. But one time out of ten, something went wrong. The witness ran. Or he started a fistfight. Or he pulled a gun. As a lawyer, Jessie didn't really belong here. But then again, Graham didn't really belong here, either. Keeley was not her case.

"Are you ready?" Graham said.

"Yes."

Jessie tried to hide her anxiety, but a crack in her voice betrayed her. Graham turned to study her face. "You have nothing to prove to me."

"I know. I want to do this."

Graham sighed. "Okay. Let's do it, then."

The detective climbed the steps to the front door and pushed the doorbell. Jessie stood beside her. When there was no response, Jessie almost laughed. All that nervous energy, and the guy wasn't even home. But then the door opened and a middle-aged woman looked out at them.

The woman was tall and well-dressed. Her hair—brown streaked with gray—looked like it had been recently styled. Her fingernails were neatly manicured. She wore simple but expensive-looking jewelry—a necklace, a bracelet, and several rings. "Can I help you?"

Graham showed the woman her badge. "We're

looking for Conrad Deprisco. Is he here?"

"I'm his mother, Irene Deprisco. What is this about?"

"We'd like to talk to him."

"I understand that." The wind picked up, whistling in Jessie's ears. Irene Deprisco shivered, but did not budge from her place in the doorway. "I'm asking what it's about."

"It's a private matter," Graham said.

"I'm his mother."

"Conrad is eighteen," Graham said. "He's not a minor."

The woman continued to block their path. Her expression was stony. Jessie didn't think Graham's approach was going to get them very far with her, so she spoke up.

"We should introduce ourselves. This is Emily Graham, a detective from the Philadelphia Police Department. I'm Jessica Black, from the district attorney's office. It's really important that we speak with your son. He's not in trouble. We think he may have seen something and that he may be able to help us with an investigation. If he's home, we'd really like to talk to him."

The woman seemed to study Jessie for a moment, as if deciding whether she could trust her. Jessie held her breath. After a few seconds, the woman said, "I suppose I don't have much of a choice. Come inside."

She led them to a small family room and invited

them to sit down on a couch. Then she left them there. Once her footsteps receded, the house seemed unnaturally quiet, especially after the windy conditions outside. Jessie took a breath and let her gaze wander the room. The furnishings looked old and expensive. A lot of dark wood.

"This place reminds me of the waiting room in the funeral parlor where we had my uncle's ceremony," Graham said.

"You probably shouldn't share that with Ms. Deprisco."

"You don't think that's the ambiance she's going for?" They exchanged a brief grin.

Irene Deprisco returned a moment later with a skinny eighteen-year-old. "This is Conrad. You can talk to him, but I'm going to be here, too."

Jessie was relieved when Graham didn't object. Persuading the woman to even let them into the house had been a challenge. It might not be wise to push her any more than they already had. She might push back, by demanding that they leave or calling a lawyer.

Conrad bore little resemblance to his mother. Where she was all stiffness and formality, he was a slouching teen with tousled hair, stubble on his cheeks, and bare feet that extended from the torn cuffs of his jeans. Everything about him looked laid back except for his eyes, which seemed to watch Jessie and Graham with nervous caution. "What do you want to know?" He had a husky voice Jessie thought had probably served him well with his female classmates.

"Have you ever been to a restaurant called Bistro Cannata?" Graham said.

"Of course not!" his mother interjected. "Is this a joke? Conrad could barely afford an appetizer at a place like that."

"No offense," Graham said, "but your family appears to be fairly well off."

"My husband and I are well off," Irene corrected her. "Conrad is an unemployed kid. He's not dining at the city's finest establishments."

Jessie listened to the woman, but her attention was focused on Conrad's face. The kid had flinched at the restaurant's name. She leaned toward him. "Conrad, we know you were in the parking lot behind Bistro Cannata on Friday, October 14, the night Councilman Corbin Keeley was shot."

"That's ludicrous," his mother said. "You must have my son confused with someone else."

This was possible. All they really knew was that Conrad's *car* had been in the parking lot—and they didn't even know that for certain. But Conrad's reaction when Graham had spoken the name of the restaurant seemed to indicate that they had the right person.

"We have you on video," Graham said. "From the surveillance camera of a jewelry store next to the parking lot. We know you were there, and we know you witnessed the shooting."

Conrad's mother rounded on her son. "Is this true?"

"No," Conrad said. He shook his head vigorously, but he avoided making eye-contact with anyone in the room. "It wasn't me. I've never been to that parking lot. I swear."

"You *were* there," Graham said. Her voice sounded harsher now, edged with anger. "You were sitting in your car, a silver Nissan Sentra." Graham rattled off the license plate number, and with each digit, more of the color seemed to drain from Conrad's face. "Do you know what obstruction of justice is, Conrad? When you know something about a crime, but you refuse to cooperate with the police, you can be arrested and put in jail. Is that what you want?"

Conrad looked at Jessie and Graham, then at his mother. An expression of helplessness entered his eyes.

Graham let out an exasperated sigh. "I guess we're going to have to place you under arrest."

"Now hold on a second," Irene said. She threw a protective arm in front of her son. "You've obviously made a mistake. If I need to call our lawyer to sort this out, I will."

"That's fine. Your lawyer will tell you the same thing I am about obstruction of justice. In fact, your lawyer will probably explain that you can be arrested, too."

"Me?" Irene Deprisco's eyes widened with indignation.

"Wait!" Conrad's gaze bounced nervously between Graham and his mother. "Mom, maybe I could talk to the police in private?"

"Don't be ridiculous."

"Please, Mom. Just for a minute."

"Ms. Deprisco," Jessie said. "Could you please get us the documentation on your son's car? If you're right and we've made a mistake, that might help clear it up."

The woman hesitated. She obviously wanted to stay and protect her son, but his pleading eyes, along with Jessie's logic, seemed to sway her. She excused herself to retrieve the documents, giving Conrad a look of warning on her way out.

As soon as she left the room, Jessie and Graham leaned toward the kid. "What is it you're uncomfortable telling us in front of your mother?" Jessie said. "Does it involve drugs?"

Conrad shifted his gaze to his bare feet. "It's not like I'm a junkie or anything. I enjoy a little weed now and then. It's relaxing, you know? And I can't smoke at home or my parents would flip. I mean, you met my mom. Imagine."

"I understand," Jessie said. "We're not looking to get you into trouble. We're only interested in the shooting. I'm an assistant district attorney and I am giving you my word that you will not be prosecuted for your marijuana use on the night of the incident."

Conrad nodded, seeming to relax a little. "Okay," he said. A relieved breath hitched out of him. "Thanks."

"Did you see something that night?"

"Yeah." His face darkened, as if from an unpleasant memory. "Yeah, I did."

"What did you see?"

Conrad let out a nervous laugh. "I saw everything."

27.

"Okay, counselors." Judge Armstrong reclined behind the desk in his chambers. He clasped his hands over his chest and looked at them with a serious expression. His judicial robes hung from a hook on one of the wood-paneled walls, and dressed in a white shirt and red tie, he looked more like a businessman than a judge. That seemed appropriate, since he was all business now. "I read your briefs, which I appreciate both of you working on during your weekend, so let's cut the rhetoric. I think the law favors Ms. Black on this one."

"Judge, with all due respect," Hughes said, "I'd ask you to think about what's fair to the defendant here, not just the letter of the law. Ms. Raines is entitled to a fair trial. We've had no time to prepare for this surprise witness."

"You've had just as much time as we have," Jessie said. "As soon as we discovered the existence of this witness, we provided immediate notice."

"On a Sunday," Hughes said. He turned to the judge, his expression imploring.

Jessie said, "Just because you don't like what he has to say isn't grounds for excluding his testimony."

The judge raised his hands for quiet. "Mr. Hughes, have you reviewed the notice and discovery provided by the Commonwealth?" When the defense attorney did not answer immediately, Armstrong said, "I know you have, given the detailed arguments in your brief. There is precedent for introducing evidence at a late stage—especially crucial evidence like an eyewitness present during the commission of the act. You haven't provided any argument to dissuade me from allowing this potentially critical evidence to be presented to the jury."

"Well, obviously, we reserve this issue for appeal," Hughes said. "In the highly unlikely event that we don't win this trial." He shot Jessie a look that said he fully intended to prevail. She met his gaze without blinking.

The judge nodded. "I think the jury has waited long enough. Let's get to the courtroom."

Conrad Deprisco had shaved his stubble and combed his hair. In khaki pants, a light blue button-down dress shirt, and a navy sport jacket, he had a clean-cut, boy-next-door appearance. He looked trustworthy.

Jessie saw her own impressions of Conrad reflected in the faces and body language of the jurors, who pivoted toward the witness with open expressions. A good start. She wasn't about to get comfortable, though. Conrad's nice clothes and boyish face wouldn't get him very far once Hughes started pounding on him. Still, first impressions mattered, and she intended to make the best of the kid's.

"Hi, Conrad," she said as she approached her witness. "Could you please tell the jury where you were on the night of October 14?"

"I was in my car in the parking lot behind a restaurant called Bistro Cannata."

"Did you witness anything unusual that night?"

"Yes. I witnessed a woman shoot and kill a man."

A surprised murmur rippled through the jury box and the gallery. "Can you describe for the jury your line of sight to these two people?"

"Clear line of sight. No obstacles between us."

"Do you recognize either of those people here today?"

"Yes," Conrad said. He stared at Brooke Raines, who stared back at him with a look of disbelief. "The woman is right there." Conrad pointed at the defense table.

Judge Armstrong leaned toward his court reporter. "Let the record reflect that the witness has identified the defendant, Brooke Raines."

"And the person you saw Ms. Raines shoot was a man?" Jessie said.

"Yes."

Jessie showed him one of the Commonwealth's exhibits, a smiling photograph of Corbin Keeley. "This man?"

"Yes."

The judge commented for the record again.

"Thank you," Jessie said. "Conrad, you say you had an unobstructed view. On a scale of one to ten, with one being the least sure and ten the most sure, how sure are you that the woman you saw was Brooke Raines and the man you saw was Corbin Keeley?"

"Ten," he said without hesitation.

"Could you hear anything?"

"Yes. I had the driver's side window down. The parking lot was quiet. I heard everything they said, and I heard the gunshot. It was so loud I thought it might burst my eardrums."

"Objection," Hughes said.

The judge nodded. "Sustained. Mr. Deprisco, just stick to the facts."

"Before you tell the jury what you witnessed, I have a few other questions for you," Jessie said. She'd reached the trickiest part of her direct examination, and she needed to tread carefully. She had just prepared the jury to hear what had really happened in the parking lot on the night Keeley died. And then she'd paused. This was the point at which she planned to reveal Conrad's drug use—while the jury's curiosity and attention were still strongly focused on learning what he'd seen. If she played the moment right, the jurors' attention would glide over Conrad's marijuana use in their eagerness to get to the answers they cared about. "I need you to explain what you were doing sitting alone in your car in a parking lot at night, with your window down."

"I was smoking weed."

"You were smoking marijuana," Jessie said. "You are aware that's a crime under the laws of Pennsylvania?"

"Yes."

"Objection," Hughes said. "Aside from the fact that the Commonwealth is clearly leading the witness, I have no doubt that Mr. Deprisco has been assured of his immunity in exchange for testifying today."

"That's a question you are free to explore on cross," Judge Armstrong said. "Your objection is overruled, but I urge Ms. Black to take better care in forming her questions in a less leading manner."

"Yes, Your Honor," Jessie said. "Conrad, would you please tell the jury what you saw and heard?"

"The first thing I heard was the sound of high heels clicking on pavement. I looked up and this pretty woman—the woman over there—walked around the side of the restaurant and came into the parking lot."

"Was she walking or running?" Jessie said.

"Walking."

"What happened next?"

"The woman walked maybe six steps into the lot, and then the man came around the building, too. He was kind of jogging, I guess. Like he wanted to catch up with her."

"Then what happened?"

"He said, 'Wait,' and she stopped and turned around and faced him. He said, 'Can we finish dinner?' She didn't answer. Then—"

Jessie lifted a hand, gesturing for him to pause. "Can you describe his tone of voice?"

"Objection," Hughes said. "His tone of voice? Seriously?"

"Overruled. I'm going to allow Mr. Deprisco to answer. Go ahead, please."

"He sounded ... friendly, I guess," Conrad said. "Like he was trying to be nice so she'd go back to the restaurant with him."

"Did he raise his voice?" Jessie said.

"No."

"Did he sound threatening?"

Hughes was on his feet again. "Your Honor!"

The judge nodded. "Ms. Black, I think you've made your point. Let's move on."

"Thank you, Your Honor. Conrad, after you saw Mr. Keeley follow Ms. Raines into the parking lot and try to talk to her, what did you see and hear next?"

"She was looking for something in her bag. He took another step closer to her. She pulled out a gun."

"Go on," Jessie said.

"He sort of froze in place, staring at her. Like he was so surprised, he wasn't sure what to think."

"Objection," Hughes said. "Mr. Deprisco had no idea what the victim was thinking."

"Sustained," Judge Armstrong said. "Stick to the facts, please—just tell us what you saw and heard."

"What happened next?" Jessie said.

"She aimed the gun at his head and shot him."

Jessie glanced at the jurors and watched their faces as Conrad's version of events settled in. "Conrad, at the time Ms. Raines shot Mr. Keeley, did she appear to you to be in immediate danger?"

"Objection," Hughes said. "Calls for a legal conclusion."

"I disagree," the judge said. "Overruled. Please answer the question."

"I don't think she was in any danger," Conrad said.

"And after she shot him, what did she do next?"

"There was a rock on the ground. She picked it up and threw it at the wall of the building."

A roar of excited voices rose from the gallery. Judge Armstrong banged his gavel until his courtroom settled back into polite silence. During the brief moment of chaos, Jessie looked at the jury and saw the expressions of shock she'd been hoping for. Conrad's testimony had the potential to turn the whole case around.

"Brooke Raines threw the rock, not Corbin Keeley?" Jessie said.

"Yeah. She threw the rock."

"You're absolutely sure about that?"

"Absolutely."

"Why do you think she would do that?"

"Objection!" Hughes practically screamed.

"Thank you," Jessie said. "I have no further questions."

28.

"Mr. Hughes," Judge Armstrong said. "Your witness."

Hughes approached the witness stand and glared at Conrad with an expression that was equal parts disbelief and disgust. Conrad seemed to shrink into himself. He looked away from Hughes and stared at an invisible spot in the distance.

"Mr. Deprisco," Hughes said, "my name is Aidan Hughes. I'm the attorney representing Brooke Raines, whom the Commonwealth alleges committed a crime when she shot Mr. Keeley on the night of October 14. Your testimony seems to support the prosecution's theory of this case, but I have to say, it was pretty shocking for my client and me to hear—and for the jury, too, I'm sure."

He paused, probably hoping Conrad would say something to fill the silence. Jessie had not had much time to prepare him, but one thing she had done was warn him about avoiding certain lawyer tricks. *Only respond if you are asked a question*, had been one of those tips, and judging by his silence, he'd taken it to heart.

Hughes shrugged. "Okay, Mr. Deprisco, let's get down to it, then. A few minutes ago, you admitted that you were abusing an illegal drug on the night in question, correct?"

"I was smoking weed—"

"The answer is yes?"

"Yes."

"How much weed were you smoking?"

Conrad looked uncertain. "It was a joint. Maybe half a gram?"

"You only smoked one joint?"

"Uh, well, no, I guess I smoked two." Conrad ran his fingers through his hair, and the carefully combed strands reverted to the tousled mess Jessie remembered from their visit to his house.

"Which is it, Mr. Deprisco? One joint or two joints?"

"Two."

"Where did you get the marijuana?"

"A friend."

"Did your friend *give* you the marijuana or *sell* you the marijuana?"

"He sold it to me."

Hughes turned to the jury and arched an eyebrow. A few of the jurors shook their heads with disapproval. "So he's your drug dealer, not your friend, correct?"

"I mean, he's both."

"Does he sell drugs to other people, or just you?"

"Other people."

"So he is a drug dealer, right?"

"I guess so."

"Did he sell you just the marijuana you smoked that night—the two joints you described as containing about half a gram of marijuana each?"

"No."

"How much marijuana did he sell you?"

"Objection," Jessie said. "It's already been established that Mr. Deprisco smoked two joins during the night in question. Further details are not relevant."

Judge Armstrong nodded. "I agree. Sustained."

"Mr. Deprisco, are you being compensated in any way for your testimony today?"

"Compensated? You mean, like being paid? No." Conrad crossed his arms over his chest and straightened up. Jessie recognized defensive body language and knew it would not play well to the jury. If only she'd had a few days to better prepare him.

"Did the Commonwealth promise not to file criminal charges against you for your drug-related offense in exchange for your testimony?"

"No," Conrad said, his voice a little too loud. "I mean, it wasn't 'in exchange.' Ms. Black said I didn't have to worry about the marijuana."

Jessie felt a muscle in her jaw twitch as she struggled to maintain a neutral expression. Hughes said, "You didn't have to worry about it. That's nice."

"Objection," she bit out.

Hughes lifted a hand before the judge could rule. "I'll move on. Mr. Deprisco, you testified that after you bought marijuana from a drug dealer and you drove to the parking lot behind Bistro Cannata and you smoked two joints, you saw my client, Ms. Raines, run into the parking lot. Is that correct?"

"Objection," Jessie said. "Mr. Hughes is misrepresenting the witness's testimony. He very clearly stated that he observed Ms. Raines *walking* into the lot."

"Walking," Hughes amended. "My apologies, Your Honor. Mr. Deprisco *was* very specific on that detail, almost as if he'd been coached on its importance."

"Objection!" Jessie said.

"Sustained," the judge said. "The jury will please disregard counsel's color commentary."

Jessie fumed. Hughes was methodically discrediting her witness, and doing a good job of it.

Hughes said, "You saw my client, Ms. Raines, enter the lot?"

"Yes," Conrad said.

"After that, you saw Mr. Keeley pursue my client into the parking lot. Correct?"

"I don't know if he was pursuing her."

"He was following her?"

"Yes."

"And moving in her direction?"

"Yes."

"And, I believe you testified, jogging?"

"Yes."

"So he was pursuing her, right?"

Conrad ran his fingers through his hair again. "I guess so."

"And then you saw and heard them argue."

"They talked."

"Did they seem to be agreeing with each other? Or expressing affection for each other?"

"No."

"Did it seem more like Mr. Keeley wanted one thing, and Ms. Raines wanted a different thing?"

"Maybe, yeah."

"He wanted her to stay, and she wanted to leave?"

"I think so."

"So they were arguing, or having a disagreement or a debate of some nature, right?"

"I guess."

"And then something happened and Ms. Raines shot Mr. Keeley, correct?"

"It was like I said." Conrad's voice cracked on the word, and his gaze swept the courtroom with a hunted, almost fearful expression. "She took her gun out of her purse, aimed, and shot him—"

"How much time passed, approximately, between the moment Mr. Keeley pursued Ms. Raines and the moment she shot him?"

"I don't know."

"You don't know? Is that because your perception of time was impaired by the marijuana you'd been smoking?"

"Objection," Jessie said.

Hughes looked at the judge and spread his hands. "Your Honor, I'm trying to understand why the witness is unable to approximate the time as requested."

Armstrong nodded. "Answer the question, Mr. Deprisco."

"I wasn't impaired. I guess it was a few seconds."

"A few seconds. You guess. But you testified that you didn't think Ms. Raines was in any danger, didn't you?"

"Yes."

"It was nighttime, correct?"

"Yes."

"Was there a lot of light in the parking lot?"

"Not really, no. A few lamps."

"It was actually pretty dark, wasn't it? Hard to see?"

"I could see."

Hughes cast a skeptical look at the jury, then returned his focus to the kid. "Was it easier to see, harder to see, or the same, as if it were daytime?"

"Well, harder than if it was daytime, obviously. But I could see—"

"Was there smoke in your car?"

"Smoke?"

"You testified earlier that you lowered the window of your car, right?"

"Yes."

"Did you lower the window of your car to let out the smoke from the marijuana joints you were smoking?"

"I guess."

"So there must have been smoke in the car, right?"

"Yes."

"Are you sure Mr. Keeley didn't throw a rock at Ms. Raines?"

"I'm sure."

"But you agree it was nighttime. There wasn't a lot of light in the parking lot. There was smoke in your car. And it was harder to see than it would have been during the day. And everything happened in the space of a few seconds. But you are still telling us, and asking us to believe you when you tell us, that you could tell with absolute certainty that my client, Ms. Raines, was not in any danger, and that Mr. Keeley did not throw a rock at her?"

"Yes. I know what I saw."

"How many years have you been smoking marijuana?"

"Objection, relevance," Jessie said.

"Your Honor, if you give me a second, the relevance will be clear."

"Okay," the judge said. "Please answer, Mr. Deprisco."

"About two years."

"So it's fair to say you are an experienced marijuana user?"

"I don't know about 'experienced.'"

"Based on your two years using marijuana, wouldn't you agree that one of the effects of marijuana is that it alters your perceptions?"

"Objection," Jessie said. "The witness is not an expert on the effects of marijuana use."

"I'll rephrase," Hughes said. "Is it your testimony today, under oath and under penalty of perjury, that after smoking two marijuana joints, your vision, sense of time, attention and focus, and other senses were not in any way whatsoever impaired?"

Conrad hesitated. His eyes flicked from Hughes to Jessie. He swallowed hard.

Jessie felt a sinking feeling in her stomach. It didn't matter what he said now. He was physically unraveling in front of the jury.

"Please answer the question," the judge said.

"I don't know," Conrad said. His voice had dropped to a mumble that was almost inaudible.

"You don't know if you were impaired?" Hughes said.

Conrad licked his lips.

"Objection," Jessie said. "Asked and answered. The witness said he doesn't know." At this point, the best she could do to help him was to try to force Hughes to move on.

"Sustained," the judge said.

"Sure, Your Honor. I'm almost done. Just a few more questions. Mr. Deprisco, did your parents know you were in a parking lot smoking marijuana that night?"

"No."

"You didn't tell them?"

He shook his head. "No."

"When you saw the shooting, did you call the police?"

"No."

"Did you tell your parents?"

"No."

"In fact, you didn't tell anyone about what you had seen until Ms. Black and Detective Graham visited your house, correct?"

"Yes."

"So you weren't honest with your parents about that night?"

"No."

"And you weren't honest with the prosecutor or the police about that night, either, until they caught you. Correct?"

Conrad nodded miserably.

"Were you dishonest with the police and prosecutor? Yes or no?"

"Yes."

"But we're supposed to believe that you're being honest now, is that right?"

"I am being honest now."

"Assuming you even know what you saw, in your impaired state, on that night?"

"I know what I saw."

"Well, that's for the jury to decide. No further questions."

29.

Leary sat in his car, low in the seat. He was parked in a crowded corporate parking lot. Through the streaked glass of his windshield, he could see the entrance to the CBL building, an eleven-story glass-and-chrome tower in the suburbs just outside Philly's urban center. He had been watching the front of the building for about an hour. He was looking for two people whose faces he had on a color printout on the passenger seat next to him. The founding partners, whose photos had been easy to track down online—Jack Woodside and David Whittaker. Either one of them would do.

His plan—if you could call it that—was straightforward. Corner one of the men, ask him some unpleasant questions about Lydia Wax and the death of Terry Resta, and see how he reacted. If Leary was lucky, this surprise attack would shake something loose—something he could use to start building a case against CBL and its principals.

He knew the company was responsible for at least two deaths—those of Terry Resta and, indirectly, Lydia Wax, since her suicide had been related to her involvement in their scheme. He intended to prove this and bring them to justice.

His thoughts were interrupted when a black man in a suit emerged from the doors of the building. Leary swept the printout off the seat beside him and compared the face on the page to the face he could see through his windshield. The man was David Whittaker, one of the company's founding partners and current leaders. No question.

Leary watched Whittaker get into a car—a fancy-looking Jaguar—and pull out of his parking space. After a silent count of five, Leary tailed him. They drove away from the city.

He wasn't sure where he expected the ride to lead—to some shady warehouse, maybe?—but he definitely was not anticipating Whittaker's actual destination, which turned out to be a Toys "R" Us. Leary followed the Jaguar into the toy store's parking lot, watched Whittaker find a space, and then parked his own car a few slots away. He watched Whittaker get out of the Jag and head for the store. He seemed to recall one of the articles he'd read online mentioning that one of Whittaker's reasons for establishing his company in Philly was to start a family in the same city in which he'd grown up, so it made sense that the guy had kids. Apparently, even criminal masterminds bought toys for their children.

He decided to let Whittaker do his shopping. He'd catch the man on his way out of the store. No sense denying a kid a toy.

Ten minutes later, David Whittaker emerged from Toys "R" Us carrying a small plastic bag. Leary popped open his car door, climbed out, and walked casually in the direction Whittaker was coming from. About halfway between the store and the Jaguar, Leary intercepted him.

"David Whittaker?" he said with a friendly smile.

Whittaker stopped. He returned the smile, but Leary could tell he was struggling to identify him. Finally the man said, "I'm sorry, have we met?"

"I'm a friend of a friend," Leary said, injecting a cheerful tone into his voice.

"Oh?" Whittaker seemed to relax. "Who's that?"

"You probably wouldn't want me to say her name in public, since you paid her to kill a man."

The effect was instant and obvious. Whittaker's dark skin seemed to pale a few shades, his mouth opened, and his grip on the plastic bag tightened.

"I don't know what you're talking about."

Leary got closer, invading the man's personal space. "I think you do."

Whittaker's gaze jumped to his Jaguar, as if he were weighing the option of making a run for it. He didn't run, though. He took a breath and met Leary's gaze. "You must have made a mistake. I'm not the person you think I am."

"You're not David Whittaker, one of the founding partners of CBL Capital Partners, LLP?"

He saw the hand holding the Toys "R" Us bag

tighten like a claw, crinkling the pastel-colored plastic. A bead of sweat rolled down Whittaker's forehead, even in the chilly autumn air.

"You can't just corner a man in a public place like this and start throwing around accusations," Whittaker said. "This is harassment. It's defamation. My company has very good lawyers. We'll—"

"You'll sue me? That wouldn't be a good idea."

Whittaker straightened up. He puffed out his chest. "Why not?"

"Because truth is an absolute defense to defamation, so if you take me to court, you'll force me to publicly prove that you engaged in a conspiracy to commit murder."

Whittaker laughed and shook his head. "Is this a joke? Who the hell are you?"

"It was a clever plan, making the killing look like self-defense. You want to know where you screwed up? You weren't careful enough to hide the financial connection between CBL and your poor, helpless, scared-for-her-life murderess."

"I'm going to my car now."

"That's fine. I won't stop you."

Whittaker watched him with a wary expression, as if he were not sure whether Leary might actually do just that, then walked slowly past him, moving toward his car like a man stepping carefully away from a live landmine.

"Things will be easier if you talk to me," Leary

said. Whittaker stopped walking. A second passed before he turned to face Leary again. "I have influence with the DA's office," Leary said, which he supposed was sort of true. "Come in, talk to us voluntarily, and maybe you won't spend the rest of your life in a prison cell."

"You listen to me," Whittaker said. The man looked suddenly furious, and Leary wondered if he'd pushed him too far with the threat of prison. "I don't know what you're talking about. Your accusations are crazy. My company had nothing to do with any shooting."

Whittaker was breathing heavily now. He turned away from Leary and practically fled to his car. Leary watched him go.

Shooting? What the hell was Whittaker talking about? Terry Resta had been stabbed, not shot.

Thoughts swirled in Leary's head as he returned to his own car and slid behind the wheel. Could he have been wrong about CBL being involved? All he knew was that the company had purchased the Resta brothers' business, and that Lydia Wax had acted evasive, and then killed herself, after he mentioned the company's name to her. That was hardly overwhelming evidence. He didn't need a law degree to know that.

Or maybe CBL had been involved, but Whittaker didn't know. Maybe it had been the scheme of the other partner, Woodside, or someone else at the company.

But why had Whittaker assumed Leary was talking about a shooting?

A feeling like an electric bolt shot through him. His hands tightened on the steering wheel. *Holy shit.*

Terry Resta had not been shot, but Corbin Keeley had. What if CBL was connected to both deaths? Could it be possible? Had they pulled the same trick twice, used the same MO to eliminate obstacles to their success on two separate occasions? If so, Leary might be able to crack not only his own three-year-old case, but Jessie's current one, too.

Holy shit indeed.

30.

The cross-examination of Conrad Deprisco had been brutal, and there wasn't much Jessie could do to repair the damage on redirect. When the judge told Conrad he could step down from the witness stand, the kid was visibly shaken.

Watching him move meekly from the well of the courtroom to the gallery, where his parents sat with horrified expressions, Jessie saw the glint of tears in his eyes. A feeling of guilt and regret burned through her. She'd called him to the stand knowing there was a high risk that Hughes would hit hard on the drug use as a means to attack his credibility, but she'd decided that the risk was outweighed by the potentially game-changing evidence Conrad could provide as an eyewitness to what had actually happened that night in the parking lot. She had been wrong. Just when she'd thought she was making real progress, Hughes's cross-examination had thrown her back. One look at the jurors told her Conrad's testimony had been rendered untrustworthy, and that many of them were going to dismiss it altogether—including his testimony that it had been Raines, and not Keeley, who'd thrown the rock. Jessie had put the kid on the stand, and subjected him to almost an hour of humiliating interrogation, for nothing.

When Conrad reached his parents, his father turned away, seemingly unwilling to look at his son. His mother hugged him, but the hug looked stiff, hesitant, and she pulled away from him after only a second. Then his parents turned to leave, and he trailed after them out of the courtroom. Jessie felt a pang in her chest.

"Ms. Black?" Judge Armstrong said. She realized he'd asked her a question and was waiting for an answer.

She snapped to attention. "I'm sorry, Your Honor. Could you please repeat that?"

"I said, are you ready to call your next witness?"

The image of Conrad Deprisco dejectedly following his parents as they marched out of the courtroom refused to leave her mind. "Your Honor, would it be possible to take a short break?"

Armstrong did not look thrilled by the idea. "I'm trying to keep to a schedule here, Ms. Black."

"I know. I appreciate that." She tried to force the negative thoughts out of her mind. She needed to focus on presenting her case.

"On the other hand, maybe this is a good time for a break," the judge said, surprising her. "Let's take a fifteen minute recess."

"Thank you, Your Honor."

She caught up with Conrad and his parents in the hallway outside the courtroom, just before they reached the elevator. "Conrad, wait a second!"

The three people turned. Conrad's parents glared at her, while Conrad looked at his hands. His face twisted with embarrassment and misery.

"What the hell was that?" the kid's father said. He stepped closer to Jessie, so close she could smell the sour odor of his breath. "You walked our son into an ambush. You just embarrassed our whole family!"

"There's no point in talking about it now," Conrad's mother said. "We told him not to testify, but he thought he knew better. He's eighteen, a grown man." Her voice was so thick with sarcasm and disdain, she almost made Hughes's cross-examination seem friendly.

"Can we talk alone?" Jessie said to Conrad. "Just for a minute?"

"Yeah, okay."

She led him away from his parents, feeling their stares burning into her back as she walked. She found an empty attorney room and ushered the kid inside.

"I'm sorry I screwed up in there," Conrad said as soon as the door was closed. "I tried, but I didn't know a good way to answer the defense lawyer's questions. I guess my parents were right."

"You did fine, Conrad. You told the truth. That's what matters."

He didn't look convinced. Jessie's heart clenched as she tried to think of something she could say that would make him feel better. She came up empty. Even worse, a glance at her watch told her she was almost out of time.

"Listen, I need to get back to the courtroom. Judge Armstrong only gave us fifteen minutes. I have a few more witnesses to call today."

Conrad nodded. "Yeah, I gotta get going, too."

"Promise me you'll think about what I said. You did the right thing today. Sometimes the right thing ends with the wrong result, but it doesn't change the fact that it was right. A man was shot and killed. Your testimony could help ensure that justice is served."

Conrad sighed. "Maybe."

She watched him leave the small room, shoulders slumped. *I'll give him a call tomorrow*, she thought, *make sure he's okay.*

Then she followed him out of the small room and into the corridor, where she walked directly into Carrie Keeley.

"We're losing, aren't we?" Carrie said.

Jessie glanced around quickly to make sure no one was in earshot. Even though she was pretty sure their conversation would be private, she still lowered her voice almost to a whisper. "It's hard to say. You can never be sure what a jury is thinking, or which witnesses they find believable."

Carrie's eyes narrowed. "Come on, it doesn't take a mind reader to see what the jury thought of that guy."

"It was a tough cross-examination."

Carrie shook her head. She looked like she was holding back tears. "It was a slaughter. And the worst part is, he saw the whole thing. He *saw* Brooke Raines kill my father and then throw the damn rock to make it look like he attacked her first. That's cold, calculated murder. But no one will listen to his story because he was smoking weed? For God's sake, from the way the defense attorney questioned him, you'd think he was a drug-crazed maniac, not an eighteen-year-old guy who smoked a few joints. What is wrong with this city?"

"The trial's not over yet, Carrie."

"Whatever. It's obvious the jury thinks my dad deserved to die. They're not going to find that woman guilty no matter what evidence you show them."

Words of encouragement came to Jessie's mind, but she didn't speak them. Creating false hope didn't help anyone, and Carrie's assessment wasn't far off from her own. "If I had to guess, I would agree with you. My sense is that the jury's not on our side yet."

"Yet?" Carrie closed her eyes and her features scrunched up. After a few seconds, she seemed to regain her composure. "What's it going to take?"

Jessie put a hand on the girl's shoulder. "We still have a few more witnesses, and then we'll have a chance to cross-examine the defense's witnesses, and we'll end with a closing argument. Each of those moments is another opportunity to sway the jury. So please don't give up yet, okay? I haven't."

Carrie nodded. "My dad isn't the bad guy. People

need to know the truth."

"I'm going to do everything I can. That's a promise."

After the girl walked away, Jessie let out a long breath. It seemed that she kept making promises to Carrie Keeley, but she didn't seem to be making much progress delivering on those promises. Every step forward seemed to be met with resistance that pushed her two steps back. Carrie had been right about one thing—they were losing.

31.

His encounter with the man in the Toys "R" Us parking lot left Dave Whittaker in a panic. He fled back to CBL, where he barricaded himself behind the closed door of his office. Nightmare images and awful thoughts assaulted his mind.

The public humiliation of an arrest and trial.

Talking to his wife and children through the glass partition of a prison visitation room.

Kids ostracizing his children because of his crimes. His boys in tears.

The rest of his life spent in some hellhole, where he'd be beaten and worse for the rest of his life.

He put his elbows on his desk, lowered his head, and ran his fingers over his close-cropped hair. Everything he had, he was going to lose. His family. His company. His wealth. His life. All lost. All gone.

Was there anything he could do? The man from the toy store parking lot had insinuated that he might have options. What had he said? *Things will be easier if you talk to me. I have influence with the DA's office. Come in, talk to us voluntarily, and maybe you won't spend the rest of your life in a prison cell.*

Right, Dave thought. He knew better than to trust the DA's office. Making deals with criminals was what they did, day in and day out, and like any lawyer specializing in a type of transaction, they would make a good deal—for themselves. He, on the other hand, would be screwed.

"What choice do I have?" he said to the empty room. If he couldn't go to the DA, where could he go?

When the answer came to him, it came with an overwhelming feeling of cowardice and self-loathing. Goyle. Luther Goyle, the man responsible for all this horror in the first place. Goyle would help him because it would be in Goyle's self-interest to do so. Goyle might be a sociopath, a psychopath, but he was smart. Goyle would know what to do.

Dave closed his eyes. Had it really come to this? After all the moral agonizing he'd done from the comfort of his own safety, now that his life was on the line, and the choice between doing the right thing or the wrong thing was upon him, was he really going to choose to do the wrong thing?

I guess you learn something new about yourself every day.

He would tell Goyle about the man in the Toys "R" Us parking lot. And whatever Goyle decided to do about it, Dave would follow his lead. He would justify it after the fact. He would rationalize it. And not from the squalor of a prison cell, but from the luxury of his home.

Maybe he wasn't as good a man as he'd once believed, once hoped.

So be it.

In Luther Goyle's office, Dave Whittaker told the whole story to Goyle and Jack Woodside, from the moment he'd walked out of the toy store and been approached in the parking lot, to the moment he'd driven away, hardly able to control his car in a haze of panic.

Every few seconds, Jack cursed under his breath. Goyle remained silent until Dave finished.

"It's nothing, right?" Jack said. He turned away from the windows and looked at Goyle with an imploring expression. "Some random guy talked to Dave, spouted some nonsense that, obviously, turned out to be insanely close to the truth—but so what? If the authorities really knew anything, we'd all be in handcuffs."

Goyle breathed steadily. His iPad was on his desk, but for once, its screen was dark.

"Luther?" Jack said. "It's nothing, right?"

Goyle sighed. "It's probably nothing. But...."

"But what?" Jack said. "I don't like 'but.' You're a lawyer. When you say 'but' it's usually not a good sign."

"I received a call from Lydia Wax recently. She was upset." He rubbed the jowls of his oily face. He looked, Dave thought, uncharacteristically unsettled.

"She received a visit from a man who made accusations similar to those made to Dave."

"What?" Jack exploded. "Why didn't you tell us about this?"

"Because," Goyle said, glaring at him, "the incident seemed to resolve itself. I sent a couple of men to ... handle her. But when they arrived, she was already dead. She took her own life."

"Oh, Jesus," Jack said. "This is not good. This is really, really not good."

Dave would have agreed, but after telling the men his story, his voice seemed to have abandoned him. His brain felt fuzzy. He was hearing Goyle and Jack, but not really reacting on an emotional level. He suspected he might have entered a state of shock. He thought that might be a good thing.

"We need to find this guy from the parking lot," Jack said. "*He's* the one we need to handle. And we need to do it quickly."

Goyle nodded. "I agree. It will be messier than usual, though. We won't have time to set up a nice and tidy legal defense. But the risk of allowing him to continue what he's doing is unacceptable."

Finally, Dave's voice returned. He said, "How can we get rid of him if we don't even know who he is?"

"Get rid of him?" Air whistled from Goyle's nostrils as he exhaled. A sleazy smile crossed his face. "It sounds like you've had a change of heart since the last time we spoke, Dave."

Dave ignored the taunt. He already hated

himself—nothing Goyle said could be worse than his own thoughts. "I just don't see how we're going to be able to identify him. Where do we even start?"

"His name is Mark Leary," Goyle said, "and I already know everything about him." He looked at Dave and Jack as if they were children. "He's a former homicide detective. He was forced out of the police department, but it was for stupid reasons. He has a reputation as an excellent investigator."

"Oh God." Jack moaned. "Why is he investigating us?"

"It doesn't matter. Go home, both of you, and stay there until I call you. When I do, this problem will already have been taken care of and we'll be free to focus on more important matters, like the ten-million-dollar deal we're about to close with the city."

Jack looked relieved. He left Goyle's office with some of his swagger restored. Dave remained for a few seconds, watching the fat man return his attention to his iPad, as if Dave were not even there. He wished he felt the same relief Jack seemed to be feeling. He wished he could look forward to closing their ten-million-dollar deal. Instead, he felt like the only deal he'd made was with the devil.

32.

After Jessie called her final witness, she rested the prosecution's case. It was the defense's turn now. The time had come for Hughes to call his first witness. Word had already spread about who that witness would be, and the atmosphere of the courtroom felt heavy with anticipation.

Most accused murderers declined to testify at their own trials. The prevailing wisdom was that trying to offer testimony on their own behalf would only come off as self-serving, and was outweighed by the damage the prosecution could inflict on cross. But to support a self-defense claim, the testimony of the defendant was practically required, which provided an unusual opportunity for the press and the public to see the accused on the witness stand. They could judge Brooke Raines for themselves and decide if they found her to be an honest person or a liar.

Jessie was just as anxious as the crowd, if not more so. She saw Raines's decision to take the stand as her best chance to convince the jury that the woman's story did not add up to a valid self-defense claim. A strong cross-examination, combined with the questions she'd already raised, might be enough to get the jury on her side. On the other hand, if she failed, she would probably lose the trial. The pressure of facing off against a murder defendant on the witness stand would be high in any trial, but in this one, it felt like everything was at stake.

She took a deep breath and held it. The bustle of the courtroom seemed to fade around her, and the noises became background static. *You can do this.* Jessie held her breath for another few seconds, then let it out in a slow, relaxing exhalation. The room came alive around her again.

Aidan Hughes stood up and said, "The defense calls Brooke Raines to the stand."

A buzz of excited whispers and murmurs rose from the gallery. Judge Armstrong banged his gavel to silence the crowd. They complied, but Jessie felt an almost electric tension in the air as Brooke Raines walked to the witness stand. She wore low heels that clicked against the floor of the courtroom, and a gray pantsuit that bulged slightly at the ankle where her monitoring device was strapped. Her blonde hair was simply styled, and her makeup was minimal, but the overall effect was flattering. She looked pretty, but not glamorous. She looked *pleasant.* One thing she did not look like was a killer. Hughes had done a fine job of disguising his client as a normal person.

Raines proceeded through the swearing-in process, then faced Hughes with a calm expression as the defense attorney approached her.

"Ms. Raines, we're here because the Philadelphia DA's office has decided to prosecute you on a charge of murder for the death of Corbin Keeley, but ultimately it is the jury—a jury of your peers—who will decide if you are guilty of that crime. I'm sure they would like to hear from you, in your own words, what happened on the night of October 14. So let's start at the beginning. Can you tell us the nature of your relationship with Corbin Keeley, including how it began?"

Raines nodded, leaned forward, and looked at the jury. Her features seemed open, sincere. "I met Corbin at a fundraising party at the Children's Hospital."

"That's the Children's Hospital of Philadelphia, correct? Where you work as a nurse, caring for sick and injured kids?"

Jessie considered objecting to this obvious attempt to ingratiate Raines to the jury, but decided not to. She didn't want to irritate the jury by objecting too frequently, and she had a feeling there would be more egregious questions before Hughes was done.

"That's right," Raines said.

"And when was this fundraising party?"

"June 4. It was a Saturday."

"How did you meet Mr. Keeley?"

"The party was informal, with fun activities for kids and their parents. A lot of local politicians came to show their support. Corbin was one of them. We got to talking, and he asked me if I'd like to get coffee with him some time. I thought he was nice, and found him attractive, so I gave him my number."

"And did you meet him for coffee?"

"He called me a few days after the party and asked me to dinner. I said yes. That was our first date, I guess. After that, we started seeing each other regularly."

"You spent a lot of time together?"

"Yes. I pretty much moved in with him. I mean, I didn't give up my own apartment, but ... I spent the night at his place most nights." She blushed deeply.

"How long a period was this relationship?"

Raines turned to the jury. Her expression looked somber and regretful, but not guilty. "It ended on the night he died. I broke up with him at dinner that night. So, about four months total."

"Can you tell the jury why you ended the relationship?"

Raines looked down at her hands, which were clasped together on the witness stand. "Corbin was abusive." She lifted one hand and wiped a tear from her eye. Jessie couldn't tell if it was real or not, but it was convincing. "He was violent."

"I know this is difficult for you, Ms. Raines," Hughes said, "but it's very important that you tell the jury the details. In what way was Corbin Keeley abusive?"

Raines straightened up and looked directly at the jury. "He hurt me. Several times."

"In what ways?"

"Sometimes he got angry and hit me. On my arm once, really hard, right here." She indicated an area on her upper arm, near her shoulder. "Once he slapped me across the face and my lip swelled up like a balloon. He pushed me a few times, too. Right into a wall once. He would throw things at me, pull my hair." The woman seemed to shudder at the memories.

Jessie could feel the attention of the jurors, but she did not dare to look at them. She somehow knew, without seeing, that some of them had turned accusatory glances toward the prosecution table—that some of them were thinking, *How dare you prosecute this woman? Hasn't she been through enough already?*

"Did Mr. Keeley subject you to any other forms of abuse? I mean, besides physical violence?"

"Yes. He also yelled at me. He lost his temper a lot, called me a stupid bitch, a worthless idiot. Things like that."

"That must have been terrible. Again, I'm sorry to make you relive these memories."

Raines nodded. "It's okay. I want to tell my story."

"Tell us what happened on the night of October 14."

"Well, I had decided that enough was enough. I decided to break up with Corbin. But I was afraid that if I did it at his apartment, he might become enraged and hurt me. I thought it would be safer for me if I did it in a public place. We had a reservation for dinner at a restaurant called Bistro Cannata, and I decided to do it there."

"Why did you bring a gun with you to the restaurant?"

"Because I was scared. I was terrified. I hoped he wouldn't do anything crazy in public. But I wasn't sure he would think rationally. I brought the gun just in case, but I never thought I would have to use it."

"Have you used guns before?"

"Yes, but never on a person." She looked at the jury again. "I know it seems unusual, a woman bringing a gun to a restaurant. But I'm very comfortable with guns. When I was young, my dad used to take me target shooting. I'm good at it, but there's nothing violent about it for me. It's a sport. That's why I had a gun, and a license to own and carry it, and why I knew I could handle it safely and would use it only if I absolutely had no other choice."

"Tell us what happened at Bistro Cannata," Hughes said.

"The hostess sat us at a table and I tried to break up with him. You know, I had to gather my courage. He ordered wine, and then he was looking for the waiter so we could order our meals. I didn't want it to get that far, so I just blurted it out. I said, 'Corbin, this isn't working for me anymore. I want to break up with you.'"

"How did he react to that?"

"Badly," she said. "He managed to keep his cool in the restaurant, but only barely. I could see his anger simmering just under the surface. He said, 'Don't be an idiot.' And when I told him I was serious, he said, 'I'll kill you before I let you leave me.' And he meant it."

"Objection," Jessie said, as much to break the spell Raines was casting over the courtroom as for legal reasons, "the witness had no knowledge of what was in Mr. Keeley's mind. Also, it's hearsay."

"Sustained," Judge Armstrong said. "Ms. Raines, you may testify that you thought Mr. Keeley meant it when he said he would kill you, but you cannot testify as to what he was actually thinking."

She sat up straighter in her chair. "Like you said, it's what I thought—I thought he meant it."

"What happened after that?" Hughes said.

"I tried to calm Corbin down. I said we could still be friends, even though I didn't mean it. He just glared at me and said I was going to eat my fucking dinner. Those were his words—*'my fucking dinner'*. I was so scared I was shaking. I was making the whole table shake."

"What happened after that?" Hughes prompted.

"I said, 'I'm leaving,' and I got up. I took my bag and I walked out the door. I knew he was following me, but I didn't look back. I was too scared. I walked into the parking lot and headed for my car. Then something flew past my head and hit the wall of the building. It was a big rock. I could hear his footsteps behind me, coming fast. I knew he'd catch me before I got to the car. So I turned to face him."

"You heard Conrad Deprisco testify that *you* threw the rock, not Mr. Keeley. Is that true?"

"No, that's not true. That's a lie. Corbin threw the

rock at me."

"Do you know why Mr. Deprisco would lie?"

"I don't know. Maybe to avoid being arrested for drug use."

"Objection," Jessie said.

"Withdrawn," Hughes said. Then, to Raines, "When you turned to face Mr. Keeley, what did he do?"

"He kept coming toward me. He looked so angry. His whole body was like, radiating anger. His hands were fists. I'd seen him like that before, but never as bad. I was afraid he wasn't just going to hit me this time. I was afraid he was going to kill me. There was nowhere to run. He was coming toward me. So I pulled my gun out of my bag and I shot him."

"What did you do after that?"

"I almost threw up. I had trouble catching my breath. It took me a few seconds to get myself under control. Then I called 911. When the police came, I told them exactly what happened. Those were the uniformed police officers. Then the detective came—Detective Fulco—and I told him, too. He took me to the police station and I wrote out a statement."

"Did you ever talk to a detective named Emily Graham?"

Raines shook her head. "No."

"What did you tell Detective Fulco?"

She faced the jury. "I told him what I'm telling you. The truth. That I was defending myself."

"One more question, Ms. Raines. Do you regret what happened on the night of October 14?"

Raines's throat moved as she swallowed. She seemed consumed by emotion as she contemplated the question. "No. I believe every person has a right to defend themselves. A basic, human right. I don't regret it."

"Thank you, Ms. Raines. I have no further questions."

Hughes walked back to the defense table and took a seat. The courtroom was so quiet, Jessie could almost hear her own beating heart. A sniffle came from the direction of the jury box, but Jessie didn't look.

Brooke Raines's performance had been so compelling, even Jessie caught herself starting to believe it. She felt the rise of panic.

"Ms. Black," Judge Armstrong said. His voice seemed unusually subdued. "Would you like to cross-examine this witness?"

Jessie rose from her chair on unsteady legs. She could feel the animosity of the crowd focus on her. It was an unfamiliar feeling. Usually, it was the defense attorney who endured the scorn of the courtroom, not the prosecutor. But this time, the courtroom saw the defendant as the victim. This time, Jessie looked like the bad guy.

She had one chance, and only one chance, to change that.

33.

The jurors leaned forward in their seats. Most of them bore hostile expressions. Jessie briefly met one woman's hard, flinty stare, and returned it with one she hoped showed confidence and determination. Her role here was to expose the truth, and to accomplish that, she needed their attention. Judging by their faces, she had it. Now she needed to deliver.

She turned her attention back to the defendant. In a steady voice, she said, "Ms. Raines, you testified earlier that after you shot and killed Mr. Keeley, you 'told the police exactly what happened.' Isn't that what you testified a moment ago?"

"Yes."

"But that's not true, is it?"

"It's true."

"Really?" Jessie walked to the prosecution table, picked up a document, and returned to the witness stand. "Do you recognize this document?"

"It's the statement I wrote out for Detective Fulco."

"You wrote it on the night of the shooting,

correct?"

"Yes."

"It's your handwriting, your words, right?"

"Yes."

"In this statement, you wrote that you ran out of the restaurant, and that Mr. Keeley ran after you. Isn't that what you wrote?"

Her gaze cut toward Hughes. "Yes, but—"

"But that contradicts the eyewitness testimony from Conrad Deprisco and your own words a moment ago, does it not?"

Raines's eyes narrowed. "That doesn't mean I was lying." Her voice sounded terse and strained. She seemed to realize this and turned to the jury with a more confident expression, chin jutting. "Walking and running, there isn't that much of a distinction."

"But you changed your original story, after you realized that the evidence contradicted it, correct?"

"I realized I had misremembered what happened."

"But you wrote the statement on the night of the shooting. Are you telling us that your memory of what happened is better today than it was on the night the event actually occurred?"

"I guess so."

"Did you also misremember Mr. Keeley's drinking?"

"What?" Raines's gaze flitted across the courtroom, seeming to seek out Hughes again.

Jessie stepped into her line of sight and held up

the statement again. "In the statement you wrote out for Detective Fulco on the night of the shooting, you wrote that Mr. Keeley had been drinking wine. But when the police spoke to other people present at Bistro Cannata on the night of the shooting, no one said they'd seen Mr. Keeley drinking. As you heard during the testimony of Andrew Dale, the deputy medical examiner who performed the autopsy on Mr. Keeley, the toxicology report on Mr. Keeley indicated that he had no alcohol in his system. I noticed that when you testified a moment ago, you didn't mention Mr. Keeley drinking. So, is it fair to say that this is another example of you having misremembered something?"

"Objection," Hughes said.

"I'll rephrase," Jessie said. "Ms. Raines, do you deny that in your initial statement to the police, you claimed that Mr. Keeley had been drinking?"

"I thought—"

"Just answer yes or no, please. Do you deny that?"

"No."

"Do you deny that you are now testifying to a version of events in which Mr. Keeley was not drinking?"

"I don't know if he was drinking. I don't remember."

"We have a witness I would be happy to call on rebuttal—your waiter, Greg Clifford. Do you think calling Mr. Clifford to the stand would help you refresh your memory?"

"Objection!" Hughes said.

"I don't think that's necessary," Raines said. She was talking over her lawyer's objection, a good sign that Jessie had her flustered.

"But your story has changed, correct?" Jessie said

"Yes."

"In your statement to the police, did you claim that Mr. Keeley yelled at you in the restaurant?"

"I was describing what it felt like."

"But today, you testified that he was quiet. More inconsistencies. But you probably never expected anyone to look too closely at your story, did you?"

"Objection. Your Honor...." There was a note of pleading in Hughes's voice.

"Sustained," Armstrong said. "Save your conclusions for closing arguments, Ms. Black. If you have no more questions for the witness...."

"I have a few more, Your Honor. Ms. Raines, why didn't you break up with Mr. Keeley over the phone?"

"What?"

"You testified that you ended the relationship at a restaurant because you felt safer doing it in a public place. But wouldn't a phone call have been the safest alternative?"

"It seemed ... it seemed like something I needed to do face-to-face."

"Really? You were so frightened of Mr. Keeley that you brought a gun with you, but your concern for his feelings was so powerful that you put your life at risk to meet him in person when you could have called him? Is that what you're telling the jury today?"

"I—"

"Yes or no, Ms. Raines."

"Yes, I guess."

"And speaking of the gun, I just want to clarify something. You testified that you are very comfortable with guns, correct? That you've been using guns for most of your life, as a sport?"

"Yes."

"As part of this hobby, did you ever receive safety training?"

"Of course."

"I own a gun, too, Ms. Raines. When I had safety training, my instructor told me I should never aim my gun at a person unless I intended to kill that person. Did you ever receive similar advice?"

Jessie was taking a risk asking a question she did not know the answer to, but she figured the answer would benefit her case whether it was a yes or a no. If Raines denied having received that advice, she might appear as a careless gun owner. If she admitted to having received it, she would be showing a premeditated intent to kill.

Raines hesitated, seeming to sense the trap. Her brow furrowed. "Yes. I was taught that, too."

"But you brought your gun to Bistro Cannata. So you must have anticipated killing Mr. Keeley."

"Objection," Hughes said. "That's not a question."

"Do you carry your gun to your job at the Children's Hospital?" Jessie asked.

"No."

"So you don't carry it at all times?"

"No, I—"

"But you brought it to your dinner with Mr. Keeley. Did you do that because you were terrified that he might put you in a situation where you would have to kill him in order to save your own life?"

"Yes! Exactly! I was afraid...."

"But you weren't sufficiently afraid to break up with Mr. Keeley over the phone, or just to cut off all communication with him and report his threatening behavior to the police?"

"No, I—"

"In fact, you never went to the police for help, did you, until after you'd shot and killed Mr. Keeley?"

"No."

"You testified that Mr. Keeley gave you a swollen lip. Do you have any photographs that show you with that injury, or any other injury you claim Mr. Keeley inflicted?"

"No."

"You claim that Mr. Keeley threw a rock at you, but an eyewitness who was watching you in the parking lot testified that Mr. Keeley didn't throw the rock. He testified that *you* threw the rock after you shot Mr. Keeley. Did you throw that rock to create evidence to support a self-defense claim?"

"No!"

Jessie paused, letting the exchange hang in the air of the otherwise silent courtroom. In the jury box, the jurors continued to lean forward, but the focus of their hostility shifted—at least for the moment—to the woman who Jessie hoped now seemed significantly less innocent. She figured she'd pushed Raines as far as she could. "I have nothing further for this witness."

As she returned to her seat, the courtroom exploded with a babble of conversation. The judge hammered his gavel until the room quieted.

"Mr. Hughes, will the defense redirect?"

"Yes, Your Honor." Hughes approached Raines, who looked rattled from Jessie's cross-examination. "Ms. Raines, did you give the jury an honest account of what happened on the night of October 14?"

"Yes, I did." Her voice rose, sounding almost shrill.

"The prosecution pointed out some differences between the statement you gave police and the testimony you offered today. Is it possible that there were differences because you were so afraid, so upset on the night of the shooting, that you got details wrong?"

"Objection," Jessie said. "Mr. Hughes is leading the witness."

"I agree," Judge Armstrong said. "Don't put words in Ms. Raines's mouth."

Hughes's jaw flexed. "Ms. Raines, why did you shoot Mr. Keeley?"

"Because I was afraid for my life. I shot him in self-defense."

Jessie studied the jurors' faces. She could tell she'd succeeded in converting some of them to her side, but she needed more than some. For a guilty verdict, she needed all of them. Her instincts told her she didn't have that yet.

34.

Leary worked late. He had to—he'd spent so much time recently on his private investigations of Lydia Wax and CBL Capital Partners that he'd let his real work pile up unfinished. By cramming for hours into the night, he'd managed to catch up a little bit, but eventually, hunger and exhaustion had gotten the better of him. It was time to go home.

You don't deserve to rest. You deserve to be fired.

Leary gritted his teeth as he rode the elevator down to the ground floor of the Acacia building. *That's all I need, to lose another job. Establish a nice pattern. Jessie will be thrilled.*

The elevator doors opened and he stepped out into the lobby. It was dark, with only minimal lighting to help him find his way to the door. He walked outside, where his car was one of a handful left in the parking lot.

You won't get fired, he told himself. *Not unless you make a habit of shirking your duties. And you're not going to make a habit of it. This Lydia Wax thing is a special case, a one-time deal.*

But was it? Or a few weeks from now, would something else remind him of some other unsolved case from his past, sending him off on a quest to solve that one? Was he becoming one of those pathetic ex-cops who couldn't leave the job behind? Would spend the rest of his life as a wannabe, pretending he was still a detective?

He reached his car but didn't open the door. He looked down at his reflection in the driver's side window and shook his head. No, he wouldn't let that happen. His life was too good right now to jeopardize everything. He didn't need to live in the past, not with a good job and a wonderful woman in his present. His interest in Lydia Wax was unique, unfinished business that he'd needed to handle, but as soon as that business was done, he would stop.

He pulled his keys from his pocket, and was about to press the button to unlock his car when he felt the hairs on the back of his neck tingle. He wasn't alone.

Pain exploded in the center of his back. The force smashed him forward against the side of his car. Then there was more pain screaming across his scalp as someone grabbed his hair and yanked him backward. Through his spinning vision he saw two men. One of them—who must have kicked him in the back and then dragged him backward by his hair—now held him from behind. Leary couldn't see his face, but he could tell the man was massive. The arms squeezing his torso were thick and bulging with muscle, and he could sense that the man's head loomed far above his—the guy had to be well over six feet tall.

The second man, smaller and rangier, came in quick. He punched Leary's stomach, then his face. Pain and blood blurred his vision. He felt a cut open on his cheek.

"Your wallet, asshole!"

Leary stared, uncomprehending, and felt his mind begin to cloud with shock. He mentally shook off the numbness. *Stay calm. Stay focused.* He was being mugged. He could deal with muggers. The man reared back to hit him again, this time in the ribs. Leary took the punch and gasped.

"It's ... in my ... back pocket," he managed.

Neither man moved for his wallet. The man with the eager fists seemed to be choosing his next attack. Leary braced himself for it, and at the same time, tried to wriggle free of the bigger man behind him. Leary's arms were pinned to his side, but....

The man in front of him threw a punch to Leary's side. Leary moved with the blow, letting the momentum slam him backward into the man behind him. The vise-like grip on his body loosened, and Leary got his right arm free. He drove his fist back and up and felt it connect with the man's nasal bones. The man howled. Hot blood splashed the back of Leary's head.

Free of the giant's hold, he lurched away and pressed his back to the side of his car so they couldn't surround him again. His right hand dove toward his hip, but his fingers closed around nothing. He wasn't wearing his gun. As an executive at Acacia, carrying a weapon had simply been unnecessary, and his colleagues had seemed relieved when he'd stopped bringing it to work.

The bigger man—Leary could see his full height now, and judged him to be at least six-foot-five, and maybe two-hundred-and-fifty pounds—was bent at the waist, cradling a broken nose. Blood dripped from his cupped hands. The other man seemed to have lost interest in throwing punches. He pulled a knife from his pants and came toward Leary with the wiry, erratic energy of an addict.

Fight or run?

He hated the thought of running from a couple of low-life muggers like this pair, but with no weapon, the odds were not in his favor. "Here!" He dragged his wallet out of his back pocket and threw it as far across the parking lot as he could. "Take it!"

The wiry man ran for the wallet. Leary twisted around and grabbed the door handle of his car. Locked. He pawed his pocket for his keys and realized he didn't have them. He'd been holding them when the men ambushed him. He looked around, spotted them on the pavement six feet away.

"You got my money," Leary said, taking a step toward his keys. "Now get out of here—"

The giant advanced on him and seized his sides with rough hands. He felt his feet leave the pavement. Then he was flying. The ground rushed up to meet him and pain jolted through his knees and palms and chin. He tried to roll over to face his attackers and get his bearings. Now he was even farther from his car keys.

So much for running.

The wiry man with the knife was already coming back, stuffing Leary's wallet into his pants as he walked. That seemed strange to Leary. Criminals could be unpredictable, but as a general rule, muggers took off after getting your money. These two seemed almost uninterested in his wallet. They looked much more interested in beating the crap out of him—or worse. It dawned on him that he might be in a lot more danger than he'd initially thought. He ran his hand over the ground, searching for loose dirt or rocks, anything he could fling into the faces of the men coming toward him. His palm passed over nothing but flat, smooth pavement.

"Back off!" he yelled, hoping someone might hear him. He doubted anyone would, though. His was one of the only cars in the lot, and the building was in an area of the city that emptied out after business hours were over.

He needed to stand. He got to his feet, legs wobbling beneath him, and faced the men. The smaller man with the knife got to him first. The blade glinted, and Leary felt panic bubble in his stomach. *Stay calm.* The knife looked wicked, but Leary's leg was longer than the guy's arm. He kicked out with his left foot. His shoe connected with the side of the man's knee. The blow knocked the man off balance and he fell. Leary heard the knife clink against the pavement as the man dropped it to use his hands to break his fall.

Leary felt a wave of relief, but it was short-lived. The giant was on him in the next second, roaring curses from his blood-caked face. Leary thought the indistinct words were "I'm gonna kill you!" but the distortion caused by the broken nose made it hard to be sure.

Leary straightened the fingers of his right hand into a flat, blade-like shape, then lashed out at the giant's neck. He hit the side of the neck, a move he hoped would stun the man. It seemed to work, at least for the moment. He followed it up with the kick to the man's balls and watched the big man fold.

Both of his attackers were on the ground, but they would recover soon. Leary was breathing hard as he ran to his keys and swept them off the ground. In seconds, the men were coming toward him again, but they seemed to advance more cautiously this time.

Definitely not a run-of-the-mill mugging. These guys hadn't come for his money. Someone had sent them.

"You guys work for CBL?" Leary said. "Funny, you don't look like financial types."

The smaller man lunged forward with the knife. Leary knocked his arm aside and deflected the weapon. Its blade whistled past his left ear, but didn't touch him. Leary countered with the only weapon he had—his keys. He swept them across the man's face, scratching his eyes. The man screamed and danced backward.

Leary got his car door open and slid inside. He

pulled the door shut and locked it just as the bigger man grabbed the handle. Leary watched as the giant actually tore the door handle off of his car. Leary started the engine as the man tossed the door handle over his shoulder. The big man's fist slammed into the driver's side window. The sound was like a thunder clap in the car, but the glass held. Leary hit the ignition and pressed his foot to the pedal. The car jerked forward. The big man stumbled away.

His tires screeched as Leary sped out of the parking lot. Driving with one hand, he fumbled his phone out of his pocket and called 911.

35.

Detective Emily Graham sat behind her computer in the Homicide Division squad room, straining her brain to come up with something that could help Jessie's case. She'd come up empty so far, and it was getting late. Now, she took a deep breath of stale air. Maybe it was time to call it a night.

"You moonlighting now, Graham? Working on cases that aren't even assigned to you?"

She let out a sigh and turned. Kyle Fulco stalked toward her workspace. The detective's usually laconic expression had been replaced by a clenched jaw and a red tinge to his skin. Graham rose from her chair as he came toward her. She became very aware that the two of them were alone. She staggered back a step, but recovered quickly, planting her feet and standing her ground. She wasn't going to be intimidated by Full-of-shit Fulco.

"I'm a detective," she said. "You should try it sometime."

"A detective for the defense, maybe. Great job. You really helped them out. Hope you're charging that guy Hughes a good fee." His raised voice seemed to echo in the empty bullpen.

"Jessie asked for my help."

"Maybe I should be talking to *her* then, huh? Or maybe her boss?"

"If you're looking for someone to blame, look at yourself. Jessie wouldn't have needed to call me if you'd been doing your job. But I guess you couldn't be bothered."

Fulco's teeth flashed, and he looked like he might snap at her, but at the last moment, his face seemed to collapse into a miserable frown. He turned away from her, brought a hand to his jaw, and rubbed his mouth. Quietly, in a muffled voice, he said, "Damn it."

"It's one thing being made fun of in the department," Graham said. She was angry now and the words flowed out of her. "They call me names, too. That's how cops are. I get it. Some jerk thought he was clever when he called you Full-of-shit Fulco, and the name stuck. But do you have to prove them right, time after time? I mean, Jesus Christ, Kyle. Do you really *aspire* to being lazy?"

Fulco shook his head, and she realized she'd misread him. He was angry, yes, but there was another emotion there, too. Shame. "I wasn't lazy, Emily. I was *stupid*. I believed every word Brooke Raines told me when I interviewed her after the shooting. That's why I closed the case. I was a dope. A stooge. A total sucker."

Graham took a breath. The confession seemed to

have deflated the man. Her anger ebbed, too. "But now you know she lied to you," she said.

"Yeah." Fulco met her stare. "Now I know, when it's too late to do anything."

"It's not too late. The trial isn't over yet."

Fulco let out a laugh. "Now you sound like Jessie."

"You should try to sound more like her, too. It might do you some good."

"Yeah, I don't know. Maybe I should." To her surprise, he actually seemed to consider the idea.

36.

Leary hated hospitals—especially when he was the patient. But the police had insisted, both for his own sake and to create an official record of his injuries. He knew the drill and had come here without objecting, but he was itching to leave. Every minute spent talking to doctors and undergoing tests instead of bringing the cops up to speed on the facts reduced the chances that the two men who had attacked him would be apprehended.

Besides, he knew the muggers—or hired thugs, as he suspected—hadn't done any critical damage to him. Scratches and cuts, yes. Some bruised ribs. One of his knees ached, as did his elbow. But he was fine.

"Leary."

He looked up and saw Jessie. She brought her hands to her face. "Oh God."

"I'm all right. I'm fine."

"You look awful."

"I need to get to the police station, look at mugshots."

"I took care of that," Jessie said. "The police are

coming here."

He felt relief. "Thanks."

"I just spoke with the doctor. The tests are almost done, but it's important that they make sure you're okay. We don't want you to walk out of here like a tough guy only to collapse in your apartment and crack your head on the coffee table."

"That's not going to happen."

She sat on the edge of his hospital bed and rubbed his arm. The warmth of her touch calmed him, but her face was taut with worry. "So, are we going to talk about this new hobby of yours?"

He sighed, and immediately regretted it as pain shot through his torso. "I was just asking some questions, talking to some people. I didn't think it was a big deal."

She frowned. "You kept it from me."

"I didn't want you to ... I don't know ... feel bad for me. It seemed pathetic, an ex-cop chasing after a three-year-old case."

"You should have told me."

He nodded, wincing at the stiffness in his neck. "I know. I'm sorry. But listen—I know this is hard to believe right now, but this attack is good news for both of us."

"That is pretty hard to believe."

"Those guys were sent by someone who didn't like the questions I was asking. Questions about a connection between supposed self-defense killings and a company called CBL Capital Partners. Questions that resulted in a CBL exec mentioning a shooting when I was talking about a stabbing. You know what that means? I solved *both* of our self-defense cases. I found the bad guys."

By the look on Jessie's face, he realized he wasn't speaking clearly. "Let's talk about this when you're in a calmer frame of mind," she said.

"No, Jess, listen to me. Your case isn't just a murder. It's a conspiracy."

She shook her head. "Leary...."

"Listen. I was investigating the connection between a company called CBL and my self-defense case from three years ago. But someone at CBL thinks I'm investigating their connection to Keeley. That's because CBL was behind *both* murders. They used the same trick, making the killings appear to be self-defense. That's why they sent these thugs to take me out."

"I know that seems true to you right now. But I don't think it's the most likely explanation. It's a conclusion your brain is jumping to because you're in shock after being attacked. You were already thinking about CBL, so your brain made the connection, but it's tunnel vision. If you calm down and force yourself to think objectively for a second—"

"For God's sake, don't patronize me! I'm a homicide detective!" Yelling caused pain to bolt through his temples, but when he realized what he'd said, the embarrassment hurt more. "I mean I still *think* like one. If the men who attacked me were really muggers, they would have taken my wallet and run."

"They did take your wallet."

"But they didn't run. They tried to kill me."

"You saw their faces. Maybe they were afraid you could identify them."

"So they decide what? To stab me? Beat me to death? They're going to commit murder for the fifty dollars in my wallet? Any thug with even a tiny bit of street experience would know the risk outweighed the reward. They came to kill me."

"Okay," Jessie said. "Maybe they did. But that still doesn't automatically mean they were hired by this CBL company. A lot of people probably want to hurt or kill you."

He couldn't help but smile. "Gee, thanks."

"You know what I mean. You were a cop. Cops make enemies. Maybe someone decided to get some revenge, especially now that you're not a cop anymore and don't have a police force backing you up."

Leary shook his head. "If it was revenge, that would mean it was personal. I would have recognized them. But I didn't. I've never seen them before."

"People change their appearances. Gain or lose weight, change their hair styles. Or maybe they were the brothers of someone you put in prison, or cousins or friends."

"Why are you trying so hard to change my mind?"

"Why are you trying so hard not to consider other

possibilities? It's almost like you ... like you *want* it to be a conspiracy."

"Don't you?" Leary said. "If CBL tried to kill me, it means we're on the right track. It means we're close to—" He stopped abruptly as he saw her point. Damn. He *did* want CBL to be responsible for the attack. He was making a classic investigatory mistake—reaching a conclusion first, and then searching for evidence to support it, when he should be looking at all of the evidence and following it to a conclusion.

The sound of a man clearing his throat caught their attention and they both looked up. Two men approached Leary's hospital bed. Leary's spirits lifted at the sight of them.

Jessie made room as one of the men, a detective named Matthies, pulled a bulky laptop from his bag and placed it on the food tray clamped to Leary's bed. The tray leaned under its weight, and Leary grabbed the computer and moved it to his lap before the table could break. Matthies's gaze followed the laptop with a disapproving look.

"Maybe you shouldn't hold heavy things," the detective said. "You know, there could be something broken or torn inside you. I got beat up once, and—"

"I'm fine," Leary said, maybe a little too sharply. "Nothing broken. No big deal."

The other cop, Mannello, leaned over Leary to get a closer look. "Looks like you did ten rounds in a cage match."

"One of the guys was big." Leary opened the

laptop. Matthies sat on the edge of the bed where Jessie had sat a moment before. He leaned over the keyboard, touched the track pad, and clicked a few times. The laptop's screen filled with a grid of unflattering photos. It was the electronic equivalent of the thick, photo-album-style mugshot books cops used to show to victims and witnesses back in the old days.

Leary scrolled through a seemingly endless collection of mugshots, hoping he would find one or both of his assailants glaring out at him from the screen. Chances were good that neither was an upstanding citizen. But none of the faces matched. Eventually, he sighed and shook his head.

"None of them even look like possibles?" Matthies said.

"No." Leary was certain. If either of the two men had appeared in the mugshots, he would have recognized them.

The two detectives looked like they might press him to take another look, but Jessie, who was standing at the side of the bed with her arms crossed over her chest, said, "He would know." Something in her tone convinced them to stand down. Matthies closed the laptop and put it back in his bag.

"Okey-dokey."

"Thanks for coming so quickly," Jessie said to them. "We appreciate it."

"No problem. Cop gets mugged—even an ex-cop— it's a priority," Mannello said.

Leary and Jessie waited until the two detectives

left. Then she turned to him, a look of concern softening her features again. "What do you think it means, that their photos aren't in the system?"

"Those guys are definitely career criminals. I wasn't their first victim. If the PPD doesn't have their faces on file, it means CBL—or whoever's behind the attack—must have recruited them from outside Philly. Probably from another state."

Jessie frowned. "That would mean resources, reach, sophistication."

"Like a well-funded corporation."

"Maybe."

He caught her looking at her watch. "You should go," he said. "You have a big day in court tomorrow."

"I'm not going anywhere."

"I'll be fine here."

He could see her struggling with the question of what to do. Finally, she said, "You need to promise me you're going to stop this. No more detective work."

"I won't promise that," he said. He wouldn't lie to her. "I'm seeing this thing through to the end. I'm solving it."

He was close now. The attack told him that much. Talking to Lydia Wax and David Whittaker had made someone uncomfortable. He didn't intend to stop now, when he might be days away from solving two crimes.

"Solving murder cases isn't your job anymore." There was an edge to Jessie's voice, and he heard both sympathy and exasperation in her tone. "You're not a cop anymore. You don't have a partner, or a badge, or access to backup. You shouldn't be out risking your safety investigating a three-year-old case—or my current one. That's my job and Fulco's job, and Emily is helping now, too."

Graham was helping? Jessie had asked her for help rather than come to him? He turned away from Jessie, not wanting her to see the hurt in his eyes. "None of you found CBL," he said. There was bitterness in his voice, and she seemed to pull away at the sound of it. "*I did.*"

"Yeah, you did." She wiped a hand across her face. When he looked at her, he saw a smear of tears beneath her eyes. "And look what happened. You could have been killed. You need to rest and heal, and then go back to living a civilian life." She leaned over the bed and kissed him. Her lips, warm and soft, lingered against his, relieving him of most of the hurt he'd felt a moment before. "Please."

After she was gone, and Leary was waiting to be discharged from the hospital, he thought about what she'd said. She was right, of course. The police, while far from safe, enjoyed more protection from violence than an average person, by virtue of the department's procedures and the psychological intimidation a badge had on most criminals. As a civilian, Leary was on his own.

On the other hand, he'd always believed the best way to remain safe from a criminal was to put that criminal behind bars, or in the ground. He was good at doing that, and always had been, and he knew how close he was to doing it now. All he was missing was solid evidence of the connection between CBL and its victims. Once he found that, he was confident he could fit the rest of the pieces together and bring down the company and the evil people running it. No, he couldn't stop now.

37.

Leary left the hospital as soon as he could, spent a restless night at home, and then headed out first thing in the morning to continue his investigation. He knew he was doing exactly what Jessie had asked him not to do, but he also knew he was close to solving two murders—maybe more—and he couldn't stop now. Not even for her.

At the intersection of Broad and Market, Philadelphia City Hall rose from Center Square. Once the tallest building in the city, it was opulent and lavish, adorned with columns and sculptures and a clock tower topped with a huge bronze statue of William Penn. To Leary, the building, which was the seat of government for the city, had always looked like a castle—something more at home in Disney World than downtown Philly. It was one of the city's more famous tourist attractions, and for good reason. But Leary wasn't here this morning for the tour. He had an appointment.

He tried to ignore the sidelong glances and outright stares as he passed through security and limped across the lobby to a small waiting area. His body still ached, and although a suit and tie covered most of his injuries, he was aware of how swollen his face looked, and of the bruises, stitches, and bandages.

He had made an appointment to meet with a man named Patrick Perez. Perez was a longtime city council employee, and had, until recently, been a legislative aide to Corbin Keeley. Leary suspected that CBL Capital Partners had arranged for Keeley's death in furtherance of some profit motive, the same type of motive they'd had with Terry Resta. Resta had stood in the way of a real estate purchase because he'd been an owner of the land CBL wanted to acquire, and had been unwilling to sell. Leary didn't know how Keeley had gotten in the company's way, but chances seemed good that his role as a city councilman had played a part. Leary hoped that Perez might help him identify a connection between the dead councilman's politics and the company's business.

A few minutes later, a man emerged from the elevators and approached him. Tall and slim, mid-thirties, Latino. He had neatly-styled black hair, an olive complexion, and a blinding smile. He extended his hand and said, "Detective Leary? I'm Patrick Perez."

"Good to meet you," Leary said as he shook the man's hand.

Perez's gaze seemed to take in Leary's battered appearance. "Are you alright?"

"It's not as bad as it looks. Listen, just so we're clear, I'm not a PPD detective anymore. I'm working privately on this." Leary hoped Perez wouldn't ask what that meant, since Leary himself wasn't sure. He did not have a private investigator's license—or a client, for that matter. "Thank you for agreeing to meet with me. I know I'm taking time out of your day. I appreciate it."

"It's no problem," Perez said. "Corbin wasn't just my boss. I considered him a friend. I want to help."

Leary nodded. "Good. Is there somewhere we can speak in private?"

"I have a room for us on the fifth floor."

A few minutes later, Leary eased himself into a chair in a nondescript room. Perez sat across a small table from him.

"Do you want a cup of coffee? Water?"

"No thanks," Leary said.

"Soda?"

"I'm good."

Perez looked disappointed, and Leary pegged him as the kind of guy who was a little too eager to please. That wasn't necessarily a good thing. In his experience, the eager-to-please personality type, while cooperative, could sometimes be *too* cooperative. Useful information could get buried under an avalanche of facts and observations.

"What can I tell you about Corbin?" Perez said.

"Well, I'm specifically looking for enemies he may have had in connection with his work here at City Hall."

Perez's forehead wrinkled. "I thought his girlfriend killed him because he ... you know...."

"Is that what you believe happened?"

Perez picked up a pen from the table and twisted it in his hands. "I don't know. He never seemed like that kind of person to me. I was familiar with the rumors, of course, but I guess I just hoped that's all they were." His gaze met Leary's. "You think that stuff's not true?"

Leary observed the hopeful look in the aide's face and hated to crush it, but the facts were the facts. "I wish I could tell you the abuse allegations were fabricated, but it looks like Keeley had a history of being physically abusive. His ex-wife confirmed it, and she has no reason to lie. We don't know for certain if he acted the same way with Brooke Raines, but...."

Perez nodded glumly. "I understand."

"What I'm here to figure out is whether his history might have been used against him, as a way to kill him under cover of a credible self-defense claim."

"You mean like it was staged?" Perez looked confused. "Is that what the DA's office believes?"

"I'm helping them with the investigation. That's why I'm asking you if his political activities led to any enemies."

He watched Perez mull over the question. "It's hard to say. I mean, yes, he definitely made enemies. In politics, it's impossible to please everyone. For every decision you make, some people benefit while others lose. You know what the city council does, right?"

Leary actually wasn't all that sure. "Give me the high-level overview."

"Do you remember your elementary school social studies class, where they taught you the three branches of government? This is the legislative branch. Think Congress at the federal level, only this is city government."

"So they make the laws," Leary said.

"That's their primary function. They have meetings every Thursday morning at 10:00 AM in room 400, one floor down from where we're sitting now, from September to June, with a month off for the holidays. There are also standing committees where council members hear testimony and review proposed bills in depth."

"Was Keeley on any standing committees?"

"Sure," Perez said. "He was on several."

"As his legislative aide, were you aware of the bills he was looking at?"

Perez nodded. "Oh yeah, of course. I provided Corbin with all kinds of support—administrative, research and analysis, that sort of thing. I kept track of all of the legislation he had an interest in."

Leary leaned forward. "I'm looking for some kind of legislation or other activity Keeley was involved with, where his involvement came between a company and a lot of money. I can only guess at the details. Maybe Keeley was going to shoot down a bill funding some kind of program, or he was choosing between two different companies where only one would benefit."

"And his death now clears the way for this company to get its payday?" Perez said.

"That's the theory. Can you think of anything that fits?"

Perez leaned back in his chair. "I could come up with a hundred scenarios like that. But we're not talking about big money. Not big enough to justify setting up an elaborate murder. The only big one that comes to mind is the prison project."

"You're talking about the city's plans to build a new prison?" Leary remembered reading about it in the *Philadelphia Inquirer*. There was general agreement that the city's overcrowded prison system needed relief, but the project had stalled in the planning stage because no one wanted the new facility built in their backyard.

"Exactly," Perez said. "There's a proposed plan to construct the prison on a sixty acre tract of land that's currently privately owned. The city council is scheduled to vote on a bill that would authorize the expenditure of ten million dollars to buy the property. Before his death, Corbin was planning to vote against the bill, because he thought the site was too close to his district and putting a giant prison there would wreak havoc on his constituents' property values."

"With Keeley out of the picture, is the bill likely to pass?" Leary said.

"Yeah, it's a foregone conclusion now. The bill's

going to pass when the vote happens next week."

Leary felt his heart pound. Ten million dollars, hinging on a vote that Corbin Keeley would have opposed—this was exactly what he'd been looking for.

"Who owns the land?"

"It's owned by a manufacturing company called Ironforge. There's a factory on the property now. The land is zoned I-3—heavy industrial—which also makes it eligible for detention and correctional facilities. The factory makes machine parts. Or, it used to. Ironforge was acquired by another company last year, and the new company closed the factory down, laid off all the employees, and liquidated most of the assets. That's why the land is up for sale."

"Do you know the name of the company that acquired Ironforge?" Leary asked the question and then held his breath.

"CBL Capital Partners," Perez said. "Big player in the Philly finance world."

Leary was speechless. There it was, the connection and the motive. All of the pieces were now in place. "Thanks. This is very helpful." He tried to hide his excitement, but he must not done have a very good job, because Perez seemed to be studying him more closely.

"You think CBL has something to do with Corbin's death?" The man sat back in his chair and stared into space for a moment, as if he were chewing on the idea. "You know, I would have told you that's a crazy idea. CBL is an extremely well-respected company. But their chief lawyer—this guy named Luther Goyle? I always thought there was something off about him."

"Luther Goyle," Leary said. The name was familiar to him from his research. Goyle had come on board as general counsel and later became a partner in the firm.

"Yes, Luther Goyle," Perez said. "If you're investigating CBL, you should definitely take a close look at him."

"I'll do that."

38.

Leary spotted Kyle Fulco sitting at his desk in the homicide bullpen. He had his chair tilted back, his shoes up on the edge of the desk, and a glazed look in his eyes. Just like Leary remembered him. A few cops spotted Leary and came over to say hello and ask how he was. "Doing great. Just came to by to talk to someone."

One of the other detectives watched Leary's limping gait with a skeptical look. "You sure you're okay, Leary? I heard you got mugged or something."

"Something like that," Leary said.

Another cop said. "You look like shit."

"Thanks, Dan."

The conversation drew Fulco's attention, and Leary saw the detective's eyes widen when he realized Leary was coming his way. His shoes dropped from his desk and his chair snapped to an upright position.

"Detective," Leary said as he closed the distance between them. "I hear you're the man to talk to about the Corbin Keeley case."

"Very funny." Fulco looked sheepish for a

moment. "How'd you get in here? Do you have an actual reason, or did you just stop by to rag on me?"

"I'm not here to rag on you. I'm here because I could use your help."

Fulco's gaze looked uneasy. "My help?"

"I just got a new lead on the Raines case. Need your help running it down."

"Wait a second, Leary." Fulco looked even more anxious now. "I can't do police work with you. You're a civilian. Not only could I get in trouble with the department, but your girlfriend would kill me. I can't just allow you to participate in an investigation."

Leary leaned against the man's desk and stared down at him. "I'm not participating in it. I'm leading it, since it currently doesn't have a lead detective who actually does anything."

Fulco gritted his teeth. "I'm gonna let that go, since I heard you've had a rough twenty-four hours and—"

Leary felt himself losing patience. "Look, Kyle, I'm not asking for a favor. I'm *offering* one. I don't need you. I could track down the information myself, or reach out to another friend from the PPD. But this is technically your case, and your reputation could use some help. So, I'm giving you a chance to be part of this. If you want it, great. If not, I'll be on my way. So how about it? Do you want in?"

"I want in."

Leary's next argument was already on his lips. He stopped, surprised. "I didn't think you'd be convinced that easily."

"I've been doing a lot of soul searching lately."

"Really?" Leary leaned forward and looked more closely at the man. Maybe Fulco wasn't exactly how he'd remembered him after all. "Good."

"So what really happened? You said you figured it out, and now we're going to prove it."

"Murder for hire."

Fulco looked shocked, then wary. "If this is a fucking prank, I swear to God—"

"No prank. There's a company called CBL Capital Partners. They were going to lose out on a major deal worth millions of dollars because of a city council vote that wasn't going to go their way. Because of Councilman Corbin Keeley. They knew about Keeley's past, so they paid a woman, Brooke Raines, to kill him make it look like self-defense."

"That sounds far-fetched."

"Keeley isn't the first victim. I worked a case three years ago in which a man named Terence Resta was killed by his girlfriend, supposedly in self-defense. After his death, his business was sold to a company that wanted his land. The company was CBL Capital Partners."

"I don't know." Fulco blew out a breath. "I want to believe you, but I still can't say I'm convinced."

"I tracked down the woman, Lydia Wax. She was living in a million-dollar house in New Jersey. I visited her and asked her some uncomfortable questions.

Within hours after I left, she killed herself."

Fulco rubbed his face thoughtfully.

"There's more," Leary went on. "I also approached one of the founding partners of CBL. I asked him some uncomfortable questions, too. And the next thing I knew, I was being attacked at night in the parking lot of my office by two thugs trying to kill me and make it look like a mugging. Do you still need more convincing?"

"It's a good theory, but where's the proof?"

"That's what you're going to help me find. Keeley's legislative aide suggested I take a hard look at a man named Luther Goyle. He's the chief lawyer at CBL and also a partner."

Fulco lifted the receiver from the phone on his desk. "Let me see what I can find."

"Thanks," Leary said. "Put it on speaker."

Fulco started by trying to find any record of criminal activity by Luther Goyle in Pennsylvania and federal records. Nothing. While he listened in on the calls, Leary did his own searches on Fulco's computer, finding Goyle's work and education histories online.

"He used to be a partner at a law firm in Manhattan," Leary said. "See if New York has anything on him."

Fulco made more calls. The calls took longer this time, as Fulco needed to navigate the politics of multi-state police cooperation. After several connections and transfers, they learned that neither New York City nor New York State had any criminal records involving Goyle.

"You sure this guy at City Hall wasn't talking out of his butt?" Fulco asked. "Goyle seems like a model citizen."

"Or a very careful criminal. Remember, this is a guy who uses other people to do his dirty work, and he uses the nuances of the law to protect them and himself. He's smart."

"Okay, but where do we go from here?"

"He grew up in Connecticut."

"Yeah, but he left for college when he was eighteen. Anything he did before that would be a juvenile record."

"No harm in trying."

Fulco made more calls. Leary had run out of ideas for internet searches, so he sat and listened as Fulco did the inter-agency dance again, trying to get connected with a cop who would help them.

"Nothing for a Luther Goyle," a clipped voice said eventually.

"Okay," Fulco said. "Thanks for checking—"

"I see a file for a Candice Goyle. Looks like a homicide. She was cleared though. Self-defense."

Leary lurched forward, eyes on Fulco's phone. "What year was that?"

There was a pause on the other end. Then, "File's old. Looks like 1972."

"Who was the victim?" Leary said.

Fulco's eyes met his. "You can't think Luther was

involved. He would have been a little kid."

"A self-defense homicide? It can't be a coincidence."

"I'm looking at a database entry, not the file itself," the cop said. "I could pull up a digital copy if the record was more recent, but 1972? Those never got scanned. I can put in a request to try to find the paper file."

"How long will that take?" Leary said.

"Hard to say. No more than a few weeks, probably."

In a few weeks, Brooke Raines would be acquitted. "We don't have a few weeks. We don't even have a few days."

"I'm not sure what to tell you, pal. It is what it is."

It is what it is. Was there any less useful statement in the English language?

"What about the name of the lead detective?" Fulco said. "Can you give us that? Maybe we can talk to him."

Leary gave Fulco a nod. Good idea.

"Yeah. Guy's name is James Rowe. He's retired, though, and has been for a while."

"Do you have a number we can reach him at?"

"Sorry, I can't give out personal information like that. Besides, an old retired guy, and a case that old, what are the chances he'd even remember anything?"

"We really need to get in touch with him," Leary said.

"And I told you, I can't give you his personal information. These aren't the old days. These are days when we have cyber-security training and people are stealing identities instead of wallets. The rules are tougher now, and I'm not breaking them for two guys from Philly I don't even know."

Leary and Fulco exchanged another glance. They were both experienced enough to know they'd reached a dead end. "We understand," Fulco said. "Thanks anyway. We appreciate the information you were able to give us."

"No problem. Good luck with your case."

Fulco ended the call. "So much for research on Luther Goyle. Sorry, Leary."

"We don't have to give up yet." On Fulco's computer screen, Leary had a list of people named James Rowe who had publicly listed phone numbers in Connecticut. "You want to make some cold calls, see if we can find our retired detective?"

Fulco's face sagged. "Sure. Why not?"

He put his phone on speaker again and started calling the numbers. The first three were each the wrong James Rowe. The fourth person didn't pick up. The fifth was a woman.

She said, "No, my husband isn't a cop. But I think I know the person you're looking for. We get calls for him from time to time. He lives in an assisted living facility in Danbury. Hold on and I'll get you the number."

They called and spoke to a friendly-sounding

receptionist who explained that it would not be possible to put Rowe on the phone, given his current condition.

That didn't sound good. "He's that out of it?" Fulco said.

"Oh no, Mr. Rowe's quite alert. It's just that he can't talk because of a surgery he recently underwent on his throat. He's actually been communicating using a little dry-erase board, the poor guy."

After they ended the call, Leary looked at Fulco. "You up for a road trip?"

"All the way to Connecticut? You gotta be kidding."

Leary wasn't kidding.

James Rowe was indeed alert. He seemed thrilled to receive a visit from two brothers in blue—even if Leary technically was no longer in the family. Fulco and Leary sat with him in a pleasant, sun-filled room in a cheery facility.

I remember Candice, he wrote on his handheld dry-erase board. *Not the kind of case you forget.*

"Why's that?" Leary said.

Domestic abuse, always sickening. But this was more. Brutal. Husband punched her, kicked her, cut her.

"And she killed him?"

Rowe nodded, then wrote. *Blew his brains out.*

"I guess it must have been a pretty clear-cut case," Fulco said. "He attacked her, she got her hands on a gun, and she shot him before he could hurt or kill her, right?"

Rowe's mouth opened and he laughed, but no noise came from his throat. The effect was eerie.

"It wasn't that simple?" Leary said.

What was simple was he deserved to die. So we didn't arrest.

"Yeah, but was it self-defense?" Fulco said.

The retired detective laughed again. He shook his head.

"How can you know for sure he wasn't threatening her life when she shot him?" Fulco said.

For the first time since they'd arrived at the facility, Rowe seemed reluctant to answer. He sighed and moved his pen with squeaky movement over the board.

Son told us. He witnessed it. Rowe watched their reactions, then erased the board and wrote: *You won't find his statement in the file. We tore it up for his sake and his mother's.*

Leary already knew the answer to his next question, but he asked it anyway. "Do you remember the son's name?"

The old cop nodded, then wrote. *Luther.*

Leary looked at Fulco.

39.

Warren Williams put the folder down. "We still don't have a case."

Leary threw up his hands. He sat in a conference room in the DA's office. Around the table were Warren Williams, Kyle Fulco, Emily Graham, and Jessie. Jessie gave him a warning look, then said to Warren, "We need to make one."

"Let's review what we think we know," Warren said. He took a deep breath. "We believe Brooke Raines was hired or otherwise persuaded by CBL Capital Partners to kill Corbin Keeley so that an upcoming vote would go the company's way, resulting in a transaction worth ten million dollars. We believe that the actual plan was orchestrated by a man named Luther Goyle, a partner in the firm, but that others in the firm were likely also involved. To cover up the real motive behind the killing, and avoid a criminal investigation, the killing was made to look like an act of self-defense. This was made possible by Keeley's own character problems, and appears to be a ruse that CBL has used effectively in the past, in at least one instance. Does that sum it up?"

Heads around the table nodded.

"Okay," Warren said. "Now let's talk about what we can actually prove in court. Do we have any evidence connecting Brooke Raines to CBL?"

"No," Fulco said. "And believe me, we looked. We got warrants to search Raines's apartment, her financial records. There's nothing."

"There's Lydia Wax," Leary said. "She received a payment we might be able to tie back to CBL—"

Warren cut him off with a wave of his hand. "Come on, Leary, you know that won't prove anything in Brooke Raines's trial."

Leary wasn't ready to admit defeat yet. "When I questioned David Whittaker about Lydia Wax, he thought I was talking about Brooke Raines. CBL was involved in both killings, and Whittaker was aware of what was happening. Maybe we can put Whittaker on the stand and get him to admit it."

Jessie shook her head. "Too risky. If we call him as a hostile witness and he denies everything, where does that get us?"

"Then put *me* on the stand," Leary said. "I talked to him, and to Lydia Wax."

Warren laughed. "Even if we survived the hearsay objections, Aidan Hughes would crucify you on cross. Can you imagine? 'Mr. Leary, are you a police officer? No? A DA investigator? No? What exactly is your relationship to the prosecutor in this case?'" Warren shuddered.

Leary glanced at Jessie and saw her face redden.

He said, "That's enough, Warren. We get it."

"We need evidence," Warren said. "And we don't have it."

"Think about what it could mean for Rivera's approval rating if we demonstrate that Brooke Raines was a hired killer," Jessie said. "All the negative publicity, the protests, the questions about the next election—that would all go away. Overnight, Rivera would stop being the DA who went after a domestic abuse victim and become the DA who uncovered a sinister corporate conspiracy."

Warren glared at her. "Obviously, I would love that. But the fact remains that we can't prove any of it."

Jessie sat back in her chair. A faraway look entered her gaze, and Leary could tell she'd withdrawn into her own mind. "What are you thinking, Jess?"

"There might be a way," she said. The room fell silent and all eyes turned to her.

"I'm listening," Warren said.

"Maybe we don't need to prove our theory. We only need to make Brooke Raines and Aidan Hughes think we can. Murder for hire adds aggravated circumstances to the murder charge, which would push the case into death penalty territory. If I can convince Brooke Raines that she's facing a lethal injection, she might make a deal with us."

Leary nodded as he saw where Jessie was going. "A plea bargain. She testifies against Goyle, Whittaker, and the other people who hired her to kill Keeley, and we take death off the table."

Jessie nodded and looked at Warren. "What do you think?"

"I'm okay making a deal with her, if it means getting the ringleaders. But do you really think you can scare her enough to negotiate with us?"

"I shook her up pretty badly on cross-examination. She's not nearly as confident as she was when the trial started. Once I tell her we know about the murder-for-hire arrangement, and threaten to amend the charges, I think she might panic."

There were thoughtful nods around the table.

Warren sighed deeply. "Do it."

40.

Jessie faced Brooke Raines and Aidan Hughes across a table in a room down the hall from Judge Armstrong's courtroom. The space was tight, claustrophobic, and barely large enough for its spartan furnishings. It was also too warm, and the smell of a previous occupant's perfume lingered in the air.

The discomfort was a plus, as far as Jessie was concerned—a demonstration of the squalor of the penal system and a reminder of what was at stake. She placed a legal pad on the table. The wooden surface was oily and gouged with initials and graffiti. Raines seemed reluctant to touch it. She sat a good six inches back from its edge, and kept her hands in her lap.

Hughes didn't seem to share his client's aversion. He placed both hands on the table and leaned aggressively forward. "This deal is an insult. Life in prison? Why would we even consider taking that? Maybe you haven't noticed, but the jury doesn't appear to be on your side."

Jessie sat back in her chair. "The circumstances have changed. We know your client's real motive now.

We know the shooting was a murder for hire."

"You haven't proven it in court."

"Not yet. Have you explained to your client what the term 'aggravated circumstances' means?"

By the fear she saw in Raines's eyes, Jessie was pretty sure he had.

"You think that's enough to make life without the possibility of parole an attractive option?" Hughes bit out the words.

"That's up to your client." She looked at Raines.

"I shot Corbin in self-defense," Raines said. "I'm innocent."

"I don't think you are," Jessie said, "and if we don't reach a deal today, I'm going to introduce the jury to a lot of new evidence we've discovered about one of Keeley's upcoming city council votes and a company called CBL Capital Partners."

Hughes brayed a laugh, but it sounded forced, and the expression on his face showed his uncertainty. "If you were really confident you could do that, we wouldn't be sitting here."

"If the only person I were interested in convicting was Brooke Raines, you'd be right." Jessie kept her voice level. She needed to be convincing, and she couldn't let Hughes figure out how close his words had come to the truth. "But luckily for her, I want her co-conspirators, too. Especially the ones who set this crime in motion. *That's* the reason we're sitting here."

Hughes turned to Raines and shook his head. "I

think she's bluffing."

Jessie locked her gaze on Raines. "Easy for your lawyer to say. He gets to go home either way. You don't, Brooke. The jurors are already starting to doubt your story. Don't tell me you didn't feel their suspicion in there, when you were on the witness stand. Don't tell me you didn't see the distrust dawning in their eyes. Now imagine how those jurors will react when they learn you had a financial motive for shooting Keeley. Are you as confident as your lawyer that they will still be on your side? Do you want to take that chance on a charge of murder with aggravated circumstances? Do you know how death row inmates are executed in Pennsylvania?"

Raines blanched to a paler shade of white. Before she could speak, Hughes said, "You made your point, Jessie."

"Good. Because this is critical. Brooke, I want the people who are *really* behind Corbin Keeley's murder—people who believe they don't have to play by the rules, who think they can get away with anything. They're the people who should be on trial, facing a jury, and I'm willing to make a deal with you to get them. I'm willing to spare you from the death penalty. But if you won't help me, I'll make sure you get the sentence you deserve."

Raines and Hughes huddled together. Jessie heard the lawyer say, "We have a strong case—"

"That's what you keep saying." Raines's voice came out in a high pitch. "I saw the way those jurors were looking at me."

"Is there something you can tell me about the people who orchestrated Corbin Keeley's death?" Jessie said.

Hughes placed a hand on Raines's forearm, stopping her before she could respond. His gaze turned to Jessie. "Anything Brooke says now is purely hypothetical."

"Understood," Jessie said.

Hughes looked at his client. "Is there?"

"These people are dangerous," Raines said.

"We can protect you," Jessie said.

Raines's face twisted with misery. She looked at her lawyer. "What should I do?"

She looked helpless, almost childlike, and Jessie felt a sudden pang of sympathy for her. She forced herself to remember that Brooke Raines was no one to feel sorry for. She was a killer, and one who'd done it for money. She was as cold-blooded as they came.

Hughes sighed. "It's your call. If you turn down the Commonwealth's offer, I still believe the jury will acquit you. On the other hand, there are no guarantees at trial, and the stakes are high. If we lose, you're probably looking at an execution. You need to decide whether you're willing to take that risk."

Raines turned back to Jessie. "Can I have some time to think about it? Before I make a final decision?"

"There's no time," Jessie said. "Judge Armstrong isn't going to allow us to hold up his trial schedule any longer."

"Give her one night," Hughes said. "Let her sleep on it. We'll have an answer for you tomorrow morning."

Jessie hesitated, then let out a breath. "I can agree to that. But I need an answer first thing in the morning. Otherwise, we'll proceed with the trial and let the jury make the final decision."

"Thank you," Raines said.

Raines and Hughes rose from the table. Jessie watched them leave the room. Once she was alone, she wondered if she'd made the wrong decision giving Raines the night to think it over. Raines was under house arrest. In the comfort of her apartment, would the threat of a death penalty verdict seem as real? There was no point second-guessing herself now. She gathered her things. One way or the other, she'd have her answer tomorrow.

41.

That night, like every night since she'd become involved with this case, Jessie tossed and turned. Her mind refused to stop fretting over the details of the trial. Leary slept beside her, a motionless form in her bed. She resisted the temptation to wake him and talk to him. That would only ruin his sleep and wake her up even more. She flipped her pillow over, pressed her face to the cool side, and closed her eyes. Would she ever have a good night's sleep again?

Her phone vibrated on the nightstand. *Who could that be?* She propped herself up on one elbow and swept up the phone. The name on the screen was Kyle Fulco.

"This is Jessie." She spoke quietly, trying not to wake Leary.

"Sorry to call so late," Fulco said. "I thought you would want to know. About twenty minutes ago, the service center computer received a notification from the receiving unit in Brooke Raines's apartment. Her ankle monitor was tampered with."

"What?" Jessie sat up straight. She had a basic

understanding of how ankle monitors worked. The devices were designed to enforce house arrest. A black box secured to a tether around the person's ankle sent out a radio frequency signal at timed intervals to a receiving unit, which then relayed the information through a cellular network to a computer monitored by the police. The devices had been in use for decades, and the latest technology was very difficult to circumvent. Any attempt to tamper with an ankle monitor set off warning alarms at the PPD, which was apparently what had happened tonight.

"What's going on?" said a groggy voice beside her. Leary's head was still on his pillow, and his eyes were half-open. "Who are you talking to?"

"It's Fulco."

"I'm at her building now," Fulco was saying. "We found the ankle bracelet on her kitchen floor. Looks like she cut the tether with a knife. She's not here."

"Jess, what's going on?" Leary said. He sat up. The sheet fell away from his bare chest. She saw his bruises even in the darkness of the bedroom, large dark splotches against his pale skin. "Is it about Raines?" he said.

Jessie nodded. Raines should never have been allowed to remain under house arrest during the trial. She was a killer, and all killers were flight risks. But the bail commissioner had been lulled into a false sense of security by the self-defense claim, and Jessie had not tried to revisit the issue after the trial began, believing it would be a lost cause and that her time and energy were better spent on other battles. She regretted that decision now.

"Is there anything in her apartment that would give us any clue where she would run?" she said.

"Her keys are here, and her car is on the street, so we know she's on foot. I mean, unless she has access to another vehicle, or someone picked her up, or—"

"Is there a computer?"

She heard the sound of Fulco moving around the apartment. "Yeah, there's a laptop. I'm turning it on."

"Open her web browser and check the history." Jessie crossed her fingers. Many perpetrators—even careful ones—made the mistake of researching their crimes on the web and not clearing their search histories. She hoped Raines might have made a similar mistake, especially if she'd been rushing.

"Good idea," Fulco said. "Here we go."

Jessie was already out of bed, pulling on a pair of jeans. She saw Leary watch her for a second, then yawn and climb out of bed himself and search around in the dark for his clothes.

"What did you find?" Jessie asked Fulco.

"A train schedule for the SEPTA lines."

"Can you tell which destination she was looking up? Or which station she was planning to depart from?"

"I can't tell. The page she was looking at lists all the stations."

Jessie took a breath. Each minute that passed

reduced their chances of catching Brooke Raines before she vanished. She needed to think. Raines's apartment was located near the Penn Center area of Philly. The closest train station to her home was Suburban Station at 16th and JFK. But Suburban Station was a small commuter station with only about eight tracks. If Raines wanted access to all destinations—and a better chance at fleeing the state—Philly's main train station, Thirtieth Street Station, wasn't that much farther away, across the Schuylkill River on Market Street.

"Since you're already in the area, check Suburban Station," Jessie said. "I'll check Thirtieth Street Station."

"What do you mean, *you'll* check it? You shouldn't be running around—"

"I've got Leary with me," she said, cutting him off. "We don't have time to argue about this. Look for her at Suburban Station and check in with us when you're there."

She listened to his breathing as he hesitated, but then he said, "Be careful. I'll call you back soon." The line disconnected.

"You get all that?" Jessie said to Leary.

She assumed he must have picked up enough of the conversation to fill in the rest, because he was sitting on the side of the bed, loading his gun.

"You're carrying again?" she said.

"Two guys try to kill you, you start to take personal defense a little more seriously."

Jessie nodded. "Let's hope we don't need it."

Jessie and Leary hurried inside Thirtieth Street Station. Although Amtrak owned the building, it was also the hub for SEPTA's local rail lines, so if Raines was trying to catch a SEPTA train, there was a good chance she'd do it here. The problem was the building was huge. It covered two city blocks and, on a typical day, handled maybe twenty-five-thousand people. Luckily, it was now almost midnight, and at this hour there wasn't much activity. The maze of fast food restaurants, coffee shops, and newsstands had been secured for the night behind locked gates, and most of the people were clustered around the station's high-ceilinged center, where an electronic board dutifully listed the final departures of the night.

Jessie scanned the scattered crowd. Two half-asleep college students, some homeless people under filthy blankets. A bored-looking transit cop who paused just long enough to give Jessie and Leary a once-over.

"I don't see her." Leary looked grim.

"Maybe Fulco will find her at Suburban Station."

"Or maybe she's not even taking a train. Maybe she left that search history on her computer to throw us off the trail. Or maybe she checked the train schedule but then decided on a different plan."

Jessie chewed her lip. Those were all possibilities. Brooke Raines could be anywhere. And if they lost her now, not only would she escape punishment, but so would Luther Goyle and the other people who'd orchestrated the murders of Corbin Keeley and Terry Resta.

"Look over there!" Leary said. Jessie followed his pointing finger to a shape flitting behind a stone column in the shadows near the deserted ticket booths. "Shit, she saw us."

Leary broke into a run before Jessie could even find the person he'd pointed at. When she saw the blonde hair, she knew it was Raines running for the doors at the other end of the station.

She grabbed her phone and called Fulco. On the line, he said, "Did you find her? I hope so, because the only people at Suburban Station are a couple of homeless men."

"She's here," Jessie said as she broke into a run, following Leary. "Thirtieth Street Station. Leary's chasing her. We need help."

"I'll radio dispatch."

Jessie saw Raines shove her way through the doors at the other end of the train station, followed seconds later by Leary. Jessie followed. Cold November air hit her face, along with the sounds of car engines and the roll of tires on Route 76, surprisingly loud for the late hour. The air was damp, chilly, and heavy with the smells of exhaust and the Schuylkill River.

She turned right. Leary was a barely discernible figure in the distance. Raines was gone, swallowed whole by the murk. Jessie wasted no time. At least she had one thing going for her—at her apartment, she'd put on sneakers instead of her usual heels. Within minutes, she overtook Leary, whose limp seemed to be getting worse.

"You okay?" she said.

"Not really. I guess those guys did more damage than I realized." His speed slackened and he dropped a pace behind her as she pushed harder and left him gasping in her wake.

"Wait," he said, "don't put yourself ... in danger."

The word caught her off-guard, and she realized what she was doing—chasing a murderer through the city in the dead of night. She hesitated, losing some speed, but didn't stop. Whatever the danger, she couldn't let Raines get away.

"Jessie ... wait!"

She risked a glance over her shoulder. Leary gained on her. A moment later, they were running side by side. She looked forward again, just in time to see Raines cut around a corner. The blonde was running down the ramp toward Route 76. Jessie heard a screech of brakes, a long, angry honk. A car must have swerved around Raines.

"She's gonna be roadkill before we can ... get to her." Leary was panting.

"Come on," she said. They ran down the decline of the ramp. No cars barreled into their path, though judging by the screeches and horns punctuating the traffic sounds, Raines was disrupting traffic ahead.

They emerged onto 76. Lanes of cars rocketed

toward them at sixty-plus miles per hour. Headlights stabbed Jessie's eyes and she stumbled onto the shoulder, hands on her face, blinking away the orange afterimages.

"Open your eyes!" Leary said. "Are you crazy?"

She opened them. Cars whizzed past.

"Where did she go?" She had to shout to hear her own voice.

Leary pointed ahead, and Jessie spotted Raines running along the shoulder.

Leary said, "At least she's got the good sense to stay on this side of the highway—"

Before he could finish, the woman darted between two cars and continued her flight against the flow of traffic, presumably to make pursuit more difficult. Apparently, she had decided to escape or die trying.

42.

Leary tried to ignore the pain screaming through his body as he half-ran, half-staggered down Route 76, struggling to stay close to Jessie. He knew if he allowed himself to fall too far behind, he'd be putting her in danger. Brooke Raines was a killer, not to mention a member of a conspiracy—for all they knew, her accomplices might be out here in the darkness, too, waiting for a moment to strike. He'd already met two of them, and it wasn't an experience he wanted Jessie to suffer. The thought of anyone hurting her got his legs pumping harder. His lungs burned.

"Jessie, go back to the train station!" His voice was barely audible over the rush of vehicles.

"No!" Jessie yelled without looking back. The headlights of passing cars flashed against her face, bringing out the shape of her cheekbones and the determined set of her jaw. He knew he wasn't going to convince her to stop.

Further along the highway, Raines darted into traffic, risking her life to put more distance between them. Leary didn't intend to do the same and he hoped

Jessie wouldn't, either. He continued to run along the shoulder, struggling to catch up with Jessie. The concrete jarred his knees. Pain radiated in his bruised ribs. His face burned. Jessie was pulling ahead. He couldn't keep up.

A roar rose above the traffic, and Leary looked up into the glare of a searchlight. He blinked and saw a police helicopter in the sky, blades churning. He could hear the wail of approaching sirens, faint but getting louder. Police cruisers.

Fulco had called in the cavalry. Leary felt a rush of unexpected affection for the man. *Not so full of shit after all.* The arrival of reinforcements energized him. Jessie would be safe now, or *safer*, anyway. He lowered his head and pumped his arms. He was only ten feet behind her now, then five.

A horn blared and a Pontiac Grand Am swerved out of its lane. The smell of burnt rubber assaulted his nostrils. The Grand Am skidded and slammed into the side of the car next to it. Metal ground against metal. Both vehicles careened across the highway. Leary threw himself out of the way.

He wasn't fast enough. The rear corner of the Grand Am clipped him. The impact was a sledgehammer to his side.

He hit the ground. Screamed as the two cars collided with the concrete wall of the shoulder. Sparks rained across the asphalt. His vision blurred, then focused on a figure looming over him.

"Leary, can you get up? Leary!" It was Jessie.

Pain spiked through him. He looked up at her concerned face, seeing it through a haze. She'd stopped and come back for him. Thank God.

"I need to go," she said.

"No!"

"I hear an ambulance coming." Her voice a mixture of relief and concern. He heard the siren a second later, screaming in their direction.

He realized he'd closed his eyes. Dared not open them, afraid the pain would intensify. "Let the police chase her. Too dangerous."

"I can't risk it."

He sensed her about to leave. "At least take my gun."

"What?"

"*Take my gun!*"

He felt her remove his gun from its holster. Then he felt the warm touch of her fingers against his face, and a gentle kiss on his lips. "You'll be okay. I'll be okay. I'll be back soon."

A few seconds later, when he forced his eyes open, she was gone, and so was his Glock.

The two wrecked cars, the Grand Am and a Honda Civic, smoked no more than five feet from where he lay. The driver of the Grand Am was staring at him with wide eyes, a cell phone pressed to his face. The other driver sat slumped behind the wheel of the Honda, blood running from her ear.

Gingerly, Leary moved his hands along his body.

He found no fractures, no broken bones. A few new cuts and scrapes to join the ones he already had. The right leg of his pants had ripped apart and blood oozed from the leg underneath. It was scraped raw, but that seemed to be the extent of the damage.

Using the concrete wall of the shoulder for support, he pulled himself up. It hurt, but he could move. He could walk. He squinted into the darkness, but saw no sign of Jessie or Raines.

The sight of Leary being hit by a car still burned in her mind, but Jessie pushed away the horror of that moment and kept her eyes locked on the running figure of Brooke Raines. There would be time to focus on Leary later. Time to hold him tight and thank God he wasn't killed. Right now, she needed to finish what she and Leary had started. She pursued the woman with as much speed as she could. Her right hand gripped Leary's gun and her left balled into a fist.

A spear of brightness lanced down from the helicopter floating above. There was a circle of light, and Brooke Raines, at its center, lit up as bright as daylight. Traffic jammed as drivers swerved their cars to the shoulder or just braked in the middle of the highway. Raines was weaving between the stopped cars. Jessie ran. Heat hit her back and light almost blinded her as she caught up with Raines inside the circle of the spotlight's glare.

"Stop!" She didn't know if she could be heard over the chopping rotors, but she must have been loud enough, because Raines twisted around. "Stop, Brooke! It's over."

Raines gaped at her. The woman's shoulders rose and fell with each labored breath. Her face gleamed with sweat and the look in her eyes was wild. "It wasn't supposed to end like this!"

"It wasn't supposed to end like this for Corbin Keeley, either!"

An amplified voice boomed, *"Drop your weapon immediately and put your hands in the air."* Jessie cursed, realizing the police in the helicopter must have seen the gun in her hand. *"Drop your weapon now!"*

There was nothing she could do but comply. She tossed Leary's Glock onto the street and raised her empty hands. Her gaze never left Raines. She hoped the woman wouldn't see this as another opportunity to run.

Raines didn't run. She lunged. Before Jessie realized what was happening, Raines grabbed the gun off the ground, rolled onto her back, and fired up at the sky. The spotlight burst and they were plunged into darkness as the gunshot's report echoed in Jessie's ears.

Jessie's breath stopped. Even with the headlights of the stopped cars on the highway providing some light, her eyes were slow to adjust after the intense glare of the spotlight. She couldn't see Raines. Could barely see anything. And Raines was an expert marksman—one who'd just taken out the spotlight on a police helicopter. Jessie braced herself for the woman's next shot. Imagined a bullet through her face, just like the one that ended Keeley's life.

Above her, she heard the roar of the helicopter as it pivoted and lurched in frantic movements. Her sight began to return. Her straining eyes picked out cars and trucks, their drivers cringing low in their seats, faces pinched with fear. The sound of approaching police sirens was louder now, but still too far away.

Then she saw Raines. The woman held Leary's gun in a two-handed grip, and it was aimed at her. *Don't*, she thought. But she didn't speak the word. If she was going to die tonight, she would do it standing tall.

"This is your fault!" Raines yelled. "You should have just left me alone." She worked Leary's gun, chambering another round.

Another figure rushed from the shadows and hit Raines, knocking the woman off her feet. The two bodies rolled on the asphalt. One figure ripped the gun from the grasp of the other and threw it out of reach. Jessie ran toward them.

It was Leary. He was bleeding, but his face was a mask of resolve as he held Raines to the ground. He looked up at Jessie and managed a smile. "How's ... our case ... looking now?"

43.

Brooke Raines wore an orange jumpsuit. Shackles linked her wrists and ankles. A night in jail had left her eyes puffy and her hair tangled. Jessie thought the look suited her.

Their meeting was in another cramped attorney room of the courthouse. It looked and smelled like it hadn't been cleaned in weeks—or maybe the smell was coming from Raines.

Jessie regarded the woman and her lawyer from across the table. Aidan Hughes sat beside his client in a neatly pressed, charcoal gray suit, with his hands folded in front of him on the table's battered surface. To his credit, he didn't feign outrage over the shackles on his client. Jessie was glad. The thought of everything that had happened the night before brought a flare of anger burning through her that was hard enough to control as it was.

"Before we start," Hughes said, "I need to know if the same offer is still on the table, given the circumstances."

Jessie saw the nervousness in his eyes. She knew

what worried him. Many prosecutors, after a defendant's attempt to flee, would change the offer or revoke it altogether. Jessie would have liked nothing more than to do that now. But if she did, she would be venting her anger at the expense of justice for Corbin Keeley and Terry Resta. She couldn't do that.

"The offer hasn't changed," she said. "If your client provides us with the information and testimony we need, then we will agree not to seek the death penalty."

Hughes and Raines exchanged a look. The defense attorney nodded to his client and said, "Go ahead."

Raines turned her gaze to Jessie. She hesitated for a second, then said, "I don't know where to start."

"Why don't you tell me about the people who hired you to murder Corbin Keeley?"

Raines flinched at the word *murder*. "I only dealt with one person. His name is Luther Goyle."

"How did you first meet him?"

Raines took a breath. "You know I've been shooting for a long time. Since I was a kid. My dad got me into it. It was something we liked to do together, like a father-daughter thing. I never stopped. I still practice at a range in North Philly called Barker's, and I compete in events sometimes, although I'm not really that good, compared to the real pros."

Jessie knew all of this from the trial, but she sensed that Raines was starting with the easy facts as a way of warming herself up. Jessie let her.

"I've been shooting at Barker's for years," she

went on, "so I'm on friendly terms with the owner. He's an older guy, served in the Marines and fought in Iraq during the first Gulf War. He looks a little like my dad, and I guess that's part of why we get along. One day, when I showed up to use the range, he asked me to come into his office."

"When was this?" Jessie asked.

"Toward the end of May. I can probably get you the exact date if you need it. I'd need to look at a calendar."

"We can do that later. Let's hear the rest of the story."

"In his office, Jeff—that's his name—told me he'd received a call from a man working for a company that was looking for an attractive young woman who was a good marksman. They wanted to sponsor the woman and use her name and likeness for publicity for their company. Jeff thought it might be a cool opportunity for me, and wanted to know if he should give them my name."

"You said yes?"

Raines had a faraway look in her eyes. "I didn't think anything would come of it, but I didn't see any harm in trying."

"The company reached out to you?"

"Yes, the same day. A man calling himself Smith asked if I would meet him at a Starbucks in Center City. I agreed. But as soon as the meeting started, I knew something was wrong. For one thing, he didn't want us to even talk inside the Starbucks. There was a car on the street outside, and he wanted to talk to me in the car. For confidentiality purposes, he said."

"Did you get in the car?"

"Yes." Raines looked ashamed to admit to her own questionable judgment. "Stupid, I guess. But just getting a call had made me excited. I was already thinking about being some kind of celebrity markswoman."

"You said the man called himself Smith. Was that his real name?"

"His real name was Luther Goyle. He told me that later, after I agreed to … his proposal."

"Don't jump ahead. You got into the car with him. Was there anyone else there? A driver?"

"No. Just the two of us. But it was a big Town Car, the kind that would have normally had a driver, and Goyle sat with me in the back. So I think he sent the driver away on some errand so we'd be alone."

"You both sat in the back? He didn't drive you anywhere?"

Raines shook her head. "The car was parked legally on the street, pretty close to the Starbucks, so he didn't need to move it. The backseat was roomy, with tinted windows, plenty of privacy. I thought he was going to interview me in the car. That's what I still thought it was—an interview for a corporate sponsorship."

No witnesses to the conversation, Jessie thought. No one who could overhear a stray word. Goyle had probably been prepared to take action if Raines rejected his proposal—violent action. "You weren't afraid?"

"Not at first." Raines's lips twitched with distaste. "I wanted to believe I could be ... I don't know ... some kind of star."

"What did he say to you once you were alone together?"

"He started with an apology. He said he'd set up the meeting under false pretenses. Those were his words. That's how this guy talks. I was like, 'What?' And he said there was no sponsorship and that he'd actually come to discuss a highly confidential matter. He said I could make a lot of money. At that point I was thinking the guy was trying to scam me or worse, so I tried to get out of the car."

"Were you locked in?"

"No. The door opened. But before I could get out, he asked me in a very reasonable voice to please just give him five minutes to explain. For some reason, I did."

"You sat back down and closed the door?" Jessie said.

Raines nodded. "He had an iPad. He played with it for a few seconds, and then passed it over to me. I almost dropped the thing when I saw what was on the screen. It was a photo of a woman. Her face was covered in dark, blotchy bruises. Goyle said he wanted my help stopping the man who'd done this."

"Do you know who the woman in the picture was?"

"I didn't recognize her at the time. I'm not really into politics—especially local stuff. But it was Nina Long. Corbin Keeley's ex-wife. Goyle told me, and I recognized her later at the trial."

"How did seeing the photo make you feel?"

Raines's lips thinned as she seemed to consider the question. "Disgusted, I guess, at first. Then a little angry. How would anyone feel looking at something like that?"

"What else did Goyle tell you?"

"That it was a city councilman who did it. That he'd gotten away with it. That no one was going to punish him. Goyle was getting angry just telling me. I thought he was going to have a stroke. He's very overweight. His face turned red. He said if somebody didn't stop Keeley, more women were going to get hurt."

"Do you believe that was his real motivation for wanting to kill Keeley?" Jessie said. "To protect women?"

Raines looked at her with a sad half-smile. "I can tell what you're thinking—that he put on a show for me, tricked me, when what he really wanted was to make a lot of money on a business deal that Keeley was blocking. And that part is true, too. But I think his anger about the abuse was real. No one can fake that kind of anger."

Jessie, thinking back to what Leary and Fulco had learned about Goyle's mother, thought Raines might be right. "What did you say to him, after he showed you the picture and told you about Keeley?"

"I said it was terrible, but it had nothing to do with me, and I started to get out of the car again. Then he told me I could make a million dollars and rid the world of Corbin Keeley, with no risk of going to prison, or having to hide the money, or anything."

"So you decided to hear him out?" Jessie tried to keep her tone neutral.

"It's a lot of money."

"What exactly was his proposal?"

"He said he could arrange for Corbin and me to meet. He wanted me to date the guy for a few months—long enough for his true nature to emerge— and then shoot him when he tried to hurt me. He said with my shooting skills, there would be little risk. And he promised me there would be no legal consequences. He said I probably wouldn't even be arrested, and that even if I was, any court in the country would call the shooting justified under the self-defense laws."

"You said yes?"

"I didn't at first. I thought the whole thing was scary and weird. I got out of the car. He didn't try to stop me, but...."

Jessie waited, but Raines seemed hesitant to continue. "What were you going to say?"

She shook her head. "I don't know. The way he was looking at me, I could tell he knew I would change my mind. And he was right. I spent the whole night thinking about his offer. *A million dollars.* Life-changing money. The next morning, I was walking to work and the Town Car pulled up. He rolled down the window and looked at me and said, 'Just tell me yes or no.'"

Jessie already knew the answer, but she asked, "What did you tell him?"

Raines looked at her hands, shackled on the table in front of her. Her eyes seemed to fill with regret. "I told him yes."

"That's how it started?"

Raines nodded. Her lips quivered and a tear ran from one eye, down her face. "There was a fundraiser at the Children's Hospital where I worked. Goyle somehow arranged things so that both Corbin and I would be there, so we could meet. I flirted with him, he asked for my number, we went out a few times and then started seeing each other more seriously."

"It played out just like Goyle said it would?" Jessie sad.

Raines shook her head. Her tears were flowing more strongly now, a flood of emotion that Jessie sensed had been bottled up for months. "Nothing happened like he said it would. Corbin never raised a hand to me. He never even raised his *voice* to me. He was kind, gentle, and sweet. It was terrible, knowing that I was deceiving him. I had to close my eyes and force that picture into my head—the picture of his battered ex-wife." Her eyes cleared for a moment, and she stared at Jessie with a haunted look. "But mostly I just thought about the money."

Jessie swallowed. "And then what happened?"

"Goyle checked in with me regularly. He was getting impatient. He wanted to know why I wasn't fulfilling my part of the deal."

"Do you know why he was impatient?"

"Not at first, but when I told him I needed more time, he said there was no more time because an important vote was coming up. I told him Corbin hadn't done anything violent."

"What did Goyle say?"

"He told me it didn't matter. He said I could shoot him anyway, and with his history, the police would believe me that I'd shot him in self-defense."

"And you agreed to do it?"

"I was already in too deep to say no, wasn't I? Goyle and I picked a restaurant with a secluded parking lot. We didn't know about the security camera or the kid smoking weed in the car. I brought one of my guns. I broke up with Corbin over dinner, knowing he'd chase me outside to try to convince me not to. When I had him out there alone, I did it."

"What did you do?" She wanted to hear Raines say it.

"I shot him in the head."

"Goyle helped you plan this?"

"Most of it was his idea."

"At the time you shot Corbin Keeley, was he threatening you?"

"No."

"Did you believe you were in danger?"

She laughed sadly and shook her head. "No."

"Were you afraid for your life?"

"No."

"What about the rock?"

"I'm the one who threw the rock, not Corbin. Just like the kid said."

"Did Goyle pay you?"

"Not yet. We were waiting for the police investigation, and then the trial, to end."

The small room went silent. Jessie's gaze flicked to Aidan Hughes, who sighed.

Jessie pushed a legal pad across the table to Raines. "Write all that down."

44.

With Brooke Raines's statement in hand, the Philadelphia Police Department and district attorney's office moved in a swift, coordinated attack. As with the takedown of any large-scale criminal enterprise, the goal was to make key arrests and lock down all potentially significant evidence before the perpetrators had time to cover up their crimes or flee.

With each individual arrest and each discovery of physical evidence, the case against the whole became stronger, and more bad guys became caught in the web. In some ways, the sequence was like a series of flipped dominoes—Brooke Raines to Luther Goyle to an array of co-conspirators inside and outside of CBL Capital Partners, LLP.

Speed and secrecy were of the essence. From start to finish, the arrests and seizures took under six hours.

Jack Woodside was at brunch with his parents. The venue was Parc, an upscale French bistro on Rittenhouse Square. He'd chosen it because the food and ambiance were superb, and he could have alcohol with his eggs. He sipped a Bloody Mary, enjoying the bite of the spicy drink as he regarded the two people he loved most in the world. They were getting on in age—his father would be eighty-two in January—but with the fortune he'd amassed through CBL, he'd been able to provide for them. They lived as comfortably as was possible given their ages and health, and this, more than any of his other successes in life, warmed him with self-fulfillment and pride.

"You seem awfully happy today," his father said. "Things going well at work?"

Jack smiled as he forked potatoes into his mouth. Things were going very well at work—and were about to get even better once the city council vote went down in favor of the land purchase for the new prison. That deal would move ten million dollars into CBL's accounts, and a hefty portion of that would flow to Jack's personal fortune. When he'd founded the firm with Dave Whittaker fifteen years ago, he'd never imagined they'd reach this level of financial success. But then, Luther Goyle hadn't been in the picture back then. Jack had no problems with Goyle's methods. He respected the lawyer's intelligence and flair for creative problem-solving. He only wished Dave could feel the same way and enjoy the success they'd all achieved.

His smile must have faltered, because his mother said, "Something wrong, Jack?"

"It's nothing. I was just thinking about a friend."

His father lifted a hand and pointed his fork past

Jack. "Speaking of friends, I think some of yours are coming over to say hi now."

Jack sighed, put down his silverware, and hurriedly finished chewing. He hated being disturbed while out of the office—especially when he was spending time with his parents. He twisted around in his chair, preparing to deflect whomever was approaching with a polite but terse hello.

Three men were weaving between tables as they moved toward him. Jack did not recognize their faces. They wore suits and ties, but not nice ones. As one of them navigated around a chair, his suit jacket lifted for a second, revealing a holstered gun on his hip. Jack's stomach flip-flopped and sudden indigestion sent a surge of Bloody Mary burning up his throat.

"Jonathan Woodside?" the man in the lead said.

"Jack," he said. An automatic response. Meanwhile, his brain scrambled for traction. What should he do?

"Please stand up. You're under arrest."

He heard his mother gasp. He heard his father's brittle voice ask, "What did he say?" He heard a murmur of voices as word spread through the crowded dining room.

"What ... what is this about?"

The cop's flat stare revealed no emotion. "Stand up."

Jack grabbed his Bloody Mary and finished it in one long, urgent slurp. He felt the vodka hit him almost immediately. He was glad. He had a feeling it might be the last drink he had for a long time.

"You have the right to remain silent," the cop said. "Anything you say or do—"

"I want my lawyer," Jack said as he rose from his chair. "Luther Goyle."

"You can have a lawyer," the cop said. "But you might need to pick a different one.

Dave Whittaker's attention was divided as he attempted to play with both of his sons at the same time. No easy task with a two-year-old and a seven-year-old. The seven-year-old wanted to teach him the intricacies of the Pokemon trading card game. The two-year-old wanted him to be "an ogre" and chase him around the house. Playing with both of them demanded multitasking skills far beyond anything he'd mastered in his investment management career.

The two-year-old, frustrated that Dave was still sitting on the couch and not lumbering after him and making ogre noises, swiped a handful of Pokemon cards from his brother's collection. As his little hands bent the cards, the seven-year-old wailed with dismay.

"Maybe we should watch a movie," Dave said. Staring at the TV screen wasn't exactly the ideal way to interact with his children, but it was one of the few spots of common ground they could both enjoy.

And frankly, Dave wasn't in much of a playful mood today. He was aware of the looming city council vote—couldn't get the thought out of his head, actually—and all he wanted to do was pretend Luther

Goyle, CBL, and all of their schemes didn't exist. He'd thought staying home today, and keeping the kids home with him, would help him shut out the outside world for at least a few carefree hours, but it seemed his conscience would not even grant him that minimal respite.

"*Guardians of the Galaxy!*" the seven-year-old said.

"No!" the two-year-old said. "I no want to watch it!"

Dave sat back against the couch cushions and closed his eyes as the battle intensified. He was about to make his own selection—maybe a classic Disney cartoon would help ease his mind—when the crisp chime of the doorbell rang through the house.

The doorbell? Were they expecting anyone today?

His wife's footsteps moved toward the door. A moment later, she stood in the family room, flanked by an unfamiliar man and woman, both dressed in suits. No introductions were necessary. Dave didn't know their names, but he knew why they were here.

"Dave...." his wife said, her voice uncertain.

"It's okay." Dave rose from the couch. To the two strangers, he said, "Can we do this in another room, away from my kids? Please?"

His wife said, "Dave, what's happening?"

The man nodded and gestured toward the kitchen. To his wife, Dave said, "Stay with the kids, okay?" Then he followed the cops into his kitchen.

"David Whittaker, you are under arrest," the

woman said. Dave recognized the *Miranda* warnings from countless movies and TV shows. They blurred into a meaningless litany, like a prayer he'd heard so many times during his life it became background noise at church. Instead of paying attention to his rights, he looked around his kitchen—at the cabinets, the coffee maker, the fridge, the colorful placemats where the kids ate. He was about to lose all of this. Every little thing he'd taken for granted. He was about to lose it all.

"Mr. Whittaker?" the male cop said. "Do you understand your rights?"

Dave nodded. A tear ran down his face and touched the corner of his mouth, salty and cold. He wiped his eyes. "Okay if I say goodbye to my wife and kids?"

"Yes," the female cop said. "But please make it quick."

Operating under the power of several warrants, police searched the premises of CBL Capital Partners, LLP, as well as the private home, phone records, and bank transaction records of Luther Goyle, Jack Woodside, and Dave Whittaker Among the wealth of evidence and information uncovered were the identities of two career criminals, Ike Roels and Benjamin "Benjy" Flaxman. Mugshots of the two men, taken fourteen months earlier in upstate New York, were shown to former detective Mark Leary, who identified them as the men who attacked him in the parking lot of his office building. The two detectives in charge of the investigation of that assault, Matthies and Mannello, offered Leary the opportunity to accompany them to observe the men's arrests.

"Professional courtesy," Matthies explained. "Thought seeing us slap the cuffs on the scumbags might help those bruises heal faster."

"Thanks," Leary said. "I appreciate it. So where are these fine gentlemen?"

Mannello offered a shark-like grin. "That's the best part."

It turned out Ike Roels—he was the giant—and Benjy Flaxman—he was the twitchy knife-wielder— were creatures of habit. When they weren't running errands for Luther Goyle, they spent most of their time and money at a strip bar called Heartbreakers. The detectives and Leary drove there in separate cars, met at the entrance, and headed inside together.

After Matthies and Mannello introduced the doorman to their PPD badges, Leary and the detectives walked inside. It took Leary's eyes a moment to adjust to the gloom. Heartbreakers had a typical strip bar ambiance—dark and cavernous, thrumming with bass-heavy music, and smelling of perfume and baby powder.

"Is there anything more depressing than a strip club at 11 in the morning?" Mannello said. His partner guffawed.

Leary scanned the room. The place was mostly empty. Only one dancer worked the runway, and she looked like she might be in her late forties. She didn't dance so much as pace listlessly from one end of the runway to the other. Her body seemed to sag everywhere except her chest, where two breasts shaped like beach balls jutted out. No one seemed to be looking at her, much less tipping her. A middle aged man sat alone at the bar, staring glumly into his drink. At a nearby cocktail table, two young-looking guys seemed more interested in talking to each other than watching the naked woman.

"Depressing is one word for it," Leary said.

Two men who did not look depressed were sitting at a table at the other end of the room. As his eyes adjusted to the lack of light, Leary made out the general shapes of the men—one a massive giant, the other shorter and scrawny. The skinny one had his fist wrapped around the wrist of a scantily clad cocktail waitress. The men seemed to be taunting her as she tried to break free. Leary couldn't hear them, but he could see they were laughing.

"That them?" Matthies asked him.

"I think so, but I can't tell for sure from this distance. It's too dark."

"No problem," Mannello said. "Hang by the door here. We'll bring them over and you can give us a positive ID."

Matthies glanced at Leary and winked. Then the two detectives headed toward the thugs. Leary didn't need the wink. He had a pretty good idea what the detectives had in mind, and he was looking forward to it.

"Hey, assholes." Mannello's voice carried across the club as he and Matthies approached the table. Leary saw the detectives flash their badges. Flaxman lost his grip on the waitress, who darted away. The big one, Roels, stood from his chair.

"The fuck do you want?" Roels said.

"We want to arrest you," Matthies said. Before he could get another word out, Flaxman made a run for it. It was a clumsy attempt, since he was boxed in by tables and chairs and could have easily been stopped. But neither detective made a move to block him. He rushed past them, looking gleefully proud of his own slick moves as he raced toward the exit.

Leary extended his left arm and let Flaxman's momentum propel him full-force against it. Leary's arm connected with the man's throat, vibrating with the force of the collision. The man flipped into the air and landed on his back. He spasmed there like a beached fish, kicking the floor, gasping for breath, and clutching at his throat.

Leary crouched, rolled the skinny man over onto his stomach, and planted his knee in the center of the man's back. Flaxman struggled, but Leary pinned him to the ground, then shoved the man's face against the sticky strip club floor.

One bloodshot eye swiveled to look at him. "Y-you?"

"Good to see you, too," Leary said. "It's like a big, happy reunion. Now how about you tell me where my wallet is?"

Across the room, Mannello was securing Ike Roels with handcuffs. Matthies looked at Leary with a expectant look.

Leary gave him an enthusiastic thumbs-up. "It's them." Matthies grinned.

"I'm really going to enjoy this," Fulco said.

Jessie smiled. "This job does have its perks."

Together, they entered room 400 of City Hall, followed by six officers of the PPD as backup.

They knew Luther Goyle was personally attending today's city council meeting. The meeting was open to the public, and also recorded for broadcast. Although there was no particular need to arrest Goyle in public, Jessie couldn't deny a certain poetic justice in arresting him during the vote that had motivated Keeley's murder.

The chief clerk was in the midst of reading the text of a proposed bill. Jessie spotted Goyle sitting in the back, where his oversized frame looked uncomfortable in a narrow chair. His gaze was focused on the chief clerk, and his fleshy face bore a look of greedy anticipation. Jessie nudged Fulco.

Fulco nodded. "I see him."

They would need to weave their way through the crowded room, disrupting the formal setting in order to reach Goyle. A wooden gate separated the proceedings from the spectators. On one side of the gate, the city council president oversaw the proceedings from a raised podium that faced the wooden desks at which the city council members sat. A stenographer tapped at her keyboard. On the other side of the gate was the gallery, where Goyle sat with other members of the public to observe the meeting, crowded together in small chairs.

"Lead the way," she said.

Fulco grinned and stepped forward.

Goyle's gaze ticked toward them and she saw his eyes widen with recognition.

So you know who we are. Good.

The chief clerk was reading in a robotic monotone. "To the president and members of the council of this city of Philadelphia, I am today transmitting to the council the following bill, and I am submitting herewith for consideration by your honorable body a resolution authorizing Philadelphia to expend an amount not exceeding ten million dollars...." Jessie realized he was reading Goyle's bill. His voice cut off abruptly as Fulco, badge in hand, pushed through the crowded room toward Goyle. Jessie followed him.

"Excuse me," the chief clerk said. "Please settle down—" The president tapped his gavel to emphasize the chief clerk's command. Jessie and Fulco did not stop walking.

Goyle stood from his chair. His gaze seemed to slide from one direction to another, looking for an escape route. Not finding one, he stood frozen in place.

"Luther Goyle," Fulco said in a voice loud enough to be picked up by the room's microphones, "you are under arrest."

There were audible gasps around the room, including from several of the council members. A few of the spectators moved away from Goyle as if from someone with a contagious disease. A deputy sheriff emerged from the back wall and stepped forward to assist. Fulco circled behind Goyle, handcuffs ready. "For the murder of Corbin Keeley," he continued.

"This is.... This is ridiculous," Goyle said. He stepped away just as Fulco got close. His fleshy wrists momentarily evaded the handcuffs. "This is defamation. I'll bring a lawsuit." Spittle flew from his lips.

"Go ahead and do that," Jessie said as she moved in closer.

"What's wrong with you?" Goyle said. His face contorted. "First you prosecute a woman for shooting a man—a *monster*—in self-defense, and then you come after me? A pillar of the community?"

"You can drop the story," Jessie said. "Brooke Raines gave us a complete confession. We know Keeley never touched her."

Goyle's teeth flashed. "So what? He still beat up his wife and God knows how many other women. You're worried about justice for *him*? What kind of woman are you, to fight for a man like that?"

"I guess I'm the kind of woman who doesn't

believe people like you should get to decide who lives and dies—especially when you have a profit motive."

Fulco yanked Goyle's right hand behind his back, then his left, and cinched the handcuffs around Goyle's wrists. Goyle's face drained of color.

"Um," a voice said into a microphone. The city council president looked uncertain as to how to proceed. "Maybe we should adjourn for the day."

"No!" Goyle bellowed. "Vote on the prison bill!"

Jessie said, "Don't worry, Luther. There's a prison in your future. It's just not the one you expected."

Jessie nodded to Fulco, and together, they took Goyle away.

45.

Chance Resta emerged from his house and stood on his lawn, arms crossed over his chest. He glared at Leary. "What the hell do you want?"

Leary considered turning back. He was too tired to fight. He wondered why he'd come here at all. "I just thought, now that Lydia Wax is dead and CBL's involvement has been exposed...."

Resta scowled. "I hope you didn't come here looking for a thank you. You're three years late, Leary. *Three years!* You expect a high-five?"

Leary looked at the grass. "I don't know what I expected."

"I'll admit you might not be a totally worthless shitbag," Resta said. Then he smiled, apparently to show he'd been kidding the whole time. "Come on in, man!"

Jesus. Leary let out a breath and shook his head, smiling. "I won't stay too long."

"Oh, I know," Resta said as he guided Leary into his house. "You got a busy schedule not being a cop."

The house was neater than Leary had imagined,

but he wondered if the cleanliness was a recent development. Resta himself looked less disheveled than the last time he'd seen him. Maybe his brother's delayed justice had finally started a healing process that would help the man get on with his life. Leary hoped that was the case.

"You want a beer?"

"Sure."

Resta waved Leary toward a small TV room, then lumbered into the kitchen. Leary took a seat on a threadbare couch. He heard the sound of a refrigerator door opening and closing. Resta emerged with a Coors Light in each hand. He passed one to Leary and dropped into a rocking chair facing the couch.

Leary took a drink. "Thanks."

"No, thank you. Terry would, if he was here. I was wrong about you, Leary. You did good."

Leary had to force a smile. It wasn't that he didn't enjoy the praise—he definitely did—but it also made him more melancholy about no longer being a cop. Finding bad guys, taking them down—that's what he was good at. That's what he'd been born to do. The dull, day-to-day tedium of Acacia was all too sharp a contrast.

"I'm just glad I could finally help. I wish it hadn't taken so long."

Resta took a long pull of his beer, then wiped his mouth with his arm. His face turned thoughtful. "I was talking to some of the guys who used to work for us at the shop. After ... you know ... everything happened and I sold the business, we kind of drifted apart. But seeing the guys again, it was like old times."

"That's how it is with good friends," Leary said.

"We got to talking, and one thing led to another, and someone said we ought to try starting up the business again. No one took the idea seriously at first, but we were drinking and talking and you know how it is."

"You should do it," Leary said. "If that's what you want to do, you should find a way to make it happen."

Resta smiled knowingly and tilted the neck of his beer bottle at Leary, like a pointing finger. "You should, too. *Detective.*"

They sat in silence for a moment, each man drinking from his bottle. Leary knew that Chance Resta was right. Leary was a detective. An investigator. A cop. He had been fooling himself to think he could be anything else. He needed to find a way back in.

Jessie found Warren in his office. He had a mug in his hand, but the small mountain of used tea bags was gone and the aroma coming from the steaming cup was unmistakably coffee. Apparently, he'd ditched the herbal tea regimen. He was also smiling for a change.

As she stepped into the room, he tilted back in his chair and grinned up at her. "I would say, 'Good job,' but that seems inadequate. Sometimes it's really hard to be your boss, Jessie."

"'Good job' is fine." She smiled. "And thank you." She sat down in one of his visitor chairs.

"Rivera's approval rating is up. *Way up*."

"That's good to hear."

"I admit, " Warren said, "I thought you were going to lose this one. But somehow, you not only secured a guilty plea for what looked like an open-and-shut self-defense shooting, you also brought down a multimillion-dollar criminal conspiracy. I want you to pick my next lottery numbers. You have some luck."

"Or, you know, good skills and instincts."

"Those too. You can expect a visit from Rivera. He's thrilled."

"Maybe I'll get a raise."

Warren made a face. "Probably just a sincere thank you. But hey, that's more than you'd get from most politicians."

"He knows I still need to prosecute the cases against Goyle and the rest of them, right? It's not over yet."

Warren waved a hand. "It may as well be. You did it, Jessie. You exposed Brooke Raines as a killer, and you caught the bad guys who were lurking behind the scenes. In all seriousness, you should be very proud of yourself. Let me treat you to lunch. We'll celebrate."

"I'd like that," Jessie said, "but I already have important lunch plans."

Warren arched an eyebrow. "Important, huh? I'm intrigued."

"Carrie Keeley and Nina Long. To me, they're the most important people in the case."

"Ah."

"There is something you could do for me, though."

"No better time to ask than right now."

Jessie leaned forward. "That's what I figured." And she told him what she had in mind.

Carrie Keeley and her mother met Jessie at Marathon Grill in Center City, a casual, brightly lit restaurant. The women took turns embracing her, then led her to a secluded table in the corner. Sunlight streamed through the windows. As they took their seats, Jessie noticed that the mother and daughter both had tears in their eyes, and realized with surprise that she did, too.

"I knew you could do it," Carrie said. "I knew, right from the minute I met you at that law school thing, that my father's killers weren't going to get away with it."

"I appreciate the faith you had in me," Jessie said, meaning it. "But you deserve a lot of the credit, too. If you hadn't fought so hard for your father, I wouldn't have second-guessed the police department's work. Brooke Raines would be a free woman right now, and Luther Goyle would be closing a ten-million-dollar deal. You're as responsible for stopping them as I am."

"I don't know about that," Carrie said, "but thanks. Hey, I want to show you something." She reached into her bag and brought out an old-fashioned photo album. She opened its faux-leather cover and turned the book to face Jessie. "These are pictures from when I was a kid. I'm going to pick some of the best ones of our family. Now that my dad's body is being released from the morgue, we're going to have a memorial service. I want to ... I don't know. Show the good part of him. The part of him I'll always remember."

The photographs gave no hint of the violence that had eventually broken up the family. As Jessie gently turned the pages, she saw image after image of Corbin Keeley smiling with his wife and daughter. In one photo, Keeley pushed a very young Carrie on a swing at a playground. In another, he and Nina stood proudly behind their daughter as she blew out the candles on a birthday cake. *The good part of him.* "These are beautiful."

"Your father loved you very much," Nina said. "Whatever other faults he had, that fact will never change."

"I know." Carrie wiped her eyes.

Jessie looked at both women and felt her own tears give way to a warm smile. "I'm really glad I had the chance to meet both of you," she said. "There's a lot about my job that's sad, or scary, or just plain frustrating. But helping people like you helps remind me why I do it." There wasn't much else to say, so Jessie picked up her menu and scanned the lunch options. "So many choices," she said, "and it all looks good."

Jessie went home early that day—she figured

she'd earned it—and found Mark Leary waiting outside the door to her building. He held a bouquet of red roses in one hand and a folder in the other. "You did it," he said. "Congratulations."

"*We* did it." She took the roses and inhaled their aroma. "Thank you. These are wonderful." She kissed him, careful to avoid the cuts and bruises on his face. Her gaze went to the folder in his other hand. "What's that?"

"It's my résumé actually."

"Your résumé? That's a coincidence."

"It is?"

She opened her bag, reached inside, and withdrew her own folder. "This is an application for an investigator position at the DA's office."

He looked stunned. "I was afraid you might be against the idea. You know, the two of us working together. Mixing our private and professional lives."

She felt herself smile. "I think we might as well admit we're way past that point, Leary."

"Do you think I have a chance of getting the job?"

"I'd say you might even have an unfair advantage."

He beamed at her, and his happiness filled her with joy. "How about we celebrate a little?" she said.

"I can think of some ways to do that."

Jessie tilted her face upward and closed her eyes. A second later she felt Leary's lips on hers. His hands held her hips and pulled her tight against his body.

She was aware that they were standing outside on

a wintry afternoon, but she barely felt the cold air or the wind that whistled past their faces. All she felt was the warmth of Leary's mouth and the strength of his hands. She got her key out, opened the door to the building, and pushed him inside.

Thank You

Thank you for reading **Fatal Defense**! If you liked the book, please consider posting a review online and telling your friends. Books succeed or fail by word of mouth. Your help will make a difference.

Want more? I'm writing new Jessie Black Legal Thrillers as we speak, and they are coming soon! Be the first to know by signing up for my newsletter. You can do that at the following Web page: http://larryawinters.com/newsletter/ (newsletter subscribers also learn about special promotions and are eligible for free goodies, contests, and other cool stuff). I promise to never share your information or send you spam, and you can always unsubscribe.

ALSO BY LARRY A. WINTERS
www.larryawinters.com/books

The Jessie Black Legal Thriller Series

Burnout
Informant
Deadly Evidence
Fatal Defense

Also Featuring Jessie Black

Web of Lies

Other Books

Hardcore

About the Author

Larry A. Winters's stories feature a rogue's gallery of brilliant lawyers, avenging porn stars, determined cops, undercover FBI agents, and vicious bad guys of all sorts. When not writing, he can be found living a life of excitement. Not really, but he does know a good time when he sees one: reading a book by the fireplace on a cold evening, catching a rare movie night with his wife (when a friend or family member can be coerced into babysitting duty), smart TV dramas (and dumb TV comedies), vacations (those that involve reading on the beach, a lot of eating, and not a lot else), cardio on an elliptical trainer (generally beginning upon his return from said vacations, and quickly tapering off), video games (even though he stinks at them), and stockpiling gadgets (with a particular weakness for tablets and ereaders). He also has a healthy obsession with Star Wars.

I love to hear from readers. Here's how to reach me:

Email: *larry@larryawinters.com*

Website: *www.larryawinters.com*

Facebook:
www.facebook.com/AuthorLarryAWinters/

Twitter: *@larryawinters*

The best way to learn more about me, my writing process, and other fun stuff—as well as to stay current on my books, learn about special promotions, and be eligible for free goodies—is to sign up for the newsletter. You can do that by typing http://larryawinters.com/newsletter/ into your Web browser.

Thanks for reading!

Made in the USA
Las Vegas, NV
06 June 2022

49848810R00198